With Best Regards
from

William J. Ackerman

Keeper

of the

Wayward

Flower

W. Leonard Ackerman

Noble House
Baltimore, Maryland

Keeper of the Wayward Flower

Library of Congress
Cataloging-in-Publication Data
ISBN 1-56167-773-6

Library of Congress Card Catalog Number:
2002094839

Published by

Noble House

8019 Belair Road, Suite 10
Baltimore, Maryland 21236

Manufactured in the United States of America

A rose entwined upon the grape
    is but a weed we say
No matter what its scent or shape
    below the shears it lay.

A lily in a field of grain
    is out of place we say
It too desires the sun and rain
    but yet it must make way.

Oh, keeper of the wayward flower,
    you know your children's worth
And after our destructive hour
    they'll populate the earth.

W.L.A.

PART I

FRESH-TILLED SOIL

chapter

1

$\mathcal{E}$lla DeGraf lay in the upstairs bedroom staring at the intricate patterns of sunlight and shadow on the opposite wall. She needed something to distract her mind from the pains in her back. This would be her fifth child. They said that after the first child the others came easier, but this wasn't true. Each child had been difficult—the last as much as the first. She was not of the robust Dutch stock of which her husband often spoke. She was of Scottish blood. Not that her forebears weren't a hardy clan, quite the contrary; it was just that the women in her family were on the small side by DeGraf standards, and a bit narrow through the hips, which made childbearing difficult.

Beads of perspiration stood out on Ella's forehead, and every now and then several ran together and down into her eyes. This was very bothersome. Wiping her forehead helped momentarily, but soon the beads would form again. Why must it be so hot at this time, she thought, she was uncomfortable enough without this added burden.

Looking back at the wall, Ella tried to forget her physical discomfort, knowing she must endure and that there was still a long way to go before the baby would arrive. Old Dirk had taken the horse and buggy to the Vandenbergs to get Grace. They would be back shortly—it was only a half-mile down the road to the next farm — and Dr. Brabin would be along later. Dick had been in to see her after lunch, but that was four hours ago, and he had not been back since. She thought he might at least have come to see her at afternoon coffee; he knew that childbearing was not easy for her.

This would be her last child she told herself — five children were enough. She wasn't going to be like Dick's sister Beatrice, who had nine children. She would tell Dick after the baby was born. Yes, she would tell him — that was certain, even though he would be angry. Just this once she would stand up to him.

Ella looked back at the sunlit patterns on the wall, which seemed to form a double design, one superimposed over the other. First, there was the faded blue scroll of the wallpaper, and over this, a second pattern of light and shadows played across a section opposite her. The source was the late afternoon sun passing between the leaves of the huge maples just outside the window. As she stared, the shadows moved slowly up and down like small, long-gowned ladies dancing to a waltz. There must be a slight breeze coming up outside, but she couldn't feel it in here. The dancing ladies were ever-changing form and moving to and fro. Now, they were not ladies at all, but large-winged birds flying across a wallpaper sky. Ella saw her life in those two patterns. Her real life here on the farm was like the wallpaper design, torpid — fixed in form and place — changing only in its gradual fading with time. She felt she too was fading, yet in her mind's eye she longed to be one of the dancing ladies....or birds. She desired freedom, adventure in mind and spirit — yet here she was chained to the soil.

Ella's thoughts were interrupted by the sound of footsteps on the stairs. Sarah DeGraf stood large in the doorway. She was a very tall woman, who in spite of her age, held herself erect making her seem even taller. Her hair, now snow white, was combed tight against her skull and rolled in a large bun that sat at the back of her neck. Her face, well furrowed with wrinkles, still had some semblance of an apparent attractiveness in her youth. For a woman, her hands were large and had the look of hard toil.

"How you feelin' now?" Sarah exclaimed. "I've brought some milk from the cool cellar. Pains comin' any more often?" Sarah took a towel from a nearby chair and patted the perspiration away from Ella's forehead, neck and arms. "My, you must be hot and uncomfortable up here! We should have made a place downstairs. It's cooler there."

"Dick didn't think it would be right for me to be downstairs. I'll manage here. The pains are about every fifteen minutes."

"Well, Grace should be here shortly. Don't forget, you need anything, tap the can there beside the bed. I'll sure hear you in the kitchen below." There was a rumble of wheels in the drive out front, and Sarah went to the window. "Here they come now. Better go down to meet her." With that, Sarah left. A short while later there again was a creak on the stairs. Grace Vandenberg had arrived.

———◆◆◆———

Dr. Jeremiah Brabin was in his forty-fifth year of general practice in the township of Ridgewood. Until three years ago, he had been the only doctor in the area, but now a much younger man was taking over some of his business. Although many of his older patients refused to change doctors, the young folks were gradually making the acquaintance of the new man. For this, Dr. Brabin was grateful. He could not possibly continue the long hours of service he had taken in his stride in younger days.

Dr. Brabin was on his way to deliver another baby. The weather was hot and there wasn't any need to hurry. The phone call he had received an hour ago indicated that the baby would not be coming for some time, and Mrs. Vandenberg, who would serve as midwife, was probably already at the DeGraf's farm. She would take care of the preliminary necessities. He let the horse set her own pace along the winding dirt road. It was approaching dusk as the buggy started up the last rise towards its destination. When he reached the top of the grade, he would be able to see the DeGraf farm a mile or so down the slope at the low end of a small valley.

It had been one of those sweltering July days, and he welcomed the approaching evening and its expectant relief. As he reached the crest of the rise, he gave a slight tug on the reins and the horse stopped. The last grade had been a steep one for his old mare, and she needed a rest. Conservation of strength and spirit had always been a philosophy of his, and no doubt a good reason why he was still in active practice after so many years.

Down below, the last rays of the sun were shining across the valley. It would be dark by the time he reached the house. Two buildings stood out on the farm like a pair of mother hens—the barn and the house—while the many out-buildings were like so many chicks. The largest was the barn which stood some distance behind the house; both buildings were old, old even when Dr. Brabin had been a young man. The barn was green, not red like most modern barns, and the color was faded from too many scorching sunny days like this one. It was a rough-hewn structure that stood with its weather-beaten sides as a gaunt reminder of more prosperous days in the past. The house was a two-story frame building with white clapboard sides. It rambled in several directions and had certainly not been built all at one time, but had been added on—a wing here, a lean-to cook-house against that side, and an addition to the porch that completely crossed the front and along one side. The farm itself occupied 240 acres, but almost a sixth of it was swamp and open water of a shallow pond. Useless! A place of mosquitoes, snakes, and quicksand.

Dr. Brabin had been the DeGraf's family doctor for almost thirty years, ever since they first arrived from Holland. He had delivered all of the younger Mrs. DeGraf's children (two boys and two girls) and now he would be delivering another. He was looking forward to this visit, for he was more than a family doctor to the DeGrafs; he was also a good friend of the old folks. Dirk Sr. still ran the farm, but his son, young Dirk, or Dick as he was called, did most of the work. Dr. Brabin had shared in their health as well as their sickness, over the years.

Strong healthy children are one of a farmer's chief assets; to help with the work as they grow older. Making a living from the over-worked, heavy clay soil was no easy task. Truck and dairy farming were the DeGraf's occupation; when one failed, the other seemed to squeeze them through.

Old Dirk had lung trouble. It was a chronic condition he had developed in the old country as a young man when he worked as a stone cutter. He'd had to give up his trade and was finally forced to leave Holland for America to seek a new life, which he'd found here in farming. The old man was tough in spite of his infirmity, and had gotten by.

It was the heartache and burden of the younger Mrs. DeGraf's oldest daughter Clara that worried Dr. Brabin - worried everyone. A healthy baby when he delivered her, she had developed spinal meningitis when she was two. He had done what he could to save her, and she lived, but her mind had not developed beyond that illness. Now, a handsome girl of eleven, she was confined to a wheelchair, barely able to talk and impossible to toilet train. Her life would never advance beyond baby speech and diaper changes. Why hadn't he let her die nine years ago, the old doctor wondered. He did not know the answer. There wasn't any.

A slight jiggle of the reins and the horse started down the road towards the house while the last rays of the sun left the valley and only a dying glow sat on the horizon. He could see the lights ahead at the house and saw a lantern moving across to the barn. Dick was going out to do the evening milking. Ten minutes later, Dr. Brabin drove up the front drive, tied his horse, took a small furry bundle from the carriage seat, and went up the porch steps. The elder Mrs. DeGraf met him at the door.

"Good evening, Sarah," he said, "How is Ella doing?"

"Pains are coming every ten minutes," Sarah replied, "Grace is up with her now."

"Good, I knew I could count on Grace until I got here."

As Dr. Brabin entered the living room, old Dirk came in from the kitchen. He was considerably shorter than his wife. A stocky, barrel-chested man in his early seventies, he had a full head of wiry salt and pepper hair which contrasted oddly with a broad red-tinged beard.

"Well, well. Good to see you again, Jeremiah! My, what have you there under your arm?"

"A collie pup for Albert," replied Dr. Brabin. "I thought he might enjoy having it. Where is he?"

"He and the other children are out in the barn with Dick, helping with the milking chores. We thought it best they amuse themselves out there tonight."

"Here, will you give this to him?" Dr. Brabin passed the little dog over to Dirk. "I think I had better go up." He started for the stairs, but then abruptly turned to Sarah. "Oh, I almost forgot. I stopped in the Post

5

Office on my way out. The Postmaster had a letter for you from Holland. Thought it might be important, so I brought it along."

Sarah glanced at the handwriting on the envelope. "Ah, thank you! It's from my sister Maatje."

"You are very versatile, Jeremiah," jibbed Dirk, grinning broadly. "You not only deliver our babies, but bring us dogs and mail besides!"

"It's all part of the service," the doctor replied, as he continued towards the stairs. Then he noticed Clara sitting in her wheelchair by the large front window, staring out at the semi-darkness. He walked over and chucked her under the chin. "Hello, Clara," he said softly, "and how is my girl today?"

Clara turned her head, gave him a brief smile and in a small monotone voice replied with "Ah-h, maa-a." Dr. Brabin patted her on the head and then proceeded up the stairs.

Dirk headed for the opposite door. "Guess it's about time I went and got Albert." With that, he went out towards the barn, taking the puppy with him.

When Dr. Brabin returned downstairs, he told the elder DeGrafs that Ella was resting comfortably, in fact, had fallen asleep after an apparent exhaustive battle with the day's heat. Mrs. DeGraf and the doctor went out to the kitchen followed by Mr. DeGraf wheeling Clara ahead of him. The two men sat at the large round table in the middle of the room. The coffee pot was steaming on a black coal stove that squatted half way along the inner wall. A small blond-haired boy played quietly on the floor with the puppy, while two huge Saint Bernards, one on each side, made a living wall between him and the rest of the room. When Dr. Brabin entered, the boy came over, shyly thanked him for the puppy, and then returned to the confines of his doggy fortress. Mrs. DeGraf poured coffee, got a half loaf of honey bread from the cupboard, and sat down next to her husband.

"Hope you don't mind my adding another dog to your collection. He's hardly bite-size compared to the other two."

"Not at all," replied old Dirk. "Maybe this one will be good at rounding up the cows. Those two are useless."

"Albert seems so small beside those monsters," mused the doctor. "It seems only yesterday that I delivered him."

"Ha!" retorted Sarah. "It's goin' on six years now. Time must be runnin' together for you, Jeremiah!" Then leaning towards the doctor and lowering her voice, "He is terribly small for his age. Comes from his mother's side, no doubt. Scottish blood!"

"Do not underestimate the Scots!" the doctor exclaimed. "We English made that mistake once, but know better now. Give them a cause and they'll fight like demons. Today's British Army couldn't do without them!"

"Don't talk to me about your British Army!" shot back Sarah, clutching the letter she'd read earlier.

"Now, Sarah," broke in Dirk, "Jeremiah has nothing to do with what's happened in South Africa. Don't take it out on him." Dirk brought out a deck of cards which was Sarah's cue to clear away the coffee cups and plates. When the doctor came to visit, the old folks always played a few hands of gin rummy. It was the doctor's favorite game, and no one any longer asked whether they should play or not. Dirk would get the cards and deal the hands. It had become a tradition.

"What's this about the British Army?" The doctor wanted to know.

"Well, they're responsible for my nephew's death," retorted Sarah.

"That happened several years ago," broke in Dirk, "and she's never seen the boy, so didn't even know him"

"He was my brother Johannes' youngest," Sarah continued. "According to Maatje, Gideon was only 16 when he enlisted under General De-Wet during the early days of the War against the British. The Boer War was their fight for independence while you English were just looking for another colony. Same as here in the United States. Gideon became a Commandant and his group harassed the British for over year before he became desperately ill. His men left him at a secluded farmhouse to recover, but the British found him. They put him in a hospital and brought him back to health. Then, they turned around, put him on trial as a rebel, convicted him, and put him in front of a firing squad. Now that's British Justice for you!" Sarah fairly spat out these last words.

"Now, now Sarah!" Dirk put up his hands in her direction as though he were motioning back a charging horse. "That's what happens in war! There's no sense in you getting all riled up about it." Then, turning to Dr. Brabin, "I've got to watch her, she has a temper. These Frieslanders are a wild lot. You know they killed the first Christian missionaries that came to northern Holland? Now, nobody is as religious as they are – or so they think."

The doctor only grinned. He wasn't about to tread into this territory.

Instead, he turned to Dirk, "I hope you and Dick have had a good year so far."

Dirk drew himself up a bit before replying. The doctor knew he had asked a question which would result in no simple answer. The old man could talk about the crops for hours. Dirk thought their prospects looked quite good this year in spite of the heat and dry weather, but the cauliflower was a total failure. Dirk made it quite clear that he had advised Dick against planting cauliflower, but still his son had the urge to plant something he hadn't tried before. Each year Dick felt he would find a crop that would do better than the 'regulars' they planted. As yet, that special vegetable which would give them a big cash return, was as elusive as ever.

Dirk had to admit that the cow manure they turned into the soil each year was having its effect; the soil was more workable and productive than it used to be. Still, they were limited in what they could grow. This year it was the heat that had ruined the cauliflower, while next year it would be something else. It was best they stick with vegetables like kale, cabbage, sweet corn, beans, tomatoes, and maybe lettuce — crops which came through well most years, even if they weren't big money makers. They planted potatoes on the high, lighter ground, but the old man thought Dick shouldn't plant them every year. They had a really good crop only about one in three years. Other years, potatoes hardly paid the labor involved– the tubers just didn't size up properly.

Meanwhile, Sarah re-read her sister's letter for the third time. She would say no more on the subject for the moment, but would brood about it for weeks to come. Had circumstances been slightly different, it might well have been her son, as well as her brother's, who suffered Gideon's fate. Dirk had quipped about her forefathers being a wild lot, but they were also fiercely independent. Not a people to be easily dominated by the British, or anyone else. It was not so much Gideon's death as the injustice done and the additional suffering her relatives would undergo in the years to come. After all, Gideon had only fought for the country of his birth, and the Dutch lost the war. It was the aftermath that bothered her.

As is the way of older folks, the conversation turned to the days of youth some fifty years before. Dr. Brabin, although of English stock, was basically American. Unlike the DeGrafs, his forefathers had lived in America for several generations. His parents had moved from New England to northern New Jersey when he was a child. Mr. and Mrs. DeGraf had come from different parts of Holland. Dirk had been born and raised in a small town in the Zealand area of southern Holland while his wife had been a dairy maid from the north. Sarah had come from a large family and still had many brothers and sisters in both the old country and South Africa. They were a closely knit family, but poverty had dispersed them widely. While her oldest brother stayed to take over the family farm, two of her other brothers and one sister had left for South Africa in hopes of a better life. This they had done and prospered well. Years later, she, in turn, following marriage with Dirk, had had to make a similar decision and had wound up here in America.

When Sarah was barely fifteen, her aunt had died leaving her uncle with four small children. She still remembered how her uncle had come to visit her parents. It had been a special occasion, since he was considered wealthy, and her parents were very poor. He had arrived in a grand carriage from town and when it pulled up to their small house, she and her brothers and sisters had all rushed to see it. The children wondered why their uncle was visiting them since only the oldest remembered having ever seen him before. After the preliminary greetings, the children were sent to play and her parents and uncle went into the house and closed the door. It was not until some time later that her mother came out and called her in to speak with her uncle.

It had all been arranged before she was ushered into the parlor where her father and uncle sat drinking wine. She knew something was going on since her father drank wine only on special holidays — and this was no holiday. She was told that she would be going away with her uncle to live in town as his housekeeper. She would take care of his four children and run the household, under the same strict rules as did her mother at home. In return, her uncle would see that she got the proper clothes for living in town, her board and keep. Her uncle would send money each month to her father for her services. She herself would receive a little spending money now and then for small personal items. No more was asked— no more was given. The next morning she left with her uncle for her new life in town. At fifteen, she became mother to her four cousins and so when she married Dirk five years later, she knew all about raising a family and taking care of a household.

On the whole, her parents' arrangement with her uncle had been a good one. It had taken her away from the hard country life, and although it had perhaps given her an even harder one, town life had many advantages, and she had met Dirk. Her uncle treated her sternly, but well, and she had no serious complaints about the time she stayed under his roof.

She met Dirk three years after she moved in with her uncle. Dirk was an apprentice stone cutter. He courted her for two years and the week after he finished his apprenticeship, they married. They had four children, but two had died of smallpox the year before they came to America. It was at that same time Dirk had to quit stonecutting because of his lungs and they had both been in deep despair. Dirk always said that they had come to American because he couldn't find work in Holland. That was true, but she had wanted to come because of the death of her children. She wanted to get away— far away— and so they had.

Dick was six years old when they came, while Beatrice their oldest was fourteen and hadn't wanted to leave Holland. The dead children would have been ten and twelve, but that she tried not to think about — even now.

━━━━●▸)◄(●━━━━

Sleep must have overtaken Ella, for the next thing she remembered was a sudden series of pains. She looked to where the doctor had sat by the bed, but he was no longer there. Instead, Grace sat watching her with half-closed eyes. It was now late in the evening and much cooler.

The pains were coming close upon one another and more intense. She must have groaned because suddenly Grace was up and bending over her and adjusting the bedclothes. Ella moistened her lips with the tip of her tongue and whispered for Grace to get the doctor.

It was very late— past midnight— and in the upstairs bedroom Ella lay with the new-born infant in her arms. Everything about her had changed; her forehead was marked with suffering and her mouth was not yet freed from its strained lines of pain, but her eyes had a deep brightness in them. The broad, heavy old cradle stood ready by the bed, to receive yet another DeGraf. There was a creaking on the stairs -- a methodical tread that Ella instantly recognized. Dick was coming at last, and in the next instant, he

10

stood in the doorway.

Dick DeGraf still wore his blue and white striped work overalls which had the tangy smell of cows. He stood in his stocking feet for his boots were at the back door, as always when he came from the barn. In stature he resembled his mother's side of the family—well over six feet, with a massive frame. But when he moved, it was with an ease and agility unusual for a man his size.

"How you feelin'?" he asked, almost gruffly. "And how is the baby? The doctor says we have a healthy new boy."

Ella was propped up with pillows into a half-sitting position. She forced a weak smile, but then as Dick stood beside the bed and she looked from the child back to him, the smile broke into a radiance that won out over everything else. Dick bent down and kissed her. His massive paw took her small hand and squeezed it gently. The many haunting thoughts that had passed through Ella's mind earlier that day were swept clean. The ordeal was over. Both she and the child were well. Dick was again beside her. She squeezed back at his hand with all her strength. God was merciful indeed.

chapter

2

t was two weeks since Govert had been born and the stifling heat had subsided after a much needed rain. Ella was in the house alone with Clara, who sat looking out the window, and little Govert, who lay in his crib in the next room. Everyone else was out harvesting beans and she could see them from where she worked by the kitchen sink. All were bent over the rows except for Albert, who was on his knees. That way he didn't have to bend hardly at all. Gin, the collie pup, was dancing around his feet, chewing at the legs of his overalls. Nelson and Carlo were stretched close by, but they too, would have been with Albert if Dick allowed them in the bean patch. The big dogs would have trampled the bushes into the ground.

When she had first heard Albert call the puppy Gin, she had wondered where on earth he had gotten the name. It was not until Old Dirk told her how he, Sarah, and Dr. Brabin had played gin-rummy in the kitchen the night Govert was born, while Albert played nearby with the puppy. The boy had picked up the word "gin" from their game and soon used it for the dog. That was very like Albert, she thought, he had an active mind in that little head of his. He wouldn't be going to school until next year and already he knew how to read and write even though she's not meant to teach him so early. He had picked up words so quickly while she gave lessons to Richard and Ann that it would have been cruel not to include him.

Now Albert was standing up, bucket in hand, gazing out towards the cows in the far pasture. There was a long-legged white bird following behind the cows, picking here and there as it went, apparently feeding on insects scared up by the animals as they grazed. With some awkwardness, the bird took to the air, flapped its wings several times and made a long graceful glide back into the swamp. Albert watched a bit longer and then went back to his picking.

Ella knew the bird was some kind of heron or egret, but they were usually gray or bluish. Now it was somewhere back in the swamp and she gave a slight shudder. She hated the swamp. It was a dismal, soggy place— unsafe for man or animal. There were other things about the swamp that Sarah spoke of. She claimed she had seen lights coming from that area at night and strange mists just before dawn. Yet, nobody else had. Sarah brought many tales of unnatural happenings with her from the old country. Superstitions were stronger in Holland than here and it was not strange that Sarah would try to relive some of the experiences of her youth.

Dick had said they would have a fine harvest of beans today. The bushes were heavy laden. He and Richard would go to bed right after the evening milking, so they could be up at two o'clock to go to town with a loaded wagon. When Dick went to market, it meant that the grandfolks would do the morning milking, while Ella and Ann made the milk deliveries. Ella was not looking forward to the next morning's activities. It would be no easy task to drive the milk wagon so soon after having Govert–it seemed her strength was coming back more slowly this time.

Clara began banging her fists down on the arms of the chair and Ella went to see what was wrong. She couldn't be hungry since she had been fed less than an hour ago. Probably she had wet herself. She had. Ella wheeled her into the downstairs bedroom, made the proper changes and was back with her a short time later. She handed Clara a well-worn, but still somewhat furry, teddy bear which Clara tucked under her arm and patted vigorously; then alternately banged its head against the arm of her wheel chair and petted the fur gently back in place. All was well again.

Ella watched her oldest daughter momentarily and wondered if Clara was God's punishment to her for the thoughts which so often surged through her mind. The DeGrafs were a religious people, but she felt she was not— at least not in the same way. No matter how demanding the work at the farm they went to church twice on Sunday —morning worship and catechism for the children and then the evening hymnal service. She of course went also—she had to— but she got little out of it. The morning worship was in Dutch, the evening service in English. Although she could understand Dutch fairly well, it was completely foreign for her to pray in Dutch; it was a meaningless ritual. Why was it that people who spoke English all during the week, felt they must go back to the mother tongue in their religion? Was this the last stronghold in their lives resisting change?

They attended the Dutch Reformed Calvinist Church where the Bible was the word of God, infallible as written, and incapable of error in its definition of doctrines touching faith and morals. Reverend VandenTill held his congregation in a firm hand and did not tolerate any wandering from the right and chosen path.

The Church was hostile to the basic tenets of humanism; it extolled sobriety of expression and condemned all exuberant forms of spontaneity, any idea of art for arts sake, or the irrational element in inspiration. Ella found it hard to rationalize how such beliefs were compatible with the free expression necessary for serious art. Certainly the Dutch Masters, such as Rembrandt, Van Dyck, Metsu, Van Goyen, Terborch, and Van Gogh could not have perfected their inspired works under such dogma. They must have had to break away from the Church at least in spirit if not in patronage.

Ella questioned many things about the Church, perhaps because she had been a school teacher before she married Dick and was taught to question as well as to accept. For her this religion was austere, cold, and unforgiving. Was it this unforgiving God of the DeGraf's that was punishing her for her non-conformity? Her own spiritual breaking away? No, she could not believe this— and yet? Certainly Clara was not being punished. Her little mind was neither capable of sin nor the remorse that frequently follows it. It was the mother who suffered each time Clara cried or laughed in that baby voice.

———◆◆◆◆———

Dick swung his feet onto the floor and sat a moment at the edge of the bed before getting up and dressing in the dark. It was two in the morning. Ella had stirred when the alarm went off, but settled back again apparently asleep. He would not disturb her. She would have to get up later for the milk run. Dick took the alarm clock with him as he headed for the stairs. He would put the coffee and all on the stove, reset the alarm for five, and return it to the bedstand when he aroused Richard.

Richard was their first-born and would carry the family name. The boy had taken easily to farm life, and even as a small toddler had followed his father's footsteps in barn and fields. Now at twelve, he was a real help, for he could hitch a horse, milk a cow, or follow behind a plow in the fields when needed. In stature there was no doubt that he took after his father. It was only right that he would take over the management of the farm when the day came–but that was still many years off.

The coffee perked, the eggs and sausage fried, and the rolls warmed. Dick went up and woke the boy. This was another thing about Richard. He was quick to get up in the morning, even at this early hour. Soon they had finished eating and were on their way to the barn to hitch the horse and wagon.

The cool night air flowed by them as they rumbled along the dirt road towards town. Now the nights were pleasant for sleeping, making one feel refreshed in the morning. He would have to think about getting the next cutting of hay stored in the barn loft. Then, there were the corn and potato crops. Still so much to do, and so little help to do it with, but in a few years that would change. The boys were growing up.

Dick enjoyed living on the farm. It seemed his whole life had been spent here. He hardly remembered anything about the old country--except for a few events which had become embedded in his mind. He would never forget the time of the big storm from the sea. Their house stood on the landward side of one of the main sea barriers. Huge waves had swept to the upper parts of the dike and the spray surmounting it came crashing down on the house roof. The periodic rhythm of the waves was such that they knew exactly when the next downfall of sea water would come. He remembered how later his father and a neighbor were up on the roof repairing the damage. The other occasion he remembered was a week later. He'd seen a gathering of men on the dike standing around something they'd hauled out of the sea, and a young boy's curiosity had welled up in him. Not being able to make his way through the closely gathered circle, he had gotten down on his hands and knees and crawled between their legs towards the center. There. he suddenly came face to face with a dead man. The man who lay on his back had apparently drowned in the storm and had been worked on by the sea, until bloated, he'd floated to the surface. Dick would always remember the man's face. He had come only inches from it. It had shone in the morning sun like chiseled alabaster. He'd seen death a number of times since, but never so vividly. Death was a part of life and could not be separated from it, because life fed upon death, even as they on the farm depended upon the butchering of animals to supply their needs. Dick accepted death, and although he rarely thought much about it, he was not afraid of it. Perhaps that early experience in Holland had hardened him to it.

It was still completely dark when they arrived at the Paterson market at four o'clock. Dick pulled the wagon around and backed up to the platform near the great doors of the storage warehouse. The produce merchants would be coming out through those doors when the market opened two hours hence. Merchants were human like the rest of them and some tended towards laziness. If they found good produce near the head of the platform, they would not bother walking the length of the long loading area looking for something better. Often those at the head of the line would be pulling away empty before the first buying took place at the other end.

With hours to wait, many farmers would have their boy tend the wagon while they went to a nearby tavern. There, a few glasses of strong liquor and some friendly talk was a sure cure against the morning dampness. Dick was often tempted to follow these footsteps, but rarely did so. It took considerable dickering with the produce merchants to get the best price and a clear head was essential. A head fogged with drink could be disastrous, for the merchants were quick to perceive a farmer who had been drinking—and even quicker to take advantage of him.

Richard sat dejectedly in the wagon. Going to market was a lonely business for a boy at least until six o'clock. His father never was one for much talking and the ride into town had been a quiet one. It was damp, and now a light fog was settling in which made him wish he was still home in bed.

———◆◆×◆———

They sold all their produce of vegetables and dairy products in a little over an hour and a half and had gotten good prices for everything. This put Dick in a good mood. Unusually talkative, he told Richard that instead of going directly home they'd detour by Ridgewood and stop at Dumen's. Dumen's Bakery was an old customer on the DeGraf milk delivery route. It was good business to buy bread and cakes there when he was in town.

Stopping at Dumen's would give them a chance to warm up, have a bite to eat and a drink before proceeding the rest of the way home. He let Richard drive the team, while he sat back and counted the money they'd made.

Mrs. Dumen offered them hot chocolate, rolls and several kinds of cake. These helped remove the chill of the morning dampness. She commented that Ellen and Ann had been by earlier on their milk delivery and how fast Ann was growing. Praise always came easy for Mrs. Dumen which she readily dispersed to her customers. It never hurt business.

She went on to comment what a grand young man Richard was becoming. How much like his father and what a big help he must be on the farm. These were all words Dick and Richard had heard many times before, but it always pleased them nonetheless.

Then it was off and homeward. Again, Dick let Richard drive. The highlight of the trip came later when Dick told him he'd take him hunting that fall if he behaved himself in the meantime.

It was the following week that one of those late summer storms came up from the south, long after the DeGrafs had gone to bed. Ella had been sleeping fitfully and heard the first rumblings of thunder far down the valley. The storm was moving slowly because it was well over an hour before its fury was upon them. A sudden loud crash of thunder brought Dick out of a sound sleep.

"That must have struck close by!" Dick no sooner had the words out when a second deafening crash sounded through the house. "We'd better get up and wait this out downstairs. Have the children get dressed."

Soon, the entire family was gathered around the kitchen table. Ella let Nelson and Carlo in from the porch. They were soaked from wind-blown rain sweeping in to where they'd sat just outside the door. The only light in the house came from a lantern set in the middle of the kitchen table. The rain was coming down in almost solid sheets and, at times, violent gusts drove it against the side of the house so that the windows rattled from the force of the wind-driven deluge. Flashes of lightning lit the kitchen with a bluish-white light that was momentarily blinding to eyes not accustomed to such brightness.

To Albert, it was a fascinating yet spooky affair. The dreadfully fascinating part was the waiting for the next flash of lightning. This was unpredictable. When he thought it was coming, it wouldn't; and when he thought perhaps the last brilliant flash was over, another would come unexpectedly. The spooky part was seeing the faces around the table dimly lit by a soft yellowish glow, with shadows depending upon the position of each person in relation to that of the lamp. Then the dim light and shadows would be abruptly replaced. For a brief instant, everyone's face would be enveloped in a bright but eerie light. There was something religious about it all. The changes of light upon the faces reminded him of Reverend VandenTill's graphic depiction of the transfiguration of the dead at the final judgment. He didn't understand what that was all about, but it intrigued him. The Reverend was a good story teller, and while his stories were often scary, he told them with such fervor that they were seldom dull.

Dick went out on the porch several times and looked towards the barn — each time a spray of rain came flying into the kitchen. He felt he should go down and check the livestock, but now that was nearly impossible. Old Dirk alternately sat by the table and went to look out the window, not that anything could be seen except during the flashes of lightning. Finally, disgusted with the helplessness of the situation, he went over to the shelf by the stove and got down a deck of cards.

"How about a game of pinochle to pass the time?"

"You should be ashamed of yourself, old man," retorted Sarah. "This is a time for prayer, not card playing."

"I'm sure the Lord wouldn't mind if we do some of both," replied old Dirk.

Dick came back to the table and everyone, with hands folded, listened between thunderclaps, while old Dirk said a prayer and read several scriptures from the Bible. That taken care of, he dealt out the cards, and reluctantly, Sarah joined in the game.

"I think you show the Lord disrespect," grumbled Sarah.

"No good will come of this storm. You mark my words. Such violence as goes on outside is his doing. We should all be on our knees and praying to him for salvation at a time like this."

"Oh hush, woman," admonished old Dirk. "We show the Lord no disrespect. There's nothing wrong with pinochle as long as there's no gambling with it."

"That's not the way I see it. I'll have none of it!" Sarah slammed her cards down on the table, took up the Bible and began to read aloud. Dick looked at his father and then at Ella, but said nothing.

"All right, then we'll play three-handed," retorted old Dirk stubbornly. Thus, at one o'clock in the morning, three adults played pinochle while Sarah sat and read aloud to everyone. The children sat close by and watched and listened. Albert went over to his favorite place in the corner where Nelson and Carlo made room for him and Gin between them. He was safe with his usual companions, but wide-eyed with the excitement of all these new experiences, and of being up at this late hour.

The next morning was bright and clear. The previous night's rain had washed the valley clean and there was a cool fresh crispness to the air. Dick was still on the back porch when he saw the huge oak tree in the south pasture with part of its top missing. Lightning had struck the tree and torn a limb as big around as a man's waist from its uppermost part. Bark and splintered wood from where the bolt had followed down one side lay scattered for more than a hundred feet. The tree will probably die, he thought. This winter I'll take it down and cut it up for firewood. More important was the damage to the barn roof. A section of shingles had been ripped off leaving a gaping hole. The hay in the loft must be wet. This they would need to check without delay.

Directly after milking, Dick and old Dirk were up on the barn roof making repairs. Despite Sarah's protests, old Dirk had joined his son in nailing new shingles in place. The barn roof was no place for a man his age, but he would not have it otherwise. By noon, the job was completed and everyone was relieved to see him back on solid ground again.

Old Dirk insisted that they pull the wet hay out of the loft and spread it about the yard to dry. Wet hay in a barn loft could be dangerous. Dick did not dispute his father's "judgment", so he and the old man spent the afternoon pitching damp hay down from the loft to the ground. The wet hay would be dried and used for bedding for the cows. What was salvageable would be returned to the loft.

3

*I*t was Sunday morning and the sky in the east was beginning to show a milky stain on the horizon. The rest of the sky was black except for a scattering of stars here and there where there were breaks in an overcast sky. Lanterns had been lit in the DeGraf kitchen indicating the start of another day's activities. The rest of the house was dark. Most of the family slept an hour later on Sunday, except Dick, Ella, and Richard. Cows do not know Sunday from any other day, so milking was a daily occurrence, and late milking on Sunday was unheard of at the DeGraf farm.

The faded paint on the barn looked green only on one side of the warped vertical siding where its outward concave towards the west seemed to be trying to catch as much of the precious eastern light as possible, while the opposite curve of each board looked gray and dark, giving the building a striped effect. As the light from the east increased, the grey stripes became ever thinner until at last they were swallowed up in the morning light.

Dick and Richard had gone out to the barn and Ella cleared the table from early breakfast. She still had plenty of time before resetting the table for late Sunday breakfast for the rest of the family except Albert. He'd had a restless night and had gotten up with his father and brother.

The DeGrafs always raised a flock of chickens. They provided eggs and an occasional frier for family use. Feeding and caring for the chickens was Ellen's job. This included killing a hen now and then which had stopped laying. This was a job she inherited from Sarah. She still remembered quite vividly an episode during her training period. Sarah had picked an old hen for the pot which Ellen dutifully beheaded (a job she hated) and eviscerated it under Sarah's watchful eye. It was then they discovered the egg canal crowded with partly developed eggs. Sarah was so upset at the loss she never set foot in the chicken yard again.

Taking Albert in hand, Ella headed for the chicken yard to gather eggs for late breakfast. They were still some distance away when she heard an unusual squawking and goings on which made her break into a run dragging Albert behind her. Her first thought was that a fox or raccoon had gotten in among the chickens. When they arrived neither animal was there, but the chickens were wildly running, staggering, falling, getting up and falling again. Some, unable to get up lay where they had fallen and squawked incessantly.

"Oh! the chickens are hurting!" Albert cried, broke loose from her hand, and kneeling down tried to comfort several of the chickens flapping around on the ground. "Will they die?"

"My God!" Ellen thought *"Dick will have a fit about this."* All she could now think was that some frightful disease had suddenly descended on the flock. Ellen picked up several of the worst-off birds and examined them. She couldn't detect anything obvious except they had a peculiar smell. Then she saw something near the corner of the coop. It was a seedy purple mass. She instantly recognized it, but to be sure she brought some up to her nose and sniffed it.

It was spent elderberry mash from Old Dirk's wine making of the previous week. Now looking at the drunk chickens, the situation took on a hilarious turn, and Ellen broke out in an uncontrollable laugh. Just as abruptly, she caught herself. *Dick will probably not see the humor of it,* she thought. *However, thank God it was Old Dirk that was responsible and not one of the others. The old man could take care of himself when it came to Dick's temper.*

Quickly, Ella went through the nest boxes and gathered what eggs she could. There was nothing she could do for the chickens. Hopefully, they would sober up in due time without serious after effects. With Albert in tow and explaining the situation as best she could, they headed for the house. She would forewarn Old Dirk well before talking to Dick. She owed that to the old man.

Ella never learned what transpired between Old Dirk and Dick, but something had taken place between them. The old man was good at calming Dick and putting things in their proper perspective. He'd had plenty of experience over the years with Sarah, who was also known for her hot temper.

After a day or two of giving everyone the 'silent treatment' Dick returned to normal communication. The chickens were off their feed for two days before they returned to normal. The only bad effect was that they stopped laying for a time which caused some grumbling about a shortage of eggs for breakfast those mornings.

It was several days later that Ella decided the Crawford peaches were ripe enough for canning. This was her favorite peach. The fruits when mature were perfectly round with a suture that scarcely marred the symmetry. The soft tints of red and yellow made them the most beautiful of any peach she'd seen. Most importantly, the deep gold yellow flesh practically melted in the mouth which made them a joy to eat fresh and also good for canning.

Among the grand mixture of fruit trees Old Dirk had purchased some fifteen years earlier from a traveling tradesman, this was her favorite. Many of the farmers in the area were replacing their old Crawfords with the more productive Elberta, but Ella didn't like it nearly as well. The flesh was more coarse in texture and not as sweet tasting.

Their small orchard (all from Old Dirk's original purchase) consisted of three peaches: Crawford, Muir (strictly for canning) and the white fleshed Iron Mountain. They also had three apples: Baldwin, Jonathan and Rhode Island Greening, and three pears: Bartlett, Clapp Favorite and Kieffer (Ella's least favorite).

In addition to having canned fruit during the cold winter days when no fresh fruits were available, they would have a few baskets extra now and then for sale at market. It never amounted to much, but was welcome for the extra money that was hers to spend.

Today they were picking the Crawfords. For this she had Ann and Albert for helpers. Old Dirk, Dick and Richard worked in the barn. Sarah stayed at the house knitting socks, while she watched Clara and little Govert. It was a rare day that didn't see the whole household involved in the farm activities in some way.

The peaches were picked at three levels. Ella picked those up as high as she could reach. This was followed by Ann, not much shorter even at eight years old, and lastly Albert, the shortest and smallest of the group. When finished, there were still a number of fruits beyond reach so Ella gave Albert a lift so he could climb up after them. She could easily have gotten them herself with a step ladder, but knew letting Albert get them would give him a feeling of importance—a favor few of the others bestowed on him.

Harvesting completed, they carried their produce to the cookhouse. This was a small building attached to the back of the house. Large scale cooking and canning in the summer was rarely done in the house itself. Accepted practice was to use the cook house to avoid overheating the house.

While the canning jars and lids were being sterilized on one part of the stove, the fruits were quickly steamed to make the skins peel easily. The peeling job was assigned to Ann who sat on a tall stool with her legs dangling to the floor. Already, she showed signs of taking after Sarah. In later years she would grow to be a tall handsome woman, but now she was a skinny long-legged sapling with large hands and feet. Some said she also showed signs of inheriting her grandmother's temperament. Albert meanwhile sat low to the ground on a packing crate. He was the puny one of the family.

It was a hot unpleasant job, punctuated periodically by complaints from Ann claiming she'd wind up as boiled and cooked as the peaches. Finally, the peach halves were all packed in the jars and cooked to Ella's satisfaction. All-in-all, it had been a successful day. They had canned three dozen jars. These would be much appreciated during the bleak winter months.

The Dutch Reform Church, attended by the DeGraf and Vandenberg families, sat at the edge of a small oak grove some fifteen miles south of the DeGraf farm and a half mile less from the Vandenbergs. It was a plain rectangular wood frame structure with white clapboard sides and long narrow stained glass windows rounded at their tops. A tall, bell-enclosed steeple stood above the front entrance.

In a clearing among the oaks was the Reverend VanderTill's residence with accompanying stable. Along the opposite side of the church was a graveyard of considerable antiquity. If one stood at the uppermost end, one could see the outskirts of the village of Ridgewood in the distance.

Although the sun shown brightly outside, its rays were diffused through the thick hand-blown stained glass windows giving the inner sanctuary a greatly subdued light. The DeGrafs sat in the last row of pews at the rear of the church. This was by choice and tradition. Cornelius Vandenberg, of a more social nature, liked to be in the middle of things. Thus, the Vandenberg pew was half-way up front. The front-most pews were reserved for the six elders and six deacons. The remaining pews had been reserved over the years by individual families according to seniority and personal preference. Once a family had chosen their pew it was expected to remain theirs unless good cause was presented for change. Each family in their continuing financial support of the church paid an annual pew rental fee.

Reverend VandenTill looked down at his congregation from the pulpit with an expression of deep concern this Sunday morning. He was an exceedingly tall man with gaunt, sunken features and a long protruding chin. His frame was large-boned, but there was little meat on those bones and no fat. The man's soul controlled the body, and in his case, the body suffered because of it. An austere life dedicated to God and devoid of earthly pleasures made him lean and scarecrowish.

Rising to his full height he began his sermon with a prelude:

"I have been informed by one of our elders that several of our younger members have been seen partying in the Village where strong liquor is served. This is the path to degradation and waywardness."

Using this as the basis of his sermon, he cautioned the parents to take closer charge over the activities of their young. During the closing hymn, one of the deacons approached the pulpit and whispered in the Reverend's ear. Ella saw VanderTill's face turn white, followed by a dark shadow over his brow.

"Six boys have been found gambling in the cloakroom by Deacon Van Geldesen." The Reverend fairly spat the words out. "They are being held in my study until after the service. I will meet later with their parents here in the front pews to determine suitable punishment." The names of the six boys were announced with a final charge to the parents.

The sermon over, his shaken flock emerged into the sunlight. The buzzing between little groups pausing along the church walk was greater than usual this morning. The Reverend's words had given them cause to wonder about one another, much more than usual. Names had been given this morning, and it would not be easy to shrug off the anonymity of congregational sin. For many, it would be difficult to draw back into their ordinary weekday selves- - not so easy as the change from their starched and pressed Sunday best to comfortable old clothes- - for the Reverend's words would reach beyond the day.

Richard DeGraf's name had been given from the pulpit as one of the unholy six. Now, it was the duty of Dick and Ella to meet with the Reverend. Twelve stricken parents awaited the meting out of judgment by the Reverend and his elders. Soon the six boys, with Richard last in line, were brought in from the pastor's study. The deacon described the gambling scene to all present, and the dice and money confiscated were laid out before them. The boys were admonished to give account for themselves. The boy next to Richard raised his hand as though to speak, but Richard spoke up first. They were the youngest of the lot. In a faltering voice hardly above a whisper, Richard told how he had been excused from class to go to the outhouse, and the two boys had met there. They were returning to their classes and passing through the cloakroom when the deacon caught them. The other boy quickly confirmed Richard's story.

The Reverend looked long and hard at the two boys. He had made a great deal of this episode in his announcement and was reluctant to let any of the six escape without their due punishment.

"If you lie, we will know of it!",he admonished. "Who are your teachers? We will get to the truth of your story."

The names were given and the teachers apprehended before they left for home. Each verified that their pupil had indeed been dismissed from class, but had not returned. The deacon was asked if these two boys were playing dice with the others. He said they were not, but were in the cloakroom when he entered. The Reverend weighed the facts with his elders and then faced the boys.

"It would appear that you two young ones may represent the innocent caught in the net with the guilty. You may not have entered the game, but I suspect you paused to watch it, did you not?" Both boys denied they had. The Reverend paused and pursed his lips in thought. "Nonetheless, a bit of penance would not be out of place for the two of you." Then, turning to their parents, he addressed them. "It would be well if the fathers took their sons in hand to see that this was not the beginning of worse things to come." To assist in this matter, he recommended that the two boys come to his home for the next three Saturday afternoons where he would teach them to respect God and put them to work in his stable. With that, the two were dismissed in the company of their parents. As they left, the Reverend settled down to the other four boys—the real workers of iniquity—for them, things would not fare so easily.

After Sunday dinner Dick took Richard out to the barn. There was no anger in his voice as he emphasized his belief in Richard's innocence. He was convinced, however, that the boy had dawdled and watched the game instead of going directly back to class. He took a double length of rope in his hand, and Richard knew what it was for. Dick didn't go to the boy but waited for Richard to come to him.

"Will you stand for your whippin'" he asked, "or do I have to hold you?"

Richard submitted to his father's request and got five good lashes across the seat of his pants.

"This is not for gambling in church," Dick told the boy. "If I thought you were guilty of that, you wouldn't sit down for a month."

Tears streamed down Richard's face, but he knew better than to cry out. His father had dealt sparingly with him and there'd be no welts on his backside this time. In anger, Dick would have done far worse.

———◆◆◆◆◆———

Dick was convinced that Richard had no active part in the gambling incident and that the Reverend had gone entirely too far in calling off his name from the pulpit. Damage had been done to the DeGraf name, and it was up to the good minister to rectify that by making a statement from the pulpit regarding his hasty judgment. It was right that the man of God should be stern in dealing with transgressors, but he must also be just with the falsely accused. Dick would see to that—and he did.

That evening, before the hymnal service, Dick told VandenTill he would exonerate Richard from the pulpit, or the DeGraf family would leave the church. Families had broken from the Church for lesser matters. The Reverend was taken back by Dick's declaration, and although he admitted he may have been a little over-zealous in his accusations, Richard was present in the cloakroom and his very presence made him vulnerable to suspicion.

"There will be no guilt by association!" Dick's voice was unmistakably hard and flint-like. When the Reverend hesitated to reply, Dick turned on his heel and left. VandenTill called him back and agreed to do as Dick demanded. The Reverend knew Dick by reputation and had no desire to lose the DeGraf family from the congregation.

———◆◆◆◆◆———

Monday afternoon, Cornelius Vandenberg and his family came over for an unexpected visit. Normally, the families did not make such visits during the week, but Cornelius felt depressed and wanted to have a chat with Dick. His oldest son Neal had been one of Reverend VandenTill's unholy six, but unlike Richard, there was no reprisal from the pulpit for him. The Vandenberg name had quickly become a topic of gossip throughout the congregation. Not content to let the matter drop with the morning service, VandenTill had worried the subject again that evening—like a dog who continued to chew on a bone, after the savor is gone. The Vandenbergs had been to Church that evening, for to stay away would have invited more scandal, but Cornelius had slept poorly last night, and now he felt the need for the DeGraf's advice.

The children were sent out to play while the adults gathered around the kitchen table for afternoon coffee. Cornelius and Grace had argued, and reached an impasse. Now they were here to discuss their problem with the DeGrafs, their closest friends. Cornelius was seriously thinking of changing to another church, for he felt that the Reverend had been most unreasonable. Boys will be boys, and gambling was not the ultimate sin. Grace was strongly opposed to leaving where they had been members for more than two decades. She felt it would solve nothing. They must face the Pastor and the Congregation during these next weeks — the crisis would pass.

Dick remembered only too well his confrontation with VandenTill and his own threat at the time. He had made the declaration in the heat of anger, but once said, he would have fulfilled that threat, even if he regretted it later. Now, it was difficult to advise Cornelius to do differently in a matter where he had already taken a stand. Yet, he did not want to see the Vandenbergs leave the church. Thus, while Dick hesitated to advise, Old Dirk voiced his views and sided with Grace; the Vandenbergs must wait it out.

"As I see it", Old Dirk declared, "it was not the gravity of the gambling which aggravated the Reverend so much as where it had occurred." VandenTill was concerned that the news of this event might reach his superiors, and they would think him derelict that such a thing had happened right under his nose. It was this and not the magnitude of the sin that riled him to the boiling point. The next few weeks would tell whether the news reached the District Council in New York.

The opinion of all at the table was against Cornelius' rash decision, and so he conceded to the wisdom of staying with the Church.

———◆◆◇◆◇———

The children divided into several groups in the yard. Peter Vandenberg and Richard played mumblety-peg along the driveway and wanted Neal to join them, but he declined. Neal was two years older than Richard and sat on the porch railing where he watched them from a distance. His eyes followed their game with a brooding resentment. His gaze of deep concentration was mixed with emotions of bewilderment and contempt.

Albert asked to join with his brother and Peter, but was roughly told to play with the girls. Dejectedly, he went over to where Ann and Catherine were skipping rope. He stood with his hands in his pockets watching them. As the youngest of the group he didn't fit in anywhere. Catherine, seeing his mournful expression, stopped skipping and much to Ann's objections, loosened the one end of the rope from the fence post and put it in his hands. Catherine smiled across at him in encouragement and soon he was smiling back at her. He had found a place in the games, even if it was with the girls.

chapter

4

Except for a few hard frosts, September was unseasonably warm. Dick had completed most of the autumn chores and his feeling of well being spilled over into warmer relations with the family. There had been several trying days, but all in all, even he had to admit it had been a good year. As Old Dirk became less able to handle the heavy work, Richard was gaining in strength and skill. Where one left off, the other had begun, which was as it should be in the succession of farming through generations.

Old Dirk's rheumatism was bothering him more and more, and he often got up in the night to go to the kitchen. There, he would make himself some coffee, and pull a chair near the stove to sit by its warmth. Although it was not yet cold in the rest of the house, the stove's warmth seemed to help his rheumatism and that's where Ella would sometimes find him sleeping in the morning.

At three o'clock one October morning, Dirk went to the kitchen and sensed something was wrong. Aware of it when he entered the room, he couldn't quite place what it was. There was something in the air; a sweet pungent scent that didn't come from the stove—that was a different smell. Finally, he went to the back door and when he opened it, a burning sensation hit his nostrils. Towards the barn there was a reddish glow.

"My God! The barn's on fire!", Old Dirk shouted and clanged the dinner bell with all his might. Dick came stumbling down the stairs two steps at a time, but the old man was already racing for the barn, completely forgetting his rheumatism. "We must turn the cows and horses loose!"

The fire was still confined to the hayloft, yet from inside there was a stamping and bellowing of horses trying to get free from their stalls. Even the more docile cows were setting up an uproar. Old Dirk was out of the barn leading the brown and white mare when Dick and Richard arrived.

"Pop, you and Richard go below and get the cows out. I'll get the other horse." With that, Dick bolted into the flaming building.

As Ella reached the back steps, the fire broke through the barn roof. With a roar that shook the air about her, flames shot up into the sky making the whole yard as bright as daylight. Dick emerged from the barn with the terrified black mare. The horse lunged and Dick had all he could do to keep his footing. As he cleared the entrance, a shower of sparks fell down on horse and man. The mare reared on her hind legs jerking Dick off his feet, and then she toppled sideways, kicking him as she went. The wind knocked out of him, Dick went limp. The horse scrambled to her feet, reeled and bolted back into the flaming building, dragging Dick with her. As the rope flew back into the barn, it caught on the door hinge and snapped, leaving Dick half in and half out of the doorway. Dazed, he raised himself to his knees and Ella, grabbing him by the arm, headed him out of the doorway. Dick half turned to go back after the horse when a portion of the loft floor came crashing down where he had been.

"Where's Dad and Richard?" she screamed in his ear.

"They're – they're down with the cows," he gasped breathlessly.

"Forget the horse! It's not worth your life to go back in there."

Ann came up behind her mother, still dressed in her nightgown. The glare of the fire reflected harshly across her young face and body.

"Get back to the house with the others! Get everyone out on the porch!" Ella commanded. "Stay there! There's nothing you can do here!"

Ella pulled him by the arm and they were off around the barn to the lower entrance, Dick holding his side where he had been kicked. The cows were out and scattered down in the fields, but there was no sign of either Old Dirk or Richard. They must still be inside—both plunged into the burning building.

"Richard! Dirk!" both cried through the blinding smoke.

"Here, Pa," hollered Richard. "Gramp's pinned beneath a fallen beam and can't get out."

Old Dirk was unconscious. His legs were pinned beneath a fallen beam and small flames were licking about his shirt. Ella beat out the fire with her hands.

The main part of the fire had not yet reached the cow stalls. They could hear the horse screaming above, crashing into partitions, falling, rising, and crashing again. Then, one fearful scream and the mare came hurtling down through the floor at the far end of the cow stalls. There was a violent explosion of fire as it rushed through the opening from above. The sudden light and heat made the entire lower level like noonday and hot as an oven. Against this the three struggled over the limp form of a fourth.

"Move that beam!" she screamed. "I'll pull him out from under." As they strained on the beam, the 113-pound woman dragged Old Dirk clear, and without stopping, continued to slide him towards the rear door. She had a strength totally beyond that of her small stature.

"Get out of there, or we'll all die!" she bellowed at them. She had Dirk almost to the door before Dick and Richard caught up with her. Choking and gasping for breath, they barely reached the outside when a large section of floor came crashing down on all that was left below. A sheet of flame shot out the doorway catching up with them, setting all afire in its path. With one gigantic heave, Ella pulled the old man clear and all three rolled on the ground to put out their flaming clothes. Ella got to her feet last; the blowtorch heat had hit her full in the face—the others in the back. She stood momentarily, stared at the inferno, and collapsed.

"Quick, boy, pick up your mother, I'll take Gramps!" Man and boy, each carrying a limp form in their arms, staggered away from the crucible heat towards the house. Sarah, who could not bear to stay at the house any longer, met them halfway. One look and she knew that there was no need for questions.

The flames were still raging in the night sky when the Vandenbergs arrived. Cornelius had been only half asleep when through an otherwise quiet night, the first faint sounds of the holocaust reached his ears. The glow in the north sky told him instantly what had happened. Now he and his family came racing up the roadway to the DeGraf's.

The barn stood as a crimson skeleton against the night sky. The heavy beams underlying the loft and girding the sides, stood stark in their flaming splendor like the ribs of some mighty mammoth picked clean by colossus vultures. Deep in its final death throes, the whole structure collapsed, sending a thousand pieces of searing white fragments flying through the air and down around the Vandenbergs, the yard, and the house.

Cornelius leaped to the ground, tethered the horses securely out of the worst of it, and yelled to his sons.

"Stamp those new fires out, or house and everything will go up in flames!"

Neal and Peter jumped from the wagon and beat out the small fires that had started about the yard. Richard came off the porch and began extinguishing flames in the grass with his feet.

"Look, Pa!" shouted Neal, "there's a flaming board on the porch roof!" Quickly, Neal shinnied up a porch column, gained access to the roof, and put out the fire. The boys were too busy to notice the small figures at the back of the porch. Cornelius ran to where Richard was doggedly fighting the flames running through the grass.

"Where is everyone?"

Richard's eyes were glazed, his face smudged with soot, his hair singed, and his clothes blackened and charred. His body was moving mechanically by reflex, with little mental awareness.

"Folks're inside with Grandpa. He's bad off—real bad off!" He choked out the words in a hoarse whisper.

"Look at your arms, boy! They're badly burned. You need attention. Come in with me." Cornelius took hold of the boy and headed for the house. "Keep check on things!" he called back to his sons. "Watch the house that no fires start on it. We're going inside."

As Cornelius gained the porch steps, he saw Clara sitting in her wheelchair, her hands holding onto the baby's crib as though protecting it. She was gazing at the burning building—her face shining in the flickering red reflections of firelight—there were no signs of fear, but a glow of delight, instead.

Grace and Catherine had gone directly into the house. Grace knew this was no time for ceremony. Quickly she went from room to room. Dirk lay unconscious in one room with Sarah kneeling over him trying to remove charred pieces of clothing and sobbing softly to herself. One look told her that the old man was terribly burned. Grace's voice rattled a series of instructions to Catherine and then she went to the next bedroom not knowing what to expect. Ella lay across the bed unconscious— a mass of charred clothing and a patchwork of scarlet red and blackened flesh. Ann and Albert were struggling to lift their father to the bed from the floor where he had collapsed. Tears streamed down Ann's cheeks, but Albert only stared in dry-eyed horror as they futilely pulled at the arms of the slumped form at their feet.

The noon sun searched its way through the smoky haze that hung over the DeGraf yard. What had been a magnificent old barn, now lay in a smoldering heap of rubble. As though unconcerned with all of this, a group of cows and a single horse grazed in the pasture far below the smoking debris. Ann busied herself about the kitchen making meals which were neither breakfast, lunch, nor supper. Time had lost its meaning and food was only what kept the body going. Cornelius and his two sons slumped at the table, weary from the activities of the last nine hours. No one spoke, but all turned towards the stairs at the sound of steps, hoping for some word from the doctor who had been upstairs the past four hours. It was not Dr. Brabin, but Catherine. She had been given the task of caring for Richard, while her mother and doctor were doing what they could for the others. Catherine came to where Ann stood by the stove.

"You must be exhausted!" she whispered. "Why don't you lie down, I'll finish up here." Ann, bone-tired, gratefully accepted, and slowly made her way upstairs. After she had gone, Cornelius turned a questioning eye towards her daughter.

"How are things goin' upstairs?" he asked.

"I don't know very much, Pa," she exclaimed. "Granddad DeGraf looks awfully bad, but I mostly took care of Richard. He's burned about the back and arms, but otherwise he's all right. He's sleeping now."

There was another creak on the stairs and soon Grace entered the kitchen.

"Cornelius, you and Neal come help Dick downstairs. We're moving him to Clara's bedroom. He thinks he can walk by himself, but he's got several broken ribs, as well as his burns. The doctor says he should have assistance. Catherine, take a tray with some food up to Dr. Brabin. The poor man's been up there since early morning with nothing but tea."

Grace and her men returned to the kitchen, where she poured some coffee and fixed a plate of food for herself.

"Poor Old Dirk, I'm thinking he's not likely to make it," Grace finally said. "He's barely conscious. It's not just his burns. The doctor says he has internal injuries."

"And Ella?" queried Cornelius hesitantly.

"She's badly burned about the face and throat. It'll be a long time before she's up and around."

The menfolk helped themselves to food and drink from the stove. They weren't really hungry, but it was something to do while they waited.

It was mid-afternoon when Dr. Brabin came down to join Cornelius in the kitchen. The two Vandenberg sons had gone home to do the milking and other chores that had to be done. Dr. Brabin's face was haggard with fatigue. Catherine poured coffee for him as he dropped into a chair by the table. He gulped down the hot liquid and stared across at Cornelius.

"This household is going to need a lot of help. I've done everything I can. The rest is in God's hands." He paused a moment and then continued. "Someone should go fetch the preacher. Dirk is in a bad way."

Cornelius had no keen desire to see the Reverend, but agreed without hesitation. He raised to go, yet the doctor had more to say.

"The preacher should see Ella, too," Dr. Brabin sighed half to himself. "You mean - - -"

"No, Ella has a good chance unless infection sets in, but she's been severely burned. She was a very attractive woman—that will now be gone. When she realizes this, if she doesn't already, the preacher might help."

Cornelius left for the Reverend VandenTill. He was gone only a short while when Grace quietly came into the kitchen.

"Doctor, Old Dirk is dead!" she whispered. "Will you come up and help comfort Sarah?"

Grace moved in with the DeGrafs for the two weeks following the barn fire. There was much to do— the care of the living and the burial of the dead. Cornelius made the arrangements for Old Dirk's funeral; it was a simple service with a closed casket. Animosities between Cornelius and the Reverend were forgotten and all went smoothly. The family had suffered enough.

Old Dirk was at peace, the Reverend said, he'd led a good Christian life, a faithful church member, and had sinned against no man. Undue mourning would be unfitting for one who even now was in Paradise. Sarah took all these words to her heart, but still the tears came; quiet tears that did not break forth for all to see, but softly ran down her weathered cheeks when no one looked her way. Dirk had been her only love, and the years would be lonely without him. She hoped God would not leave her to be alone for long.

A new grave was dug in the little cemetery that lay behind the Church, which many years before had been divided for the members of the

Congregation. There was room for the entire DeGraf family including the children; Old Dirk would be the first to lay within the family plot. After the Reverend finished the service, a small procession of pallbearers carried the coffin out the front of the Church and around to its final resting place. Here, Old Dirk was laid within sight and sound of Sunday services. It was entirely fitting that it be so, for God's child thus, in the end, returned to his house to seek the peace and tranquility of eternal rest.

Sarah joined Grace in caring for Ella and Dick. She was not experienced in these matters, but she had to keep busy to ease the grief that sat heavily upon her. Richard, the least burned, was up and about within a few days. Dick was up within a week, but it would be some time before he could use his scarred hands. In the meantime, the children did what they could of their father's chores, so all was not left to the Vandenbergs and neighbors to do. For Ella, the healing process was slow. She had taken the brunt of the flames, her burns were extensive and painful, and although they gradually eased as the weeks went by, the fire had left its mark. She would be able to cover much from the casual eye by wearing high-necked, long-sleeved dresses, but the left side of her face she could not hide. This would, for the rest of her life, be a remembrance of that dreadful night. She alone, had not been able to attend Old Dirk's funeral and she felt remorse because of it. Her prayers were with him. The old man had always been kind to her and more than once he had championed her differences with Dick to settle the rough places between them. He had been a stabilizing influence on the family, and now she wondered how things would fare without him.

The DeGraf cows were stalled at the Vandenbergs. They would be cared for there until new facilities could be completed, but that would have to wait until spring—this was a time for healing, not building. The winter months were hard, and new life had to be breathed into the household. Grace and Catherine did much to accomplish this. Without Grace, the task of reconstruction would have been unsurmountable. Catherine, on the other hand, became the light that brightened those dark winter days and made it bearable. Still a mere girl of eleven, she brought a radiance into the house that dissipated much of the gloom that surrounded her elders. A handsome girl with a ready smile for everyone, she busied herself following in Grace's footsteps, but where her mother brought efficiency and comfort, Catherine gave an even more precious gift, for she brought a pleasant charm that lingered. Thus, a child led the way where adults had been unable to grope.

There had been much time for thinking during the months after the fire. Dick had time to reflect on his life and what the fire had so quickly done to him. So much of what he'd worked for had been swept away in that one night. Was this then God's answer to his efforts? Was he to be humbled for some misdeed? He knew not where he'd erred. He was hard on others, but also on himself– this was essential for survival on the farm—an arduous life meant difficult decisions for all. The fire changed him. He had to accept so much assistance from friends, he would be indebted for years to come. This hurt his pride. His broken ribs and burned hands kept him from doing those chores he'd taken for granted. He hated being an invalid. A month after the fire, he began milking his own cows again. He forced his hands, still sore from burns, to perform what to him was duty. Cornelius would follow and finish stripping each cow; Dick's hands could not complete the job without having the milk turn pink with his blood.

◆━━◆━❋━◆━━◆

Spring finally came and with it an anticipation of activity. A new barn must be built. Dick made mild protests to Cornelius' plans for a barn raising, but he himself knew there was no other way. Wagonload after wagonload of lumber arrived and was stacked about the yard. Then, one Saturday morning, men skilled in stonework came and repaired the old foundation; the new barn would be built exactly where the old had stood.

Word went out and the day was set for the big occasion, the first Friday of April. That Thursday, women for miles around cooked and baked their best. As the sun broke the horizon, the wagons came up the dirt drive. Horses were unhitched and let out to pasture. They would stay the day. Forty men and boys joined in a great work force. Soon, timbers were sawed to length and nailed in place, more sawed, more placed— and so it went, as the new framework took shape.

At ten o'clock, the first contingent of wives and daughters arrived. Coffee and cakes were served on tables improvised from planking; hustling heavy timbers brings on a hunger and a thirst.

Dick worked along with the best of them, his hands now well healed, and he was feeling better than he had in a long time. The DeGraf family worked beside neighbors in a way that brought new life to all of them. They had dwelt too long within themselves and this was a time for socializing, as well as work. Now, they were encouraged— no forced— to mix with friends in a combined effort that broke the barriers of self-concern.

Grace reigned supreme in the kitchen. It was she who directed the women's work and Ella did not challenge her, although this duty was rightfully hers. She was still conscious of her face and when talking with the women, she instinctively turned her head so that her right side faced them. As the morning drew on and more women arrived, this became impossible, so at last she did not bother. All about her knew of her condition; there wasn't anything to hide. In accepting her, they would have to do so as she was— scars and all.

By late morning, the barn's framework was completed and the first siding begun. The materials and most of the labor were furnished by others. The wood had been purchased at cost through a loan by members of the church. They had refused Dick's offer of cash from his small reserves; he would need it for replenishing his livestock and the dozens of other expenses. It was a safe loan, for they knew Dick's reputation for paying his debts.

At noon, the Reverend VandenTill arrived. He gave a brief mealtime prayer and blessing of the DeGrafs, the barn, and all gathered there. Practical as well as religious, he knew brevity was important if the work was to be completed. The tables had been set with the plateware and silver of several dozen households, and food was brought out by the women in an almost endless line from the house. Here was such a grand assortment of Dutch cooking, that it staggered the consumptive appetites of even the most hearty of eaters.

Eating and socializing finished, the work began again in earnest. Men and boys went back to the barn while the ladies, young and old, cleared the tables and packed kitchenware into their respective carriages. Soon, there was a hammering and banging as roofing shingles were nailed into place. By late afternoon, the stacks of lumber had dwindled to a few scattered planks and in their place stood the new barn. While boards were yet being nailed on the back side, the front was receiving the finishing touches of bright red paint. From the uppermost peak a pine branch stood.

As the sun sank close to the western horizon, Dick and Cornelius left the work and soon returned with bottles of blackberry brandy and elderberry wine. Everyone was called off the building, for it would soon be dark and the day's work had been sufficient.

This was an occasion for celebration and a tradition must be kept. Fortunately, the Reverend had left hours before, so no one felt uneasy about partaking. Brandy for the men and wine for the older boys, while the youngest needs were satisfied with cold milk. All who had worked on the barn now joined together in a grand salute to the day's accomplishment. The barn stood in its brilliant red splendor and everyone was justly proud.

As the first signs of dusky grey settled upon them, the wagons left, for each now had his own work awaiting at home. Dick and Ella stood before the barn, staring at the new structure.

"It's a mighty fine barn," he exclaimed, with a tired grin.

"Yes," she answered, "God bless all who worked here today. We could never have made it otherwise."

"I know!" he replied. "We are fortunate to have so many friends. In those dark days after the fire, I almost gave up. Now, I believe we'll make it!"

Arm in arm, they made their way to the house as night shadows scratched out the last light of sky.

PART II

SPRING WHEAT

chapter

5

en years had passed since the raising of the new barn. They were not easy years, but they were eventful, and the DeGrafs had made a go of it. The boys had grown in stature and now the tasks fell on more shoulders, so no great burden was upon any.

A close relationship developed between the DeGrafs and the Vandenbergs. Although they had been friends before the barn fire, that tragedy brought the two families together as a working team during the DeGraf's climb back to normality, and once established, a deep and personal friendship lasted through the ensuing years. Thus, it was no surprise to the church community when Cornelius announced the coming marriage of his daughter, Catherine, to Richard. People also made knowing glances when they saw Peter talking with Ann after Church. They said there would be a double wedding, but they were wrong.

Richard had grown to manhood, and it was time he took a wife. Many said that Richard was a true DeGraf, for physically, he was much like his father—tall and powerfully built. As the eldest son, he was a good catch for any girl. The DeGrafs and Vandenbergs were pleased in the thought of uniting their families in marriage. Therefore, when Richard and Catherine became interested in each other, it was as though it was the natural and expected thing for them to do.

The Reverend VandenTill was contacted and the wedding day set; the date carefully planned to fall in early May. It was calculated that most of the spring planting would be completed and yet cultivation chores would not as yet be heavy. There were, of course, the hogs to be taken care of, but that could wait until after Richard's return from his honeymoon. Thus, the wedding would hopefully fall during a brief spring lull in a normally busy season.

The Reverend made certain stipulations which the betrothed must perform before he would unite them in Church. There were the visits by the couple to the pastor's home for talks on the solemn responsibilities of marriage. Finally, the day before the ceremony, Catherine was obliged to stay overnight with the pastor's family. VandenTill felt he had good reason for insisting she come to his home the night before the ceremony. He saw need for more stern direction in the Vandenberg household; Cornelius showed an exasperating religious laxity, and it troubled him. This was not the case, however, with the DeGrafs, where Dick maintained a firm influence on all. Richard was a deacon— the youngest in the history of the Church— so he need not worry there. It was good that Catherine was entering the DeGraf household because this would undoubtedly do much to straighten any lack of strictness in her upbringing. Nonetheless, he felt that Catherine should be well informed upon her Christian duties in matrimony.

That evening, after a simple supper, Catherine sat with the pastor, his wife and daughter as a patient attentive listener. Here she received those instructions meant specifically for her future life as wife and, in time, mother. This was not an easy task for Catherine. By nature a light-hearted young woman, she found it difficult to maintain the somber countenance expected by the pastor. She sat within the austere parlor of the Rectory, hands folded in her lap, her head slightly bowed as though in reverence. Long reddish-blond hair that flowed across her shoulders set off a finely formed face while a full crimson mouth was held rigidly in a non-smiling position. Catherine's now grave beauty was betrayed only by sparkling blue eyes which alternately looked at the pastor and down at her folded hands.

Many of the things she heard from the Reverend she had been told before by her mother bit by bit as she'd grown to womanhood. But yet, there was a difference. The pastor's words related these things, previously considered physical, to her fulfillment to God. At times, Catherine felt the pastor touched on matters which were only her concern and which she'd rather keep to herself. After some initial resistance, she gradually let herself sink down among the somber words and let them flow over her like dark quiet waters of a bottomless pool.

The Reverend and his family retired early as usual that evening. This suited Catherine well, for she was not accustomed to so many pious words except in Church, and there they were not so directly put. Lamp in hand, the pastor's wife showed her to a small upper room that would be hers that night. Here there would be quiet and solitude, quite different from affairs at her own home —or what had been her home 'til now. It was still early by her accustomed bedtime and after the pastor's wife had softly closed the door as she left, Catherine sat on the edge of the bed and pondered to herself. The Reverend's words continued to rise and ebb about her; dark, murky words that were said to make her think about tomorrow and all that it would bring. Her life with Richard came into focus.

She had known and admired Richard for as long as she could remember. As infants they had played together. He was as strong as an ox, but she well remembered his helplessness at the time of the barn fire. She had nursed his wounds then. That was when she felt the first hints of affection for him. He had had a need and there had been a welling up within her to fulfill that need. Tomorrow, she would fill another need, but that need was less clear to her. Was it to fill another need of his, or was it now her own? She was not sure. Was this really the love she thought it was, or was it that she blindly followed the needs and wishes of others— his and her parents, and his. *Last minute doubts like this must worry many prospective brides the night before their wedding*, she thought. She loved Richard, that was all that mattered. These foolish idealistic dreams that long had laid deep within her mind, fought to be heard, and she tried vainly to subdue them.

The Reverend's words again rang in her ears.

"It is the religious fulfillment of a sacred bond and not earthly passions that sustain a marriage. The longings of the flesh must be set in proper place and should not dominate the marriage bed. It is, instead, the union of two souls in communion with God that befits the bridal chamber."

Would she then join Richard in a spiritual sense? Could she adapt to his sometimes rough hard ways. She thought she longed for a gentler touch than that which he offered her. He had the physical grandeur of a young Hercules, but there should be more— or was this expectation only the girlish fancy that fought to haunt her. Each time her thoughts dwelt upon this, a shadow crossed her mind, and turned her unseeing eye to things she dare not admit.

Now she slowly raised herself and just as slowly began to undress for bed. This she would do again tomorrow night— but not alone.

The sun rose on a cloudless sky this early May morning. The pastor's wife drove Catherine home, for the pastor had other matters to attend. A short time later, Albert brought Clara over to stay at the Vandenbergs during the wedding service and picked up Peter to join the DeGraf family. Cornelius enjoyed festive occasions and extensive preparations had been made for the wedding feast at noon which would follow the late morning Church service.

Catherine was unusually quiet as her mother and Ann busied themselves about her, adjusting her gown with all its trimmings. The garment had been her mother's and grandmother's before her. Each generation had required certain adjustments to fit, to match the bride's own proportions. Everything was ready and all looked perfect except Catherine was much too serious to suit Grace. This was an occasion for rejoicing and gaiety, Grace told her. It seemed the Reverend's words must weigh heavily upon her. Grace knew the Reverend VandenTill. She had objected to the Reverend's insistence that Catherine stay the night in his home, but her words were over-ridden in Cornelius' conformity to VandenTill's demands. After much kidding and joking, Catherine was again her usual bright self.

Several neighbor women stayed behind to prepare the wedding feast. The DeGraf's would drive separately and all would meet at ten o'clock at the Church. In many respects, this was like a Sunday morning except for the importance of the occasion. Cornelius, with Catherine on his arm, came down the aisle to where VandenTill stood in majestic reverence before them. Ann was bridesmaid and Peter, best man. Some question had been raised by Ella about why Albert was not best man, but since Catherine did not have a sister to serve for her and Ann was chosen it seemed only proper that a Vandenberg reciprocate for Richard. In the first row on the left sat the Vandenberg family; the first row on the right the DeGrafs. Little Govert sat between Dick and Ella, then came Sarah and finally Albert.

The Reverend gave of his best. Funerals and weddings were of considerable importance to him, and he felt they should be handled with dignity. A full hour passed during which the ring was passed and the congregation told of the glory of God's grace upon the couple. VandenTill emphasized the sacredness of holy matrimony; these two united in God's sight, henceforth one in flesh and spirit..."and damned be he who brings uncleanliness upon the sanctity of this holy union."

Albert looked down upon the feet of those standing before him. He had been small as a child and few thought him of much promise for the farm. At twelve he had suddenly spurted into growth, and now was only a few inches shorter than his older brother. A young sapling of sixteen, he was growing so fast that he had a certain ganglingness about him. Folks said that Scottish blood ran through his veins. He was his mother's son. He did not have the stubborn stamina for long hours of heavy toll, but there was strength and agility in his supple frame.

Without moving his head, Albert looked sideways toward his mother. After a long questioning moment, he looked at those in front of him. His eyes rested on reddish-blond swirls that swam across gentle sloping shoulders covered with a white satin-like material. He saw how the rivulets of fiery gold splashed and flowed half-way down to her waist. As she turned to the side, he saw the curve of her throat. This was all he saw—a graceful line of neck and chin.

Albert closed his eyes momentarily, then blinked and saw her mouth. Where was the radiance he had come to know? It did not seem the same. From the mouth his eyes retraced their steps, and then his gaze moved down. As a sculptor runs his fingertips over the marble statue of his craft to detect the smallest imperfections, so his eyes now ran the line down to where it joined two other lines. There were no imperfections here. Albert slam-closed his eyes convulsively; his head throbbed and he felt dizzy. When he opened them again, he looked to the far Church wall and the cross that hung there. His lips moved slightly but no words came.

Again, Albert looked to his mother, but this time he turned his head to see her fully. She sat looking straight towards the standing couple, yet there was no expression on her face; he saw neither joy nor sadness there. She was his closest kin—his rock when he was small—the healer of his wounds, both actual and imaginary. Where was his rock now? She could not heal the wound that was splitting him apart. He turned back to the cross and tried not to hear the Reverend's words.

The service was over, and bride and groom were joined in front to receive congratulations from their relatives and friends. Dick clasped Richard's hand between both his own, and shook it vigorously. Ella kissed her new daughter-in-law fondly and welcomed her into the DeGraf household, her new home. Both DeGrafs and Vandenbergs circled around the newlyweds and there were kisses for the bride and hardy handshakes for the groom. Even little Govert got a big hug and kiss from the bride. Albert hung back and stood at the outer circle as friends came forward to give their respects. There would be much more of this later at the marriage feast, but almost everyone wanted to give their immediate salutations.

Cornelius, noting Albert in the background, brought him forward.

"Come, give your good wishes to the bride and groom," he said, putting his arm around Albert's shoulder. Cornelius was pleased with the day's events and his spirits soared in anticipation of the activities to come.

"Catherine, your new brother-in-law has yet to extend his greetings to you. Albert seems a bit shy in meeting the bride." Cornelius teased and poked Albert in the ribs with his elbow.

"Go on, boy!" taunted Cornelius as he pushed Albert in front of Catherine. "Kiss her! You don't mind if your brother kisses the bride, do you Richard?" Richard nodded, paying little attention as he continued pumping hands.

Albert stood motionless as though frozen in place before Catherine, which put Cornelius in his element. He was fond of Albert, but the boy's bashfulness was just too much; it was obvious he had never kissed a girl before. Cornelius laughed so that it could be heard throughout the Church, and the Reverend VandenTill raised an eyebrow in disapproval. Ella, who stood close by, put out a hand to restrain Cornelius, but it was too late. Not getting anywhere with the boy, Cornelius pushed his daughter forward, perhaps a bit too hard, and Catherine stumbled and fell fully against Albert. Instinctively, his arms shot out encircling her. As she clung to him to steady herself, he quickly bent his head and kissed her, not on the cheek as the others had done, but fully on the mouth. It was not a long kiss, but he felt such a pounding in his chest that he thought his ear drums would burst.

"Oh ho!" cried Cornelius. "The boy's got some stuff in him after all!"

There was a frantic milling about them. Richard retrieved his new bride and soon Albert lost sight of Catherine as the wedding party was off to the marriage feast.

<hr />

The tables had been set in the Vandenbergs' side yard well away from the barnyard and in the shade of large oak trees. There was a flurry of activity in the kitchen when the first carriages were sighted, coming down the road at top speed. Shouts and laughter filled the yard as the procession pulled up in front of the house. As was customary, the Reverend and his family were there to celebrate the occasion. It would not have been proper to have left him out of the wedding feast, but many would have wished it otherwise. The Reverend had a way of restraining the jubilation of his flock; with him present, it was not likely that the party would turn wild. He and his family sat with the bride and groom and their parents at the head table. A prayer was given before any dared begin, and as long-winded as VandenTill had been in Church, now he was brief in his thanks to God. It was quite possible that he was also hungry and all the delicious food spread before him made him short of speech. This was a luxury he seldom indulged in nor would he have admitted that food was anything more than that which sustained the body.

Neal Vandenberg sat at a table far down the line, and when Albert saw him from a distance, he went and joined him. The further away from the head table the better he would like this affair. Neal looked at him in surprise as Albert plunked himself down on the seat beside him.

"Shouldn't you be up there with the others?" Neal asked.

"What about yourself," Albert shot back with irritation in his voice.

"Oh, they don't want me up there. After all, I'm the black sheep of the clan. Best that I stay well apart at a time like this."

"Well, this is where I'd like to stay, if you don't mind!"

"Glad to have you. As you can see, brother Pete is hot up there with Ann. He's been damned poor company lately. You'd think he'd shit or get off the pot."

Albert raised a questioning eyebrow.

"If he's going to marry her, he ought to get up guts enough to go ahead with it. At least Richard's done 'that' much."

"What about you?" needled Albert. "I haven't seen you getting sweet on anyone. How come you're not married?"

"Not for me! I like the girls, but not to marry them. You sure you're doing the right thing sittin' with me?" he teased. "They say I'm a trouble maker. It might rub off."

"I can take care of myself." Albert fussed with his food but ate very little. He didn't feel hungry today, and the many tempting servings didn't interest him.

Mischief was building in Neal's eyes. He was twenty-three, but still had a boyish quality about him. He enjoyed a good joke, especially if it were on someone he felt was 'too good for his own britches.' In part, it was a way of getting back at those who had cast him out of their company.

"What say we have a little fun with the newlyweds?" he whispered to Albert.

"What do you have in mind?" Albert leaned closer so those at the other end of the table would not hear.

"Well, the bridal carriage is settin' in the barn. My ol' man'll be goin' out later to hitch the horse for a grand exit. Let's fix the buggy so it'll loosen down the road. I think I can set her to come loose as they start up the hill." He jerked his head towards the road out front. "Then the horse'll leave them sittin' at the bottom."

Albert liked the idea; for the first time all day he felt like doing something. Later, they watched Cornelius leave and then return, giving

Richard a slight nod as he sat down again beside Grace.

No one noticed Neal and Albert leave. They crept around the back of the barn and soon Neal was making calculated adjustments to the carriage as Albert steadied the horse.

"You know they're going to suspect something," said Albert.

"We should make a diversion so they'll overlook what we've done."

"Good thinkin'," nodded Neal. "Got any suggestions?"

"Let's steal the horse!"

"Steal the horse? My dad will only bring the other horse around."

"Steal that, too!" replied Albert now aglow with the idea. "We'll take off with them and stay away until long after they're supposed to leave."

"You'll catch hell from your ol' man!"

"Who gives a damn!" Albert was already unhitching the horse as he spat the words out.

Quietly, the unhitched horse was led around the back of the barn, where Neal picked up the other carriage horse. Albert was mounted bareback and impatient to be away. They walked the horses until clear of the open field; then Albert dug his heels into the horse's flank, and he was off in a full gallop down the road, with Neal trying to catch up with him. Finally, after a mile of hard riding Albert slowed enough for Neal to come abreast.

"Man! You ride like hell! I never thought you had it in you to race like that!" hollered Neal across to Albert.

"There are a lot of things I can do when I want to," he said, hardly glancing over at his older friend. Then in a much lower voice, "But I wonder what good it does me."

"What'd you say?"

Albert looked down at the horse's neck, flushed slightly, but did not answer. He had a question of his own.

"You don't like Richard very much, do you?"

"What makes you say that?" returned Neal giving Albert a side-wise glance, as they jogged along side by side.

"Well, you two just don't associate. Never have that I can remember. Not only that—I've noticed things."

"You're not showing much brotherly love today yourself. You know Richard's gonna kick the shit out of you for this."

"No more he won't. I told you I can handle myself. And even if he does—I don't care." Albert bit his lip and pulled a sour face.

"Hmmm, that's strong talk from the likes of you." Neal was becoming interested. He admired this new spirit the boy was showing.

"You still didn't answer me," Albert went on doggedly. "You don't like my brother. I know that! It's now important to me to know why."

"Well, for one thing, I never liked the way he picked on you when you were small. You were a puny kid, you know. I guess you've never had much love for him either."

"No, why should I? I was afraid of him then." Albert paused. "I'm not anymore!"

Albert jammed his heels into the horse's flank. "Let's ride!" he shouted; the mare responded immediately. Neal, who was considerably heavier, was no match for the burst of speed. The wind rushed past Albert's face. He was meant for horses—strong arms and light weight—his long legs clamped tight about the horse's middle. The horse's mane flew back into his face, his mouth, his eyes, and tingled thoughts within his brain. This was like something he'd seen before that day. This hair was coarse and chestnut brown; that hair was fine and shone in crimson blond. Love and hate are easily mixed, and make a potent brew. Now drunk with both, he knew not which was which. Dropping the reins, he grasped the flying mane and let it run between his long thin fingers. The horse was free to scatter all the winds in a thunder of hoof beats and flying clods of soil. He brought his face to the mare's neck and felt the rhythmic movement of her firm flesh beneath his fingertips. Tears streamed down his face and matted mane. On he rode—as though no force could stop him.

chapter

6

The sun was disappearing behind the tops of the oaks to the west of the DeGraf farm when two figures on horseback worked their way up the dirt road toward the house.

"So, you're gonna walk right in on them, eh?" asked Neal with a look of admiration.

"Yep!" replied Albert. "No use sneaking in the back way. They know what I've done. Might just as well take my medicine and get it over with."

Albert slid off the chestnut mare at the front door and passed the reins to Neal.

"Good luck, Al!" Neal called back, as he headed down the road toward home with the mare in tow.

Old Gin came prancing up to meet him, her tail wagging a greeting she kept especially for him. He reached down and patted her gently on the head.

"I doubt I'll get this kind of welcome inside," he mused to himself.

The DeGrafs were seated at the kitchen table finishing supper when Albert walked in and all eyes were on him as he came into the room. He was not a pretty sight and this was reflected in their faces. His father had a deep frown and his eyebrows were drawn down. Albert knew this expression well. It meant only one thing—trouble! His mother's face was of more concern to him; the others were of no importance at all. She looked at him with troubled eyes. The scar on her face seemed to burn a deeper red than usual, while the other cheek was pale white, but it was her eyes he searched now. Large eyes that told a tale he'd learned to read. There was concern here, yes, but there was also fear; fear for him, he knew.

"Where in God's name have you been?" roared Dick, raising up and stepping toward the stove.

"Out riding with Neal."

"Do you know you almost destroyed your brother's marriage feast?"

"It was a prank— just a prank."

"Stealing horses was one thing, tampering with the carriage another. You could have killed them both!"

"We knew what we were doing. They weren't hurt, were they?"

"No, but no fault of yours!"

"So— no harm done. We did it on impulse."

"It was Neal's idea, wasn't it? He tampered with the wagon and talked you into taking the horses. You keep away from him. He's bad medicine and will get you into worse trouble!"

Albert saw that his father was giving him an out. Were appearances that important here? Should he save face by blaming Neal? This fit the pattern of what he'd heard earlier that afternoon. He looked his father full in the face.

"It wasn't Neal's idea. We fixed the carriage together. It was my idea to take the horses."

Dick reached for the strap that hung behind the stove, folded it to half its length and let it hang loosely from his hand.

"Don't get the idea you're too old for this," he said gruffly and confronted his son, towering over him. Dick raised his arm as though to strike. Albert braced himself for the expected blows, and met his father's glare. Dick stood momentarily frozen and stared back at his son; a flash of bewilderment crossed his face. He let his arm drop to his side. The boy had not flinched, nor shown fear of punishment. From the corner of his eye Albert saw his mother give a sigh of relief.

"Why'd you do it? You've always been such a good boy. And now, suddenly this."

"It was a prank! A joke. A big wedding joke."

"I guess it was, at that," As quickly as the storm clouds had risen upon Albert's entry, now they disappeared. "Come, you're late for supper. We've got milking to do." Dick sat down and as he took up his fork he seemed to chuckle to himself. Perhaps he remembered something from his own youth just then.

Albert sat on the milking stool, his arms and hands working rhythmically as squirts of warm white milk purred into the pail between his legs. He was not conscious of his actions. His hands had long ago learned to do this task as a reflex. His mind wandered across the countryside on the roads to town. They would have ridden these roads earlier this afternoon, and he wondered where they were now. There had been no definite talk as to where Richard was going on his honeymoon. Most guessed it would be to New York City. In town, they'd catch the train and reach the city by nightfall. They would probably spend the next several days seeing the sights and spend their nights in a hotel. A shudder passed through his hands and the cow flinched. He looked down into the half-filled pail; the new-pulled milk glistened in foamy whiteness. On the next stroke he let the clean white fluid run down his hand. It was warm and frothy—right out of the cow—it was body temperature. This is what she must be like below the clothes that keep away the tanning sun. Richard would see this tonight, and more. His hands made a convulsive movement, and the cow let out a loud bellow and kicked him in the leg. She wasn't used to such rough treatment and wasn't about to take any more of it.

"What's the matter?" came a voice behind him. Ann stood leaning against a post with a cloth in one hand and a pail of warm water in the other. She'd been washing down the cow's udders prior to their being milked.

"Nothing, Bessie's not feeling herself tonight," his only reply.

"Are you going to catch it when Richard gets back," Ann teased. "He was real hot about what you did."

"Hump!" the only reaction.

"I'm not kidding! You know the carriage was wrecked. They were half-way up the hill when it let loose and came down backwards and off the road. One wheel was shattered by a rock, and they landed in the bushes and tore their clothes."

"Catherine wasn't hurt, was she?" His father had said not, but he was still concerned.

"No, but I guess she'll remember that ride for awhile. I'm surprised Pa didn't thrash the daylights out of you tonight," she said in a low voice so their father wouldn't hear.

"Hump!" again. He went back to his milking, but she wasn't through.

"You know they were two hours late in getting off? What with looking for the horses you took, and then they both had to change clothes and get another horse and carriage. Oh! It was really something!" Ann raised herself up defiantly. "You'd better not try anything like that when I get married!"

"When _are_ you and Peter getting married?" Albert looked up from his milking. A slight grin touched the corners of his mouth. "A lot of people thought it was going to be today."

Ann flushed as her cheeks burned momentarily.

"I wasn't about to share the glory with Catherine. I want my own wedding. Just as grand as hers was—or would've been if it hadn't been for you and Neal. We saw you two ride up tonight, big as ever."

"Yeah. But when?"

"When what?"

"When you getting married?"

"Late July." Now leaning forward very confidentially, "But, don't you say anything to anyone. We haven't told a soul yet—" she caught herself— "till now. I shouldn't have said anything to you. Why did I do that?"

"Don't worry, I wouldn't tell anyone," Albert said almost in disgust.

"Promise!"

"Promise—not a word."

Relieved, Ann went on about her work. Albert emptied his pail into a large milk can and moved to the next cow. Again, there was the rhythmic sound of milk streaming into an empty pail. Why was it so many things brought his mind to Catherine?

It was almost nine o'clock that evening, and they were gathered in the parlor, playing a game of dominoes. Sarah sat half dozing in an easy chair, her wrinkled hands in her lap holding a pair of knitting needles and a half-completed scarf.

"Who can that be at this hour?" questioned Ella at a rumbling sound of carriage wheels in the drive. She went to the window, but it was too dark to see. The heavy footsteps on the porch had a sound of urgency. The door flew open, and Richard strode into the room pulling Catherine behind him.

"Where's the little punk! I'll kill him!" stormed Richard. Albert stepped forward, but Dick blocked the way.

"Calm down, calm down!" Dick ordered.

"Because of him we missed the last train out!" yelled Richard to all in the room.

"You'll have to stay here tonight then. You can catch another tomorrow morning."

"It's his fault, Pa!" Richard bellowed, pointing an accusing finger at Albert. "Let me at him!"

"No you don't!" shot back Dick. "We'll have none of that here!"

"Let him try if he thinks he can take me," retorted Albert, stepping around his father to face his brother. "You'd better get lucky and knock me out quick. I'm a lot faster than you, and I'll jab you to pieces."

"I said there would be none of that! Both of you!" Dick grabbed Albert and pulled him aside. Then, turning to the women, "You'd better ready the old folks room. Richard and Catherine will stay there tonight. Move Ma's things to Richard's room. She'll be moving a couple days earlier than we figured. All of you go on upstairs. We men have a few things to settle here."

Sarah was fully awake now. She took in everything that was going on, but said nothing. Ann helped her as they made their way for the upper level.

"Now!" Dick said equally to both his sons. "I'm still head of this household. As long as I am, you two will do as I say. There's not going to be any fighting. If you're other ideas about it, I'll whip the tar out of the pair of you."

"Yeah, Pa!" stammered Richard. The fight had been taken out of him. He eyed Albert with a malicious stare, but said no more.

Dick wasn't finished. "Albert, you go on up to bed. I want you to do the milking tomorrow by yourself. If you're man enough to stand up to your father, you're man enough to do his work. Ann and I are taking the route into town."

Ella was busy at the stove and turned slightly on hearing him. Albert went over, gently put a hand to her shoulder and bent his head to meet her eyes, for he was a full head taller. There was still a touch of fear there. *Why should she be afraid*, he thought, *she was a very brave woman*. She'd proved that during the barn fire. His father owed his life to her and, in a way, so did Richard. Then, why was she afraid? Not for herself, but only for those she loved. When the chips were down she had more raw courage than the lot of them. Did he also have some of that same inner strength? He hoped so. He'd faced his father and his brother today. A first time for both.

"Don't worry about me, Ma!" he whispered as he wrapped both arms around her. "I can take care of myself, from here on out." He kissed her gently on the forehead and gave her a quick hug.

"I know you can, son," she said. "I saw that tonight. Still, be careful. Your brother could hurt you badly."

The words came to his mind, "He already has," but they never left his lips.

Albert took his snack and left for his room by way of the back staircase. He was not in the mood to pass through the parlor. He passed Richard's room on his way to his own—the door was closed— Granny was probably well asleep by now. Something instinctively drew him past his own door and down the hall toward the front of the house. The door stood ajar. He pushed it a bit further and looked in. This had been his grandparents' room and he'd seen it so many times before, but now it was different. This is where Richard and Catherine would spend their first night, and many nights to come. The double bed stood in the middle of the room, newly made, with the covers neatly turned down. He brought the door again to where it had been and quietly went back to his own room, closing the door behind him.

Once in his room, he removed his shirt, kicked off his shoes and fell back across the bed. Thoughts raced through his mind and tumbled over one another. His wild ride with Neal. What Neal had said about his brother. Were those stories really true, or was it that he wanted them to be. Anything that would make him hate Richard more; he felt a strong need for this. One thing he'd found out already. Richard was not invincible. When he had challenged him in the parlor, for that brief moment when they had stood facing each other, he'd seen his lower lip quiver. Could he then actually scare his brother? Richard, who outweighed him forty pounds and whose reach exceeded his by inches. The thought amused him. He'd take his brother on. There'd be a day.

Albert swung from the bed and sat at the small desk in the corner. He pulled the bottom drawer out and, reaching back behind it, pulled out a notebook. He would not sleep much tonight, so he would write. It was the only way he knew to valve off the emotions of his mind.

◆━━◆×◆◆━━◆

Moonlight flooded the backyard as Albert, lantern in hand, made his way to the barn. It was best he'd gotten up before any of the others. He didn't want to see or talk with anyone, and was determined to stay in the barn until they had left. He felt groggy, his eyes burned, and he was displeased with himself. It had been a bad night. He'd stayed up writing until midnight, and felt by then he would go to sleep, but it had been after one before he finally dozed off. Then, he was awake at three and couldn't get back to sleep. He knew only too well what had gone on in the front bedroom last night, and the very thought made his stomach tightened into a knot.

Going over to a feed box he set the lantern on it, pulled himself on top of the lid, and scrunched down beside the light. He removed a folded sheet of paper from his shirt pocket and read what he had written, then stuffed it back into his pocket. It was best to get to work, but he'd forgotten the pail of warm water and cloth to wash the cow's udders down before milking. They were back in the kitchen, and he'd have to get them before any of the others got up. Quickly, he raced back to the kitchen, found the pail still on the stove, and the cloth hanging over the back of a chair.

Milking was normally a pleasant job, but this morning his brain buzzed and sputtered out of control. Forgetfulness was not the worst part of it. Each time he tried to think, his thoughts settled on unpleasant things. As if yesterday's events were not enough, his mind involuntarily went back in search of all the unhappy events he'd ever known. The day Nelson had died and the heart rendering weeks that followed, now stormed his brain. Nelson had been poisoned, just how, he never knew. The second day of sickness told him the big dog was dying and he'd persuaded his father to take the dog into town to see the animal doctor. The man could not save Nelson because they'd waited too long. The following day Nelson died. Two weeks later, Carlo was dead also, not from poison, but from the will to die. The dogs had been litter mates and had never been separated in their lives. Carlo stopped eating the day of his brother's death and no matter how hard he tried, he could not keep Carlo from the slow decline that followed. Then, one morning he found Carlo curled up over the spot where they'd buried Nelson. Carlo was dead.

He had cried himself to sleep each night for over a week. When his grandfather died, he'd not grieved nearly so much, and it made him feel guilty that he should have mourned a pair of dogs more than his own grandfather. Except for his mother, he'd perhaps loved his grandfather more than any of the others, for he had never tried to force him to do what was against his nature – like hunting and trapping. Hunting he'd learned to abhor, and trapping was even worse. The traps rarely killed, but only wounded and held their prey—the killing came later.

Fishing was somehow different. It was a peaceful pastime. Granddad had often taken him out on the pond in their makeshift boat. They'd row out towards the middle and sit in the quiet of the day and watch the hours go by, hardly speaking a word so as not to scare the fish. He realized now, what he did not then, that the old man loved the solitude of the open water. and it was this and not the fish they caught, that really mattered. Albert had been a good companion, for he sat quietly and did not fidget or chatter. But Granddad was gone, so now he fished alone; the others felt it a waste of time.

Other thoughts crowded Albert's mind, but each turned sour as milk left spilled in the sun on a hot summer's day. Work was the only answer, and he set about milking with a ferocity totally out of keeping with the task.

<hr />

Ella got up her usual time and stopped by Albert's room to arouse him but the door stood open, he wasn't there. Had he gotten up and gone to the barn already? She stepped out the back door and looked toward the barn until she saw a movement of light, which told her that he was probably washing down the cow's udders. She wanted to speak to the boy alone, but that would wait until after the others had left. Returning to the kitchen, she started to prepare early breakfast, for Dick and Ann would soon be down. She guessed that they would be well on their way by the time Richard and Catherine got up. What happened yesterday was unfortunate, and she'd never seen Albert act the way he did. He was belligerent, which was unlike him. She knew there was more here than met the eye. Her foot struck a folded piece of paper that skidded across the floor and under the stove. It was a sonnet, written in Albert's hand. She sat down at the table and started to read:

> "I dream of times in days now passed
> When all the world was brightly cast,
> When o'er the fields the sun did shine
> In radiant beams almost divine.

> "But now the fields are drab and gray
> Although the sun shines all the day,
> It seems as if the gloom of night
> Has penetrated noon day's light.

"The birds have ceased to sing the honeyed note
The pond no longer laughs about the boat,
The wind has ceased to whisper midst the pines
Now that you are gone, disenchantment's mine.

"Your fire-tipped hair has given up its sun
Your sea-dipped eyes, no longer bright and gay;
That foam white face is overcast with gray
Now that love has lost - bitter hate has won."

There was a familiar footstep on the stairs, and she quickly folded the paper and put it in her apron pocket. A moment later, Dick entered, dressed for his trip into town.

"You'd better awaken Ann. I'd like to get an early start," exclaimed Dick.

Ella did as her husband bid her, but her mind was pondering about Albert; yesterday's events, and now the paper she held in her pocket. The early breakfast was soon over and some time later she heard the rumble of the wagon wheels going out the drive. It was good they'd gotten off without further incident, for if Albert had come in, there could have been a reopening of discussions best left alone. The boy probably was purposely staying at the barn this morning.

The sun was well up above the horizon before Richard and Catherine came downstairs. Ella had their breakfast ready for them when they entered. Catherine offered to help, but Ella refused assistance.

"This is your time to be a lady of leisure," she said "God only knows, as you do yourself, that it won't last long. You might as well enjoy it while you can."

Catherine smiled. She knew. She had not been raised on a farm for nothing.

Ella set out a third plate and joined them at the table. She had not eaten with the others, preferring to eat with her new daughter-in-law.

"Ma, I think you ought to have a talk with Albert," started Richard. "I believe I had a right to be mad at him last night, for what he did. I can't understand why Pa wasn't harder on him. If I'd done something like that, I'd have gotten thrashed. Pa never laid a hand on him."

"I intend to talk to Albert this morning after you've gone," replied Ella. She wished to change the subject and was sure Catherine did also. She looked closely at the girl and addressed her, ignoring her son.

"I know I have said this before, Catherine, but I do hope you will be happy living here with us. I welcome you with all the affection I could ever possibly show my own flesh and blood. It looks as though we will lose Ann to your brother. I will not begrudge the Vandenbergs that loss, because I have you."

Catherine looked into the soft brown eyes of the older woman, extended her hand, and Ella clasped it between her own.

"If I can help you in any way," Ella continued, "please don't hesitate to come to me."

"I will," replied Catherine, her smooth young features beamed in sharp contrast to the scarred worn face across the table.

"We must be going if we're to catch the mid-morning train," broke in Richard.

It was but a few minutes after Ella heard the carriage go out the drive that she heard a step on the porch and the door hinges creak. Albert had come in from the barn. She smiled at him when he sat down, but quickly busied herself at the stove with her back to him. What she had to say she preferred to do this way.

"I'm glad we're alone," she started. "There are some problems on my mind that have been bothering me. Perhaps you can help."

"I'll be glad to, if I can. You know that."

"It's hard for me to say, but you've not been yourself lately."

"You mean about what I did yesterday? Gee, Ma! I've gone over all that with Pa."

"That's only part of it," Ella turned and looked squarely at her son. "Are you in love with Catherine?"

Albert's face dropped, his hands suddenly trembled.

"What makes you say that, Ma?"

"I know you, son. Better than anyone else in this world. You are more my blood than any of the others."

"I—I didn't realize it showed. I thought I'd kept it from everyone — even you."

"I've suspected it for some time," her voice remaining calm. "After yesterday and this morning, I was sure."

"This morning? I've been out in the barn all morning. How could—"

"I found this here on the floor. This removed my last doubts." Ella took the paper from her pocket and unfolded it on the table.

"Last night's poem!" Albert gasped and, in reflex, grabbed at his overall where it had been.

"Their marriage must have hurt you very much."

"I love her, Ma!" Albert fought to hold back the tears.

"But you're only sixteen. This is the time you should only 'start' noticing girls, going out with them and having a good time. Love doesn't come until later—after you've met the right one."

"I've already met the right one," he sobbed stubbornly.

"You just think that now. Catherine is five years older than you are. That makes a lot of difference when you're so young."

"Not to me, it doesn't. I've loved her for as long as I can remember."

"Does Catherine know? Have you told her?"

"No! I'm sure she doesn't."

"You've got to pull yourself away from this idea. It's going to be very difficult. Catherine will be living in this house. You'll see her every day."

"I know, I know." He held his head in his hands. "Don't think I haven't thought about that. Too many times." Then abruptly, "Do you think anyone else suspects?"

"No, I doubt it, but I've watched your eyes follow her. I can't help but think she is aware."

"Oh God! why did she have to marry Richard. Why couldn't she have wailed for me?"

"Now, now." Ella affectionately put her hand on his shoulder. "She's in love with Richard. She married him. It's no use talking that way."

Albert groaned. There was a long silence. "What do I do, Ma! Tell me. What do I do!"

"There's no easy answer, son. Perhaps we haven't let you go out enough and meet people your own age. Maybe if you met some nice girls at church."

"That wouldn't help."

"You've got to try. I know you're upset but you're going to have to control yourself, especially when Catherine is around. This could be very dangerous. You could get hurt badly - and Catherine, too. Don't destroy her marriage."

Albert pushed the food away. He wasn't hungry. He wanted to go back to the barn and be alone, but his mother wouldn't let him until she was satisfied they'd finished.

"I want you to promise me that you'll be very careful when near Catherine. I have faith in you. Don't give me cause to question that faith."

"I'll try, Mom, I'll try." Albert brought his sleeve up and wiped it across his face. "I'm going back to the barn before the others get up." He slowly walked out the door and back toward the barn. His mother's eyes followed him. They were tired, troubled eyes.

chapter

7

The newlyweds were gone for three days. No one knew for sure where they'd gone, and although most of the family assumed it was New York City, Sarah guessed it was Philadelphia. Philadelphia was farther away, but had advantages: Dick's sister Beatrice and her family were there and it was possible, in spite of the crowded conditions, they could stay there overnight and thus save on hotel expenses. As things turned out, Sarah was right.

There was considerable tension in the DeGraf household when Richard and Catherine returned. A brotherly disharmony which had smoldered for years, suddenly burst into flame on the evening after the wedding. Dick was determined that his sons would get along without open warfare, so he bore down heavily on both.

Dick planned a large vegetable planting so there would be plenty of work for everyone, including Catherine, since she was now a member of the family. Several of Beatrice's children would be making the trip from Philadelphia as soon as school was out, and Dick did not believe in having them idle. This had become an annual summer pilgrimage for from four to six of Beatrice's flock. They would arrive in worn, tattered clothes, but each Fall before they returned home, Ella would see that all were well supplied with clothing for another year. Keeping such a large family properly dressed was a problem for Beatrice, especially since her husband did not make much money.

The previous spring, Dick had taken Richard's suggestion that they plant an area near the house to strawberries. Most of the family had thought it ridiculous to take a two-year risk on such a perishable crop. It was bad enough to have a failure in those precarious months after a planting . . . but strawberries! If they did well the first season, the blossoms could easily be frozen out during the second. Then, what about the market? They had never sold fruit before, only vegetables. Richard felt they would have a high cash value, which meant a lot to Dick. He was still looking for that highly prized, but still elusive crop which would give them a big return. Perhaps strawberries were what he'd been looking for all these years. At least they would soon know, for the plants had done well and now had a heavy set of blossoms. Barring a late freeze, they would begin harvesting in another month.

When time would allow, Albert went for long rides on horseback. Sometimes he would ride alone and at other times with Neal. Dick had no objection to the boy taking the brown mare; it helped keep her in condition. He was a horse lover himself, but rarely had time to indulge in the pleasure. Perhaps this again was a sign of his turning away from his old hard ways. What he didn't know, was Albert's frequent rides with Neal.

One evening when they were alone, Ella approached Dick about Albert. She pointed out that the boy was growing older without the social life he deserved. She thought that Albert should join the church choir now that his voice was no longer changing. Also, he should be allowed to go to other social functions, even if it meant excusing him from some of his chores. Dick agreed that if the boy wanted to go to choir, that was up to him. As far as other social affairs, he saw no need for overdoing in that direction. Certainly, the Reverend had pointed out the evils of that life many times. Thus, it was decided that Albert would join choir, more at his mother's insistence than any desire of his own. Choir practice was on Thursday nights. Both Ann and Catherine belonged, so there would be three DeGrafs up front behind the minister on Sunday mornings.

Each year, the DeGrafs raised a few hogs for home and market use. In the spring, the sows would have their litters. One of the sows had rolled over on her young and crushed them. She was a bad mother, would be slaughtered, and replaced for the next breeding season. Ordinarily, Dick would have done the butchering much earlier, but with the wedding this job had been postponed.

Hog butchering was a family affair. It was hard, dirty work and it took all hands. This was a job Albert found particularly offensive. He had a strong aversion to the killing of animals, no matter what their kind. When younger, he had been excused from the actual slaughtering part but now that he was approaching manhood, Dick could excuse him no longer.

A crude board frame for holding the hog during the sticking was hauled out into the yard. Next, there was a large iron barrel for scalding, and stout oak tables for butchering. The women and little Govert would do the cutting and curing of the meat.

"Let Al stick the sow, Pa," Richard suggested with a grin. "He might just as well get right into the business end of it."

"Please, Pa, No! I'll help hold her, but don't ask me to kill it."

"You've got to learn sometime, Albert." Dick handed him the long pointed blade.

Dick and Richard put the sow in the holding pen, then got on opposite sides and brought the head up high to expose the underside of the throat. Dick pointed to the proper place for the knife thrust, but Albert stood motionless.

"I can't, Pa. Please!"

"Of all the lily livered—" Richard broke out in disgust.

"Never mind! If the boy can't, he can't." Dick growled, and grabbed

70

the knife out of his son's hand. "Here, you help hold the beast then."

Dick sought out the jugular vein with his fingers and plunged the long knife into the sow's throat; there was a huge squirt of blood as he hit the vein he'd sought. The animal gave an ear shattering squeal and lunged forward. They held on a few moments and then the sow broke loose running and squealing across the yard spurting blood as she went. She staggered some twenty yards, reeled and fell, gave several kicks and then lay still. Now the scalding and scraping began.

The three men gutted and quartered her and set the sections for the women to take over. Ella looked at Albert as he swung a hind quarter onto the table. Albert's face was ashen, yet beads of sweat stood out on his forehead.

"You feel all right?" she asked quietly across the table.

He nodded affirmatively but saw Catherine's searching look.

Did his face really betray his feelings about this business that clearly? Then, without warning, as Albert began to cut into the hind quarter, he retched from the bottom of his stomach and spewed his breakfast over the table and its contents.

"My little brother hasn't grown up much, has he? He sees a little blood and he upchucks," roared Richard with laughter.

Albert charged at his brother. There was still some fight in him, but his experiences had taken its toll. Richard easily stepped aside as Albert's fist grazed past the side of his face; Albert lost his balance and stumbled. Dick grabbed the boy and held him firmly.

"Now Albert, don't let Richard rile you. I know you have no liking for this business, but these things have to be done. You'd better go wash up. Ella, how about starting coffee? We'll be along shortly."

———◆◆◆◆———

The slaughtering of the hog acted like salt in the festering sore of relations between the brothers. In the weeks that followed, few words were spoken between them, and any time Richard caught his brother's eye and he was sure their parents weren't looking, he would grab for his stomach and pull a face as though he was vomiting.

Albert took to horseback riding regularly, but now it was always alone. Frequently, he would be home barely in time for supper. After the evening milking, he would leave for the pond and fish or go to his room. Either way, he shunned contact with everyone. The lamp in his room burned until the late hours; he was back to his writing. This is what sustained him now.

Ella tried desperately to bring the boy out of his abjection, but he would not respond to anything she could say. She wondered how long he could stand the double conflict that she knew was going on within him. Perhaps if he got away from the farm, away from Richard—and Catherine.

"I believe Albert needs to get away from the farm," Ella approached Dick that evening as they prepared for bed. Dick glanced across at her with a questioning look, but let her go on. "This situation between our sons is going from bad to worse. I fear for what will happen! The whole family is being torn by their feuding. I think I should write Beatrice. Four of her children will be coming with us for the summer. Why couldn't Albert go to Philadelphia and stay with her?"

"What would he do there?" questioned Dick. "Unless he got a job!"

"Why not? Perhaps Gordon or Beatrice could get work for him. He could pay them board, though goodness knows we've never taken a cent for having their children here."

"I would miss Albert," replied Dick. "He's a very good milker. He's faster and more thorough than anyone I've seen hereabouts. Yet, I agree, something must be done. The boy is not himself lately." Dick paused and thought. "I will sleep on it. We will talk about this again in the morning." Dick reached over, turned down the lamp, and got into bed.

——◆✦✦◆——

The next morning Richard, Albert, and Gin went to bring in the cows from pasture for milking. Dick told them he would be along later. He wanted to talk with Ella about their previous night's discussion, for the more he thought about it, the more sense it seemed to make.

The ground was still wet, and as the brothers entered the lower pasture,

72

the sod squished underfoot. Mist was spilling out of the swamp into the pasture like foam from a boiling pot of porridge, obscuring everything to waist level. They could see the backs of the cows, but legs and lower bodies were enswarthed in whiteness. They walked in three medias— squishing ground, white foam, and damp sticky air. Gin bounded ahead, could be heard but seen only occasionally through the rolling milky froth. The barking took on a tone of urgency and Albert scrambled forward to investigate. A large section of the fence bordering the swamp was down.

"The cows have gotten into the swamp." he yelled to Richard.

"Then we'll go in after them!"

"Shouldn't we get Pa first?"

"We've got tits to pull when we're through here. What's the matter? You scared?" Striding to the fence line, Richard grabbed one of the long poles standing there, before Albert could answer.

"No – but they'll come .. " Albert hesitated, then followed Richard's movement and soon they were both in the swamp carrying the poles horizontally before them as taught by their father. The black muck sucked at the bottom of their boots every step of the way. Cautiously, they made their separate ways among the bogs testing each step for firmness. What was foolishness to the younger, was one-up-man's-ship to the older: bravery sometimes needs an audience even if that audience is not respected. Three dark shadows moved slightly ahead of Richard, and he circled behind them to head them toward the fence opening. Gin had accompanied Albert in going still further into the swamp. He would not be outdone by Richard and Richard not by him; each was allowing disdain for the other to exceed judgment and sanity.

Richard gave a yell at the cows and two took off toward the barn, but the third bolted straight toward him. He made a frantic swing with the pole to stop her, but wet with dew, it flew from his hands and hit the cow on the rump. The cow bellowed and stampeded in the slime and muck as Richard cursed loudly.

The safety of the pole was gone, and realizing his predicament, Richard remained still while he surveyed his situation. He must retrieve that pole. Peering intently, he thought he saw the end of it, then the mist obscured it again. Albert was somewhere behind him working cows back toward the fence. Richard was about to call for help, but stubbornness overcame fear. Damned if he'd ask for assistance. Cautiously, he edged his way forward making sure that one foot was solid beneath him before putting his weight on the other. He waited again for the mist to shift and then saw it less than twelve feet before him. The ground ahead looked good. What had he been so concerned about? He took another few steps—then, his feet abruptly sank out beneath him. Instinctively, in spite of what his father had told him, he struggled to get one foot loose and then the other. His churning brought him down past his knees and half way to his crotch.

"Help! Al! Help! I'm stuck!" screamed Richard. Now, in desperation, he struggled harder.

Richard was not in sight when Albert heard the scream. He knew what had happened. Quicksand!

"Go get Pa! Gin! Go get Pa!" Gin was off toward the house as fast as her old legs could carry her through the muck and slime.

"For God's sake! Help! Al! Help!" Richard's voice reached a pitch of hysteria.

Albert clambered over bogs in the direction of the voice, without caution of testing the ground before him. He scrambled and slipped and scrambled again until finally he came up to his brother. Richard's eyes were wide with terror. There were long narrow trenches in the goo where his fingers had scraped at the sides of the hole he'd sunk into past his waist. Albert felt his way toward the edge of the quicksand hole; if he lost his footing, both would be lost.

"Don't struggle so much. You're making it worse for yourself!" he commanded. Richard only clutched at his brother. With his open hand, Albert slapped him across his face; the hands let go. He placed his pole down along the edge of the sink hole, knelt down upon it, and grabbed Richard under the armpits and pulled. With all his strength he pulled, but he only stopped Richard's downward movement. He must get greater support.

"Your pole! Where's your pole!" he shouted in Richard's ear. Richard's eyes rolled to the opposite side of the hole. Albert had to get it, but how far did this quicksand extend? He could not take his own pole with him, for Richard clung to it for his very life. He would have to chance it. He skirted what he thought was the boundary, and was back again.

In spite of Richard's violent protests, he pushed his own pole further across the hole. Then took Richard's pole and placed it across his own, forming a large cross with Richard to the side of their intersection. Bracing his knees on the two poles, he again grabbed Richard by the arms and pulled. The air was cool and damp, but as he pulled, beads of sweat rose out on his face. He closed his eyes and pulled harder, until he thought his arms would jerk from their sockets. Gradually, Richard's body moved upwards, inch by inch.

"Grab both hands along a pole and pull when I do," Albert shouted. "As I edge you up, bend yourself flat." When Richard's waist cleared the sucking black slime, Albert reached over his back and clamped down on the belt. Finally, the seat of his pants cleared and then the upper part of his legs. Changing his position, he helped pull his brother over the intersection of the cross until at last the two lay in the muck at the side of the pit, exhausted and panting without knowing or caring for how long. The fight was over and they had won against the swamp.

Dick stepped off the porch steps as old Gin came running and barking. He reached down to give the dog her usual pat on the head, but she continued to dance and bark, telling him something was wrong. Dick realized this when she took off in the direction of the lower pasture, and Dick followed. As they neared the broken fence, he heard noises from beyond. The mist still hung heavy but he could see cows, in both the pasture and the swamp. There were no signs of his sons.

"Richard! Albert! Where are you?" Dick called, cupping his hands around his mouth.

"Out here in the swamp, Pa," came the answer. It was Albert's voice.

"Where's Richard?"

"Here beside me."

"Why doesn't he answer?"

"He's exhausted—but he's all right."

"Thank God you're both safe." Dick grabbed a long pole from beside the fence as his sons had done earlier.

"Be careful, Pa! There's quicksand out here."

"I know, I know!" Dick could walk the swamps better than anyone else. He knew what he was doing and soon was standing beside his two sons. Albert was up on his knees. Richard lay on his back, raised up on his elbows, staring blankly at the spot where he had almost been swallowed up.

"Anyone hurt?"

"No, but pretty well scared," Albert replied.

Dick looked down at them; his eyes flashed from one to the other and saw where the slime stained their clothing. He knew what had happened without asking.

"Why in heaven's name did you come in here in the first place? The cows would've made their way back for milking in due time."

"Yeah, Pa. I tried to tell . . ." Albert stopped, shrugged his shoulders. "I guess we just got excited."

"Stupid!. You took an awful risk for nothing," admonished Dick. "Can you both make it back?" They nodded. "Then let's get out of here."

Dick took the lead, and the boys followed in his footsteps. The sun had barely cleared the Eastern ridge across the valley.

———◆◆◆◆———

Clean clothes, strong hot coffee, and a rest sitting beside the kitchen table, did much to revive the brothers. The story was told of the happenings in the swamp and for the first time in a long while Richard and Albert agreed on the details of an event with neither trying to undercut the other. Richard was quiet spoken and sober after his close brush with death. Ella looked from one son to the other and a new hope rose in her heart; perhaps now there would once again be peace and harmony in the house. But then—there was the other matter—and her eyes moved toward Catherine. Would this situation also resolve itself in time?

Meanwhile, the cows had not been milked, and such tardiness was normally unheard of on the DeGraf farm. When Dick and his sons finally went out to the barn, the cows were all bunched up by the gate waiting to get in the barn and feeling very irritable. Their udders were full to the point of discomfort and their mournful bellows let everyone within earshot know of their plight. As Dick had predicted, there were no longer any cows in the pasture, let alone the swamp.

Everyone helped with the milking except Ella, who stayed inside with Clara and Sarah. They took extra wash cloths, for the cows needed a good going over after their wanderings in the swamp. Albert had finished his third cow and was about to move to the next, but as he began to raise himself, he suddenly fell back. A shot of pain went through his back, and he found he couldn't move. He tried again, but it was no use.

"What's the matter, Al?" Catherine asked, coming over from the next cow.

"I can't get up from the stool. Something's wrong with my back."

"We'd better get you up to the house. You've probably pulled a muscle."

It looked like the morning's milking was never going to get done. Dick and Richard helped Albert to his feet.

"Can you make it to the house, son?"

"I think so." But it was obvious he needed help, so leaning on Dick and Richard, they made their way on up to the house, with Catherine opening doors before them.

"What now?" Ella asked, as if the day's events had not alredy been sufficient.

"Albert must have hurt his back in the swamp," explained Catherine. "We'd better get him to his room. He needs to lie down." Ella followed them upstairs where Dick and Richard stretched him out on his bed and then returned to the barn.

The women carefully removed his shirt and had him lay on his stomach. Catherine felt over his back and asked where it hurt; she had learned doctoring from her mother.

"I can't feel any vertebrae out of place. I'm sure he's pulled a muscle. That's going to be painful for awhile. I think Mom Vandenberg better have a look at him. She'll know whether we should get the doctor. In the meantime, he needs to get undressed and stay in bed."

"I'll get him undressed!" exclaimed Ella. "You get back to the barn." The tone of her voice left Catherine little choice but to leave.

"That was a brave thing you did this morning," Ella said affectionately, when they were alone.

"Thanks, Ma! It wasn't easy!"

"I realize that, but you couldn't have done otherwise."

"I'm not so sure. When I first heard him scream, I hesitated. For a fraction of a minute, I hesitated. Then, I was all right." A long pause. "I wonder if he'd have done the same for me!"

"I'm sure he would have," Ella replied, but her voice lacked conviction. "I think it best you get some rest and don't move any more than you have to until Mrs. Vandenberg has had a chance to look at you. I'm driving over to fetch her shortly." Ella softly closed the door behind her as she left.

Albert lay back and gazed at the ceiling. As long as he lay perfectly still, his back did not bother him but to move even slightly - - that was something else. He thought about his mother. She must think that now everything would be patched up between Richard and himself. He wasn't so sure. He'd saved his brother from almost certain death, but that didn't change his attitude. He'd done it almost by reflex and would have done the same for any living thing, a dog, a cow, or whatever. It was as simple as that - or was it? He thought back over things as they'd happened how he'd been unsuccessful in getting Richard out until he'd gotten the second pole, and made a huge cross of them over the sink hole. The act had been a logical one for greater support—but the cross? Was there any significance to this? Was God trying to tell him something? Had this been a divine test, imposed on him. Of late, his hatred for his brother had all but consumed him. He'd actually wished him dead. A perfect candidate for a Cain and Abel episode. Instead, he had saved his brother's life—he'd been his brother's keeper.

How close he had come to play the role of Cain. A shiver ran down his back, and he winced momentarily in pain. What of the cross? Was Richard to be his cross? His tormentor? Even after he'd saved his life? No, even Richard must now accept him for what he was without continually trying to cut him down. To be accepted for what he was, that was all he asked. But what was he? Was he really any better than Richard, whom he chastised for his sins— his brutishness, his hypocrisy? What about his own sins? His violation of the tenth commandment. *"Thou shalt not covet thy neighbor's wife. . . brother's wife."* Certainly, he had sinned there— and would continue to sin.

Ella brought Grace in to examine Albert. Her diagnosis was the same as Catherine's; her recommendation, a good liniment rub twice a day and bed rest for several days. Ella invited Grace to stay for lunch, but she had to return home; with Catherine gone, who else was there to fix the meals? She hoped Ann would soon be joining her household.

During lunch, Richard expressed concern about Albert's back. The full impact of how close he'd come to death in the swamp, flooded over him that morning while milking. Albert had proved himself a man. He would now treat him accordingly. It had been decided in the barn that Catherine would nurse Albert back to health. Her mother had taught her about such matters, so it was only natural. Ella protested. She was quite capable of taking care of him herself. When even Dick insisted otherwise, Ella was forced to relinquish to their wishes. She did not dare press the point.

"You're going to be my patient," Catherine beamed, as she brought Albert a tray with his lunch. "I hope you are sick enough to need it, but well enough to appreciate it." She was teasing him as she often did, and he enjoyed it.'

"Oh, I'll be up in a day or so," he flushed, looking up at her.

"I hope not too soon. It's been a long time since I've had a chance to baby anyone— and I've never had the chance with you. As soon as you finish your lunch, I'll rub your back. I hope you're going to be a good patient and mind." She placed a small finger to the end of his nose, and he flinched.

"I'll be as good as gold." He ate his food while she sat on the edge of the bed watching him.

"I don't know about that. At one time I'd have believed you, but now, I'm not so sure."

"What do you mean? I'll do anything you say."

"Well, you weren't very nice the day of the wedding." Now she looked at him quite seriously. "I thought you liked me."

"I do!" The words spilled out by reflex.

"Then why did you mess things up? Or was it Neal?"

'Don't blame Neal, but I didn't do it to hurt you. I never intended that. It's just— oh, I don't know! I guess I was just mixed up. I was angry at Richard."

"You two've been angry at each other a lot. Especially lately, or is it that I notice it more now that I live here?"

"Oh, we've always had our differences."

"Well, I hope that's all over now. You saved Richard's life this morning.

I know he's grateful. You can't really dislike him, after what you've done."

"No, I guess not."

"I do wish you two would be friends." Catherine was pleading now. "It has hurt me deeply to see the way you've tried to tear each other apart this last while. You both mean so much to me, I'm torn in the middle."

"I— I hadn't realized," he stammered. "I never meant to hurt you!"

"If you mean that, then promise you'll make up with him. He is your brother." Catherine laid her hand on his arm, and he felt her soft touch all through his body.

"I'll try, I promise," he replied

"Now, finish your lunch."

Albert finished as directed, and Catherine moved the tray to the top of the bureau. "Take off your gown and roll over on your stomach." Albert flushed; he had nothing on under his nightshirt. Catherine saw the redness come to his face.

"Oh, now," she soothed, amused at his bashfulness. "I won't impose on your modesty. You have the sheet to cover you. I just want to get at your back." Cautiously he tried to slip the nightshirt over his head, but couldn't, so she helped him. "Your back really pains you, doesn't it?"

"Yeah, a little."

"Now ease over on your stomach." She took the liniment and gently started to rub it in. "Tell me when I touch a particularly sore area." Her hands moved rhythmically along the shoulder blades and down to the small of his back. Albert closed his eyes and every nerve felt her hands, and with them came a feeling of indescribable warmth and pleasure. *Was this what love really felt like*, he wondered. It didn't occur to him that the liniment was going to work on his aching muscles. Catherine continued with steady soothing motions, and a gentleness far greater than she'd learned from her mother. Finally, she said that would be enough for now. She would do it again that night. Almost abruptly she left.

"Ask Ma if Gin can come up to keep me company," Albert asked as Catherine started out the door. She looked back at him, smiled, and nodded that she would.

A few moments later, Albert heard the pat of dog's feet as Gin came up the stairs accompanied by other footsteps; Ella entered with the dog.

"How are you feeling?" Ella asked and came over and kissed him on the cheek.

"Oh, I think I'll make it. It's not really that much to make such a fuss over."

"We want you to be better soon. I hope Catherine is taking good care of you." Ella gave her son a questioning look. *Catherine had been upstairs for quite awhile,* she thought.

"Oh, the best, Mom," returned Albert with a grin.

"Not too good, I hope," a tone of caution in her voice. "Be careful."

"I'll be careful," with exaggerated confidence.

"Get some rest, you deserve it." Ella turned and left.

Albert reached his hand over the side of the bed and patted Gin on the head and tickled her ears. There was a thumping of tail against the side of the bed. What a mess he was getting himself into. Just before he'd promised Catherine that he'd try to get along with Richard. He hadn't realized that by striking out at his brother, he was also striking her. How could he now react to Richard the way his instincts told him to. But that was not the worst of it. There was his promise to his mother about Catherine. She had reminded him of that promise just now . . .be careful.

chapter

8

That evening, Albert was writing in bed when his mother brought his supper to him. Peter had stopped by after lunch and taken Ann home to help Mrs. Vandenberg and to spend the night. Catherine was needed in the barn. His mother sat at the edge of the bed while he ate, exactly as Catherine had done, but it wasn't the same.

"I spoke to your father yesterday, about your going to Aunt Beatrice this summer." Albert paused in his eating, looked at her questioningly, but didn't say anything. "This was, of course, before what happened in the swamp. We all hope that things are now changed for the better between you and Richard. Still, there is the other matter. It's best you go away for awhile. I'll miss you, but it's for your own good."

"Why, Mom? Don't you trust me?"

"Of course! But it must be very hard on you. Living in the same house with her. I've watched the effect it's had on you, and it's not good. We all have our breaking point. I don't want to see you hurt." Ella looked down in her lap, because she didn't want to see the wounded expression in his eyes.

"When will I leave?"

"If your father still agrees, in two weeks. When Beatrice's children are due."

". . . and when will I come back?"

"In the Fall, perhaps. But then again, I've tried to talk your father into letting you go to school there. You have your future to look to. You've gone about as far here as our schools, and I, can teach you."

"Richard never went beyond eighth grade."

"Richard will take over the farm some day. That is his right as the eldest son. He doesn't need more education. You will have to find your own place in the world."

"Pa needs me here."

"Your father can do without you. When you and Richard were small he did it all himself. Now that Richard is older, they'll manage. You have a talent that none of the others have. I don't want to see you waste it."

"What talent?"

"You have a keen mind, and there's your writing, of course. I know you spend many hours at it, sometimes long after the rest of us have gone to bed. I've seen examples of your poetry."

"Poem you mean." Albert drew himself back as though his mother had violated his personal property. "You haven't . . . "

"No. I've tried not to pry." Ella smiled and put a hand on his arm. "I clean your room and you've been careless at times. You've left papers out you've probably meant to hide. I have a deep concern for you, and it's that concern, not prying, that has made me read what you've left open."

"Then you've seen other poems of mine. . . .and other writings?"

"Yes. They show a talent that needs to be developed. School in Philadelphia will do that for you. You were writing when I came in before. Was it another poem?"

Albert nodded.

"May I borrow it?"

"What will you do with it? You wouldn't . . ."

"Of course I won't show it to Catherine, or anyone else. I'd just like to have it awhile. I'll return it."

"Take it." He dug beneath the books on the bed stand and gave it to her. Ella put the paper in her apron pocket. She would read it when she was by herself; she loved her son and also what he did.

"I'd better go back down now. Shall I take Gin with me?" The dog was curled up fast asleep at the foot of the bed. Albert nodded.

"Come on, Gin. Time to go." The old dog raised her head at her name and then followed Ella downstairs.

His mother had dropped a bombshell in his lap. She wanted him to go to Philadelphia. He liked the idea of going to school there, but leave here? Leave Catherine?

------◆◆⦂◆●------

"I thought you might be asleep," Catherine said, when she came in around nine. "I don't want to disturb you, but if your back is to get well, we'd better have another go at it."

"I slept earlier."

"Did this morning's treatment do any good?"

"It felt much better afterwards. Real warm and cozy."

"Good! That's the way it's supposed to feel." She helped him remove his nightshirt; he turned on his stomach as he'd done earlier, and again her soothing hands did their work. It was a pleasant feeling, and he wouldn't care if she continued all night, but entirely too soon she was finished. "This time I'm going to give you a special treatment. This is only for good patients, and you've been very good today."

"What's that?"

"An alcohol-ointment rub. It will make you feel clean and refreshed. You'll sleep better tonight for it. Move over on your back. This is for your chest and arms."

Albert did as he was ordered. Now he looked up into her face as she bent over him and began to rub the alcohol on his arms. At first, it was a cold sensation, but it became a warming one as she rubbed the ointment in. The vigorous movement of her arm gave a certain sway to her upper body, and he tried not to make his gaze too obvious. She was looking down at him with a delightful smile; a relaxed pleasant smile, that seemed to say she was thoroughly enjoying her work. Her bosom rocked gently to and fro, and he could see down the neckline of her dress—a long way down. Apparently, she was not aware of how much she exposed herself, for he could clearly see the cleft between her breasts and half a sphere on either side to where the nipples were. The rest lay hidden. As her hands moved across the expanse of his chest, she paused and a quizzical smile made the edges of her mouth turn up.

"What's the matter?" he said.

"Oh nothing. I was just thinking how different you and Richard are. One would hardly guess you're brothers."

"How's that?"

"You're different in so many ways. In temperament, in voice, and manner—and now I see, in body."

"In body?" Albert blushed.

"Yes, Richard is large and muscular, and has a massive crop of dark curly hair upon his chest and arms while you have little. Only a light blondish fuzz covers here." Catherine drew her hands over his chest.

"It will grow in time." he said defensively.

"No, it will never be like Richard's. Why should it be? You are Albert. Even your skin is not the same."

"What's the matter with my skin?" slightly annoyed now.

"Don't misunderstand me. It's just that your skin is like ..."

"A girl's!" Albert said it himself before she could.

"Oh don't take offense. I like you as you are. All men need not be hairy, just as all women are not the same. We women hide a lot with our clothes, you know."

Albert wasn't so sure of that just now. Catherine was leaning over him even further than before. He wondered that she didn't realize just how much of her he could see. He had never seen so much before. He turned a bit to the side so she wouldn't guess, but the focus of his eyes remained down the full length and breadth of her bosom. Perhaps it was wrong of him to see her as he did, but nothing could make him look away. This was a beautiful part of Catherine he'd only guessed at before. She moved, and his mind came back to their conversation.

"You make me sound like a sissy—effeminate." He turned his face away.

"Please don't. That's not what I meant at all. You're just as much a man as your brother, though younger, we must admit. It's only that I was struck by these differences. You are but of a gentler type."

"I thought you meant . . ."

"Dear boy," her hand moved across his brow pushing the blond hair back toward the pillow. "I love you just the way you are; don't try to change. But, I must go now or the others will begin to wonder."

Catherine bent across the bed and kissed him on the forehead. Her bosom momentarily pressed in against his chest. It was soft as he knew it would be. He half raised his arm as though to bring her closer, but it fell back to his side. As she rose to go, her hand moved to his and gave it a slight squeeze. Then she was gone. Only after she'd left did he realize the stiffening in his groin. God, he hoped she hadn't noticed that beneath the sheets.

＊＊＊

As usual, Ella was the first to come downstairs the next morning. She had thought more about her talk with Albert and was surprised he hadn't objected more strongly to her suggestion. Perhaps his attachment to Catherine could be broken with no serious consequences. If he were once away, he would learn to forget her, especially if he met some girls his own age. In Philadelphia there would be plenty of chance for that. When she wrote Beatrice about Albert's coming, she would mention his need for a more social life, and she knew Beatrice would steer him in the right direction.

The big question was whether Dick would still agree to Albert's going. Now that the brothers' feud seemed over, Dick would probably see no need for it. Albert had not been obvious in his actions, thank God. She had observed the others closely. It would seem to her that only she was aware of Albert's secret. But Catherine herself, she was the focal point of all that welled up emotion. Certainly, Catherine was not so dense, that she didn't perceive the feelings Albert tried so hard to hide.

Ella poured herself a cup of coffee and sat down at the table; it would be awhile before Dick came down. She glanced at the coffee and smiled to herself, for it struck her that coffee was the DeGraf's strongest vice. In some families the father was a drunkard, a gambler, or ran around with other women; liquor and sex were vices that could break a family apart.

Here the vice was coffee. The coffee pot was always on the stove, and Dick drank ten to twelve cups a day. No matter what the occasion, at mealtimes, after milking, or just sitting down for a little chat, there was something about this bulky round table and a cup of steaming hot coffee that set many things right again. Now, Ella was again partaking in that custom as she unfolded the paper in her pocket and began to read the poem Albert had written.

"I wandered through the cottonwoods
And o'er the fields of grain,
I peered into a stream's great heart,
But all was yet in vain.

I looked upon the wildlife
That in the woodland dwell,
A buck and doe stood watching me,
But all seemed not too well.

For I was feeling sad at heart
And did not look around,
To see the turtle at my feet,
Or feel the soft moss down.

Across my path a shadow flew
And then a whippoorwill,
But I seem'd not to hear its call,
For everything was still.

At last I sat upon a bank
Beside a flowing stream,
Yet everything seemed dull to me,
And nothing like I'd dreamed.

Then suddenly 'twas bright again
And I could hear and view,
I felt a hand upon my cheek,
I knew that it was you.

Now nature took her mask away
And to me did atone,
By showing all the wondrous things,
That I saw not—alone."

It was a good poem, she thought, *not filled with bitterness as the other had been.* He'd written this yesterday while convalescing and no doubt the hand upon his cheek was Catherine's. The boy had talent. There was a sensitivity that cried out within him. She must see that this creativity was channeled in the right direction; not wasted in hopeless longings. This love the boy bore for Catherine was sensitive she knew - like the poem. It was the blossoming of adolescence within that was searching for a lovely thing, a pure and lovely image for the eye and heart. That eye and heart now dwelt on Catherine, striving to express itself. Catherine was testing its sincerity for knowing, or unknowing, she could push those feelings beyond the brink, for after all he was almost a man, and there was a point beyond control for even him.

------◆◆◆◆------

The day after he returned from a visit to his sister in Connecticut, Dr. Brabin phoned and said he'd like to stop by to see Sarah and the family. The doctor had given up his practice, at the age of eighty-three, to the 'new' man, as he called Dr. McCormick. "New" was a relative word as used by Dr. Brabin. Dr. McCormick had been practicing in Ridgewood for fifteen years and didn't feel he was really 'new' any more.

The last year had been quite an adjustment for the old doctor, for his whole life had been taken up with his practice. There hadn't been time for much else, even the trivial matter of getting married; Dr. Brabin had been a bachelor all his life. Now there were pangs of loneliness, and perhaps a certain feeling of uselessness because his patients no longer needed him. He took to making frequent calls on the DeGraf's which at first were the result of certain small excuses—to check on Sarah's arthritis, to inspect

88

Dick's shoulder after he had strained it one time—but finally the fabrications no longer seemed plausible, so it settled down to purely social calls. Ella saw the doctor's pretense from the start and in those first months had helped provide reasons for him to stop by. She complained to him of her burns, but to no one else. These burns had so long ago healed that both she and the doctor knew the game they played.

When the doctor phoned, Ella invited him to Sunday dinner and to stay thereafter as long as he pleased. She told him of Albert's back and her concern. He could look at that during his visit. When Sarah was told the doctor was coming, her face lit up. The doctor always brought much news about goings on and now that he was returning from Connecticut, there would be even more.

Dick enjoyed kidding his mother about the doctor. He said she had gotten sweet on the old man, and grinned to see her indignant protests at even the suggestion of such a thing. After all, she would say, she was eighty-one herself and hardly had any maidenly ideas left in her. Ella would try to cool Dick's jibing for he never did have a delicacy of touch in pursuing this sort of subject. Although he meant well, his humor was blunt and, at times, even coarse.

Dr. Brabin was in good voice during the Sunday dinner. Today, he was the family's source of news for he'd just returned from New England, with a stop-over in New York City. His sister, a widow, had tried to talk him into moving in with her, but he did not think he cared for Connecticut that much. There was no one besides her there that he knew anymore; those he'd known from his youth had long since died. On the other hand, those friends he had were here in New Jersey. It was here he would stay for those remaining years he had left. Countering his sister's request, he had tried to talk her into coming back with him, but she, like him, had declined.

When dinner was over, the menfolk and Sarah left for the parlor. Ella and Catherine went about clearing the table for washing up. Ella excused herself momentarily to see Albert where he sat propped up in the parlor easy chair. Dr. Brabin was talking when she entered.

"Have you heard the news from Europe?" he asked, looking to those seated about him, but the response was negative. "I heard about it in New York Friday. Serbia claims that Austria's Count Berchtold has betrayed the peace treaty between their countries and both are now mobilizing for war. The situation does not look good. It is a powder keg that could go off at the slightest provocation."

"Ah, yes," said Dick. He glanced over and noticed Ella standing by Albert's chair listening to their conversation. She held something in her hand. "But those Eastern European countries have been squabbling off and on for years. I don't take much stock in such rumors."

"There may be more to it this time," continued the doctor. "The Austro-Hungarian Army has the backing of the Kaiser, and Russia has sworn herself as Serbia's defender. That could mean war between Germany and Russia. There was much talk about this in New York."

"That's a long ways off. I don't see why the city people make so much of it. Here, we farm our land and do not worry about what men do a half-a-world away. It would be well if the city folks tended more to their own business."

"Perhaps," Dr. Brabin replied, "but Europe is over-run with alliances. If war once starts, who knows where it might end."

Ella spoke softly to Albert so as not to disturb the others in the room. "I know your birthday's still a month away, but I bought you this gift," she said. "It seems you might have good use for it now, so I'm giving it to you ahead of time." Ella handed Albert a book. He turned it over in his hand and read the cover - *The Works of Ralph Waldo Emerson*.

"Gee, Ma, thanks!" Albert raised himself up and kissed his mother.

Dick wanted to talk business with Richard, so he asked his son to take a walk with him along the back pasture. The Sunday afternoon walks were pleasant. It gave him an opportunity to casually inspect his fences and decide on jobs that needed doing during the coming week. Also, there was the business of the family finances. Dick relied more and more on Richard to help handle the records of income and outlay. This was an area where Richard excelled and Dick always had trouble.

Dr. Brabin and Sarah went out on the front porch, where they could be alone to talk over old times. Talk of their generation would be of little interest to Albert, and they preferred their own company. Albert had his new book and so was well content with the arrangement. He settled back and had begun to read when Ella came in again wheeling Clara ahead of her.

"Do you mind if we leave Clara in here with you? It will be easier on us in the kitchen."

"No problem. She won't disturb me," Albert responded. He had a way of keeping Clara occupied with no great hindrance to himself.

Ella and Catherine busied themselves with dinner cleanup. There had been little opportunity for them to speak privately for with so many in the family there was generally someone else about. Ella wanted to talk, although she wasn't sure where she would begin, or where it would lead, but that would come as it may. She now had the chance and she would make the most of it.

"Have you found your stay with us a happy one?" Ella asked. "I realize all has not been as we would like at times. I've been much concerned about the bad feelings between Richard and Albert. We shall hope that that is over."

"Their feuding has been my only worry since I've come here," replied Catherine. "I do hope that now they'll get along."

"As their mother, I've tried not to take sides, but you, as Richard's wife, will naturally see his point of view."

"Oh, I wouldn't say that! I'd tried to talk to Richard about the way he's treated Albert, but he wouldn't listen. They've both been wrong, but perhaps Richard's more to blame."

"You do not defend your own husband, then?"

"Not in this matter. Richard is the older and should show more restraint. They've both been very childish."

"Well, I pray that now my sons may learn to live together peacefully." Then abruptly, "You know it is very possible that Albert will be going away to his aunt Beatrice as soon as his back is well again."

"Oh, I didn't know," exclaimed Catherine a little taken back by the change in Ella's voice.

"Yes, his father and I have talked it over and think it best. He has his future to look to, and schooling in Philadelphia will be good for him."

"Then he'll be away for quite some time." There was a slight catch in Catherine's voice, which Ella perceived, as she had been on the watch for it.

"Yes, possibly for several years. He will, of course, come home holidays."

Catherine stared down at the dishes in the sink. This news had come without warning, but she did not betray any feelings, if she had them, on the matter.

"I'm glad it's finally settled between Peter and Ann," Ella went on, again changing the subject. "Everyone has been holding their breath for them to announce their engagement. Peter is such a shy boy. I didn't think he was quite going to make it at dinnertime."

"No, Peter never has been very bold in front of others," responded Catherine absently. "In that respect, he is quite different from Neal."

"In some ways, Peter reminds me a great deal of Albert," returned Ella.

"Oh, I don't think so," Catherine spoke out spontaneously, but her mind was not on the subject. "They are quite different, I think."

"I mean in their shyness with girls," remarked Ella. "Don't you think Albert is overly shy?"

"Perhaps, but there his similarity with Pete ends."

"Oh, they seem quite similar to me. What I've seen of Peter, he is much like my own son."

"Oh, no! Ma. How can you say that? You, of all people. Albert's quite unlike anyone I've ever known." Catherine caught herself. She turned and saw Ella looking at her with cold, piercing eyes.

"You're very fond of Albert, I take it then," Ella's voice was flat.

"Yes, of course. Why shouldn't I be?" Catherine exclaimed defensively. She wasn't sure of the purpose of this last twist in their conversation, but she saw in Ella's face she was testing her.

"But you are happily married, aren't you?"

"Of course. I don't understand."

"Oh, never mind. It was just a fleeting thought of an old woman."

"Now wait, Ma! You started this with a purpose. Let's finish it. What do you want of me?"

"Nothing!" exclaimed Ella. She was sorry she had started her questioning and was embarrassed about how to finish it.

"I believe I can guess," Catherine's voice came slow and deliberate. "You think I'm in love with him, don't you?"

"Yes!" came the answer.

"But Ma, he's only a boy! I love Albert as a sister does her brother. He is a sweet and gentle boy who needs affection. This is why it's hurt me to see how he and Richard have torn at each other. I love them both, but in different ways, of course."

"Is that all?"

"What else?"

Ella had no answer for this. She had already said too much and now realized the futility of her purpose. Had she really expected to ensnare Catherine into a confession? ... And, if she had, what then? The whole business took on an absurd aspect, and she wanted desperately to untangle her own web of conspiracy and resolve the situation.

"I didn't mean what I perhaps implied, but you must indulge a mother's sense of protectiveness. Call it over-protectiveness, but you too will have this feeling for your own one day. You'll find that no matter how hard you try to love them all the same, there will be one who'll be closest to your heart. Albert's been that one with me."

Catherine bit her lower lip and stared out the window. Ella had tried to lay a trap, several traps she now realized.

"I hope I've answered the question in your mind." Her voice was low and husky with restrained emotion.

"Yes, you have." Ella was showing a certain weariness now.

"But, one word more. You speak of Albert as only a boy, but don't be mistaken. He's more a man than you may think."

Ella found she had spoken prematurely in her remarks to Catherine about Albert's leaving for Philadelphia. When she spoke to Dick again the next morning, he unexpectedly balked at the idea. The two were getting along as brothers should, he said, the urgency of Albert's trip no longer seemed apparent. Ella was exasperated. She had so counted on getting Albert away that she had taken Dick for granted. This was a mistake she rarely made, but her emotional involvement had warped her usual good judgment.

It wasn't that she didn't fully trust Albert, she kept telling herself. It was just that she was well aware that the Vandenbergs were not as straight-laced as were the DeGrafs. She, of course, wore only high-necked, long-sleeved dresses even in summer to hide the scars. Yet, even before the barn fire modest dress had always been customary. From the day of her arrival into the household, Catherine had brought with her the Vandenbergs' customs.

Ella was fully aware that Catherine has a beautiful body. Although her clothing by Vandenberg standards would not be considered provocative. It seemed to her it accentuated that beauty. *Or was it just jealousy on her part*, she thought. *After_all, unlike herself, Catherine had nothing to hide*. None of the others had commented on this. Even Dick had never so much as raised an eyebrow on seeing Catherine about the house. Certainly, these men weren't blind!

She was certain that Catherine was completely conscious of her physical assets and not ashamed of them. Catherine wasn't a prude or religiously austere, for which Ella was thankful. There were enough of those among her associates at church. What bothered her most was the vague impression that Catherine tended toward being somewhat of an exhibitionist. This could be disastrous if at all directed toward Albert.

Ella had never been so persistent with Dick before. Previously, when Dick said a thing was to be so, she accepted it, but she did not do so now. Since the tactic to separate the two brothers no longer seemed valid, she spoke of Albert's future. Richard's inheritance of the farm some day was pushed—pushed hard. Dick conceded that Albert would have to make a life of his own elsewhere. Then, she continued, Albert would need a better education than was available to him now. She, as a former school teacher, had done her best to supplement the meager local schooling. Albert needed more. It was only right that he should have the opportunity to go to Philadelphia and at least be allowed to take the entrance examination at the University. That's all she asked!

Ella not only badgered Dick from sunup to sundown, she discussed the situation openly with Sarah, Dr. Brabin and even the Reverend VandenTill. She convinced them all to side with her against Dick's reluctance.

Dick wearied of the conversation. He had never seen his wife so tenacious on a subject. Finally, it was agreed that Albert would go to Beatrice's but not until school started in the fall. Dick would need the boy during the summer, and there was no point in him loafing the next few months away in Philadelphia. At the conclusion, when Dick announced his approval, Dr. Brabin grinned and took Sarah aside where he reminded her of his statement of many years before. *Give a Scot a cause and he will fight like a demon!*

Tuesday morning Albert came downstairs shortly after his father and brothers had gone out to do the milking. It was lonely staying in his room all day, and he was anxious to get busy again. Dr. Brabin had told him to stay away from a milking stool, so he thought he'd hoe the vegetable garden. The rain of the previous week had been good for the crops, but it had also made the weeds grow rank.

Hoeing was much like milking to him, although he preferred the latter. It was a job which kept the body occupied, yet one could develop a rhythm of movement while the mind was free to wander. The still quiet air of early morning was refreshing; there was a solitude and freedom here he could never feel within his room. At this hour, the colors seemed richer than later in the day —the grass was darker green, the crimson heads of clover brighter, even the short bristly crowns of the lowly dandelion were a deeper gold in the morning sun—not washed out as they so often seem when the sun is high. He set to hoeing a row of corn. Along one side the buttercups had come, and he cut one off and took it in his hand. The deeply lobed leaves had a feathery quality about them and tiny hairs covered all the stems; atop each stem, a beautiful cup of gold. It seemed so delicate a plant—and yet—here it was invading the garden rows. The beauty of the buttercup competed with the utility of the corn. How could anything that seemed so gentle, so fragile, still be so out of place. For out of place it was, and must be rogued to save the corn.

The morning air was cool and heavy dew wet down all the foliage. A glistening drop of moisture hung from the tip of each young corn leaf and sparkled in the morning light like small jewels, waiting for someone to gather them and make a necklace. He would have liked to make such a necklace for Catherine. How they would set off her lovely throat. Yet, no skill of his could make a necklace of dewdrops. Like so many other fantasies of his mind, the practical world did not permit them.

Deep in thought, he went back to the rhythmic swing of the hoe. From a distance to the south there was a steady roar which interrupted the silence. It grew louder by the minute. Albert stopped, leaned on the hoe and looked down the road the direction of the sound. An automobile broke out into the open, spewing a cloud of blue smoke and tearing along faster than any horse could trot.

"What in heaven's name. . ." The auto was coming to this farm. Albert set the hoe down and started walking towards the house. He recognized Cornelius in the driver's seat as the car swung into the driveway.

Richard was already in the driveway as Cornelius jerked to a stop. It was a Model T touring car all sparkling new with shiny black paint.

"Where's your Dad?" hollered Cornelius above the sound of the engine.

"Down milking," replied Richard.

"Go get him, boy! Go get him!" Richard obeyed and soon returned with Dick.

"What do you think of her?" chuckled Cornelius in jubilation.

She was a beauty and Dick unhesitantly said so, while Cornelius beamed with pride. He was the first farmer in the area to own one. It was a two-seater, with leather upholstery and dash.

The recent rains had settled the road dust so the car still shone with its original newness.

"Climb aboard!" insisted Cornelius. "I'll take you for a spin!"

"Well--ll, I'd like to ..." started Dick, "but I'm in the middle of milking."

"The cows can wait! It won't take long!"

"Go on, Pa!" spoke up Albert. "I'll take over your milking."

"No, you won't!" chimed in Catherine, who had come up behind them. "Remember what the doctor said. I'll take over for Dad."

Dick climbed in the passenger's seat as Cornelius mounted the driver's side. The engine roared, and with a squeal the friction clutch engaged, the car lurched forward, and they were off down the drive. As they came by the side of the house, the kitchen door burst open and Ella stood on the porch as though petrified. Dick stuck his hand up as they went chugging by, but Ella only stared as if she were too perplexed to wave.

"When did you get her?" Dick yelled to make himself heard.

He turned and looked back just in time to see Richard and Catherine go back to the barn and Albert head toward the garden. They would work without him this morning; he was going for a ride.

"Picked her up in town yesterday afternoon. I ordered her two months ago."

"How come you didn't tell me about it?"

"Wanted to surprise you. In fact, I didn't tell anyone, not even Grace, 'til yesterday. She's kind of angry about it."

"How fast do you think it'll go?"

"Oh, I haven't opened her up yet. They told me not to until she's properly broken in. On a good stretch of road she should do about twenty-five."

"Twenty-five miles an hour! As much as that!" Dick was impressed. He had never ridden in an automobile before, and was thoroughly enjoying himself. He'd admit this to Cornelius, but never to his family, especially his sons; they'd think he'd gone soft. Dick knew the car must have cost a lot of money, but he wasn't about to ask. It was none of his business. Yet he was curious. A car was a nice thing to have, but it was a luxury. It did, however, start him thinking. Maybe some day. For now, he'd be satisfied with a good horse and carriage.

In no time they were pulling into the Vandenbergs. Neal and Peter were in the barn milking, just as his own family was at home. Today, the young ones worked while their fathers played.

"Let's go in for a spot of coffee," shouted Cornelius, even after he'd turned off the engine. "Then I'd like to show you a couple of new heifers that look real good to me."

"I see Cornelius had to show you his new contraption," remarked Grace sarcastically, as they came into the kitchen.

"Yes, it's really a fine car," replied Dick. "One of these days, I hope to get one myself."

"You might speak to Ella before you do." Grace glared at Cornelius.

"Oh, I expect I might." Dick half smiled. He didn't want to get in the middle of any family feud.

"Oh, by the way, if you can spare Ann tomorrow, I'd like her to go into town with us. We've got to do some shopping and I'd like Ann to help me. I miss having a daughter in the house. Sons are no company at all these days."

"By all means," returned Dick. "Ill have one of the boys drop her off first thing in the morning. Keep her as long as you want— anytime."

"Well—if Ella doesn't mind."

"Oh, she wouldn't mind." Dick hadn't consulted with Ella, and she might have had other plans for Ann, but that never occurred to him.

chapter

9

Thursday after supper, Albert went out and hitched up the horse for choir practice. They would pick up Peter on their way to church, with Catherine and Albert serving as chaperones for the newly engaged couple. *This was a bit ironic*, Albert thought. *He and Catherine of all people. He guessed that perhaps in his mother's mind it might be the other way around.*

When they pulled up at the Vandenbergs, Peter was waiting on the porch. Albert drove with Catherine beside him, and Ann and Peter sat well apart in back— until they were out of sight from the house. It was Catherine's duty as senior member of the group to maintain discipline between those shortly to be married. This made her feel quite matronly, and out of character, for she was only a year older than the two now cuddled together in the back.

The choir director was well pleased to have another tenor in his group since they were always in short supply. In choir, the women far outnumbered the men, and among the latter, basses were always more plentiful than tenors. Albert was assigned to his place, and practice began.

Following rehearsal, there was coffee and cakes and a time for socializing. Everyone quickly separated into several groups. First, the older folks—the married ones, who congregated close to the refreshment table, for food and talk were <u>their</u> main interests. Far to one side of the room the young men gathered, some too bashful to more than look at the girls from a distance and others more interested in talking with their own kind. Far to the opposite side was a much larger group. These were the young ladies who had not yet reached an understanding with a fellow and who hoped that tonight some favorite from the other side would take the long walk over and speak to her. For the young this could be a very lonely business. A young man had most of the advantages, since he could approach almost any girl if he but dared, while a proper lady could only wait and hope. The last and final group were the mixers, couples who had passed the long ordeal of first acquaintances and were now 'going together'. Peter and Ann immediately gravitated to this group, which was the most active place for gossip about who was going with whom and rumors of those likely to do so soon. Now Ann had an engagement ring on her finger, which had been noticed as soon as she entered the building. The news had spread so fast that all the women knew before rehearsal was over. The group immediately descended upon Peter and Ann to learn all the facts about their future plans. The wedding date? Will it be here in church? .... Ann was overjoyed with all the attention, but Peter only blushed and stammered.

Albert joined the group of young men and fully intended to stay with them until it was time to leave. This is not what his mother wanted him to do; he was to socialize, but not on this side of the room, and she'd ask him about this tomorrow. His mother was pushing him and he resented it. Grudgingly, he went over to the refreshment table—a half-way station in the center of the room. It was a fueling place to get up enough courage to go the rest of the way across that very wide room. He was suddenly hungry, took some coffee, a piece of cake and looked, between sips and bites, to where the single girls were. They talked among themselves, but certain ones would frequently look in his direction. Then, he saw a girl he hadn't seen before, standing apart from the others. She was about Catherine's size with long dark hair and a very solemn face. She wasn't enjoying herself very much, that was evident, and he felt sorry for her. Should he go over and talk with her, but what would he say? How could he talk to a girl he'd never seen before? He continued to munch his cake until it was gone and then took another piece. There was a large buxom girl standing next to her, and he wondered if they were friends. They didn't seem to be talking to each other, just standing there. On impulse, he headed in their direction.

The large girl saw him coming, and he was still some distance away when she flashed a broad smile and stepped forward. He smiled back while keeping his attention on the smaller girl. Before he reached her, the large girl blocked his way and introduced herself as Bella. She noted that Albert was new in choir and hoped he liked it, and would come regularly. She had a large voice to match the proportions of her build. Out of politeness he answered, while trying to edge by her to reach the dark haired girl. Each time he tried to talk with the smaller girl, her companion pushed forward, thrusting her oversized bosom at him to get attention. He seemed trapped, and was sorry he'd ventured over. Then, instinctively he turned and saw Catherine coming his way.

"I believe it's time we were leaving. Are Ann and Peter ready?" he called to Catherine.

"They will be soon. We really should be going, if you can break away" There was a teasing note in her voice and an odd smile on her lips. "I see you've met Bella," Catherine looked to the large girl, "but I don't believe I've met your other friend."

The dark haired girl introduced herself. Her name was Margie.

—◆◆◆◆◆◆—

Albert set the mare on a steady pace once they were on the road away from the church. He glanced over at Catherine, could see the queer upturn of the corners of her mouth, and knew he was in for a kidding about what had gone on back there. Catherine loved to tease him, and if anyone else were to treat him as she did he would be offended, but from Catherine he relished it, and came back for more.

"You seemed to hit it off very well with Bella DeKamp. I wasn't aware that I had such a Don Juan for a brother-in-law."

"I was trapped. I hadn't even meant to talk to her."

100

"I'm glad. She's a nice girl, but I don't think she's your type. At least, I wouldn't have thought so, but perhaps I've misjudged you. Maybe you like them loud and buxom."

"No, thank you. Too much for me."

"Oh, I don't know," there was a tinge of laughter in her voice. "She's a lot of woman and she'd be an easy catch. She's looking for a fella, and getting desperate."

"I'm not interested."

"All right then, what <u>were</u> you doing over there amongst the girls? You know I looked all over for you. That was the last place I expected to find you." Catherine glanced behind her. There wasn't the giggling there'd been on the way out, and she was sure they were quite oblivious to what was being said up front.

"Was it the dark haired girl then?"

"Well- -ll, yes. I went over to speak to her."

"Oh ho! You are a fast worker." She moved closer and poked him in the ribs. Albert turned and saw the impish expression. She hadn't had this much fun with him since before her wedding.

"Oh, not really. I had to spend my time somehow while waiting for the rest of you."

"Ha! You won't get away with that with me. You must have liked what you saw to make that trip across the room. Many boys take months or even years before they try it. You did it on your first night. I'm really proud of you." She exclaimed with mock praise and gave him a quick hug.

"Oh, not really," he said again and blushed in spite of himself.

"What was her name? Margie? I didn't catch her last name."

"I didn't even know her first name until you came up. I just felt like talking with her, that's all. No special interest."

"That's how more serious things get started."

"Don't worry, there's nothing to it."

"Oh, but I think it's good. I know your mother will be happy to hear about it."

"Oh?" Albert turned to look at her. The sudden change in her voice caught him by surprise. There was a noise from the back seat as Ann became aware of her surroundings. They were approaching the turn-off to a pond along the route.

"Can we stop awhile?" she asked. "We'd like to watch the moonlight on the water."

"Both our folks will be up when we get back," replied Catherine. "They'll think I've neglected my duty if we come in late."

"Oh, we can say that choir was extra long. We left before most of the others."

"That's because we have further to travel than most."

"That makes no difference. Please, Catherine. We needn't stay long. Peter and I so seldom get a chance like this."

"All right but your mother will be on my neck if we get in late."

"Oh, Ma's not strict."

"Ah, but Pa is!"

Ann had no reply to this. Albert turned in the lane to the pond, pulled up and tethered the horse.

"We're going down by the water. See you later," yelled Peter as he and Ann scrambled off down the bank into the darkness.

"They want to be alone for awhile," Catherine said with a half smile. "I guess you're old enough to know about such things."

Albert made no reply. He knew Ann could take care of herself and what they did was of no concern to him.

"Since they don't want our company, let's go over and watch the water from above. Do you realize we're alone? You and me, an old married woman, here in the moonlight." There was a soft tantalizing purr to her voice. "I'll bet you wish I was that dark-haired girl now."

"Not really."

"Albert! Is that all you can say? I'm disappointed in you. Where's your feeling of romance?"

"Maybe I don't have any."

"I know better than that. Come, put your arm around me. Pretend I'm Margie." She took his arm and put it around her waist.

"You're teasing me."

"Don't you like to be teased? You always have. Now use your imagination and try to think I'm Margie."

"I don't know. . ."

"Oh come now. I'm probably a poor substitute, but I know you have a vivid imagination."

"But. . ."

"I'm trying to teach you a little about what to do when you're out with a girl. It's all in fun. Maybe you'll learn something."

"I'm not so sure."

"Now, if a girl is a little afraid of you, she'll sit like this." Catherine removed his arm, pulled away from him and sat very stiffly with her head held slightly aloft. "Do you think I— I mean Margie—has cause to be afraid of you?"

"Gosh, no. Why should she be?"

"Oh, one never knows, but enough of that. Now, if a girl really likes you..." Catherine put his arm back around her, snuggled up against him, and put her head on his shoulder so that her hair brushed against his face. A shiver ran through him, but she pretended not to notice it. When he made no further response she drew even closer and looked up into his face with eyes that sparkled mischievously. "Now, what would you do?" came a soft, challenging voice.

Albert waited no longer. His arms came up around her back and he pulled her in tight against him. He bent and kissed her on the cheek, softly and quickly. He started to raise away but then moved to her lips, now slightly parted, and pressed down with his own. Her hands went to his chest to push him away, but they never completed the movement. Instead, she drew them up around the back of his neck. It was a long and passionate kiss. Finally, Catherine strained back and broke the spell.

"Oh! My!" she sighed breathlessly, "I guess you need no lessons. School's over!"

"I—I'm sorry. I didn't mean...."

"Nonsense! Why should you be sorry? I brought it on myself, on purpose."

"But why?"

"Your mother warned me that a man lurks beneath that boyish frame of yours. She didn't underestimate."

"My mother told you about me?" Albert gasped. "What did she say?"

"Oh, that was just women's talk. I see now more of what she meant." Albert was momentarily speechless.

"You won't tell me?"

"No." The jesting tone in her voice returned. She wasn't sure this was the time for teasing but it was the safest way she knew. Albert's head slumped forward dejectedly. "I see I've hurt you. I didn't mean to."

"It's not you. It's my mother. She promised she wouldn't tell you about me." He bit his lip almost convulsively. "That's why she's sending me away to Philadelphia."

"What?" Catherine stiffened. "You mean you'll be going away because of me?"

"She knows how I feel about you. She's afraid I'll get hurt —we"ll both get hurt."

"Oh-h-h," Catherine drew in a deep breath. "Your mother didn't really say how you felt." She paused. "How <u>do</u> you feel about me?"

"You'd probably laugh at me."

"I'll never laugh at you. Tantalize you, tease you, yes. In fun, of course. But when you're serious, I'll never laugh." Catherine put her hand to his face and turned it to meet her own. She kissed him on the forehead.

"You— you know, I'm very fond of you," he stammered.

"Yes, I know."

"It's really more than that." The words caught in his throat.

Catherine waited patiently for him to go on. "I'm deeply in love with you," he finally blurted out the words he'd never meant to say. He expected she would suddenly go rigid and cold—or even slap his face. Instead she took the words as calmly as if he'd told her she had nice hands, or that the weather was hot.

"I love you too, Albert," she said softly. "I could never hope to have a better brother-in-law."

"But, you don't understand. This isn't the same. I love my sister Ann, in a way I guess, but my feelings for you aren't the same. They run much deeper."

"Like a lover. Are you telling me you want to be my lover?" She was trying very hard to tease him again, but she couldn't give it the light and airy touch she meant; it lay flat before them.

"Oh, I could never hurt you," he stammered and flushed. "I didn't mean in a lustful way."

"I know you didn't," she squeezed his hand in her own. "I've treated you badly tonight. Please forgive me, but I had to bring this out in the open. You've tried to hold it in too long."

"You mean you knew?"

"Dear boy," she ran both hands through the blond curls about his forehead. "You are a boy to me, although you try so hard to be a man. Do you think I haven't felt your eyes on me, whether it's across the kitchen table, or as I walk into the room? Whenever you're nearby, I have the feeling that you're watching me."

"Then you've known all along."

"I've known for quite some time."

"How long?"

"Since my wedding day, when you kissed me in church."

"Oh God!" He put his hands up to his face and covered it.

"You're a strange boy, Albert." She put a hand on each shoulder, held him at arm's length, and looked directly into his face. "I often don't understand you, but I think I know the feelings you've tried so hard to hide."

"Is that all you think of me—as strange?"

"No. Heavens no! I love you very dearly."

"I know. You said that before. Like a sister loves a brother."

"How else? I'm married now, but not to you."

"I wish it were otherwise."

"Oh come. You'll forget all about me once you've gone to Philadelphia. You'll see."

Albert would not answer this, but his face was glum. Catherine gave a quick sigh, she hoped she'd settled things without being too rough on him.

"We must go," she finally said. "It's getting late. Come on, let's find Ann and Peter."

Quickly they walked down towards the pond. "Peter! Ann! It's time to leave." Catherine called as loudly as she could. She didn't want to come on them unexpectedly, with Albert there. When they reached the shoreline they heard movement in the water ahead of them.

"We're coming! We're coming!" came Ann's voice. A moment later Ann came splashing up to shore with Peter in close pursuit. Ann had tucked her dress up so that it was just below her hips. Peter had rolled his pants as high as they would go but still they'd gotten wet.

"Look at the two of you. You're a sight. Ann, have you no modesty at all?" Catherine said sharply, but Ann only giggled. Peter scooped Ann up in his arms and laughing and stumbling came ashore.

"Aw, Sis. Don't be so prim! We're just having fun."

Catherine said no more. All four marched up to the carriage and quickly were on their way. Ann and Peter dried their feet and Peter tried to squeeze the water from his pants.

Catherine entered the bedroom and quietly changed to her nightgown in the semi-darkness. Richard was asleep and she didn't want to disturb him, but as she slipped into bed, the movement on the springs awoke him.

"That you, Kate?"

"Yes."

"How was choir practice?" Richard sat up, rubbed his eyes, yawned and looked across at her. "How did Albert make out? Did he enjoy his first session at choir practice?" *There was a tone of sincere interest in his voice*, she thought. "He really surprised me. Would you believe, after practice, he actually went over and talked with a couple girls?"

"No-o-o! You're kidding!" a tone of disbelief.

"Seems we've underestimated your little brother."

Richard reached over, kissed her, and rolled back on his side. Soon his heavy even breathing told her that he was again asleep; she, however, could not sleep. The evening's events disturbed her. She did not like the idea that Ella knew of Albert's boyish admiration; especially that Ella considered it so serious that she'd taken steps to send him away. Now she realized the full implications of that earlier conversation. Ella had know of Albert's feelings and was testing her for hers, had tried to trap her into revealing herself—and so crudely, too. She would have expected more subtlety.

If Ella was playing games with her, she would play a few of her own; it wouldn't be difficult, now that she knew what was going on. Ella had said that Albert would go to Philadelphia soon after Beatrice's children arrived, and they would be arriving Saturday. Still, there had been no further word about Albert's leaving from either Dick or Ella. Something must have gone wrong. Then it struck her that Ella may have used Albert's immediate departure as one of her ploys. Could Ella be that devious? No, she thought not, but she must face the chance that Albert would stay on. What was she to do about him?

She knew now that Albert was deeply infatuated with her, even more

106

than she had realized, but what harm was there in that? It was an adolescent phase he'd soon outgrow, and then his attention would shift to a girl his own age. Margie perhaps. In the meantime, she could not callously brush him aside, even if she wanted to. That was unthinkable. She owed him too much, for had he not responded to Richard's need in the swamp? Richard, who he had every right to hate. Were it not for Albert, she would now be a widow. If he could do as he had done for Richard, then she must do her best to help him now.

Many years of instructions from her mother had taught her how to heal the sick, the infirm, and the crippled. It had always given her great pleasure to help others, in respond to their needs. Albert seemed to need her in a different way, and about this she was at a loss. *Albert was very dear to her*, she thought, *but she'd never thought of him as a lover— not her lover*. He was still a boy and had a lot of growing up to do. Was it a mother's instinct that made her want to fondle him? Here was a problem she wasn't sure just how to cope with. This would take time to think out, but not now, perhaps tomorrow when her mind was less confused.

She had to get to sleep, it was well after midnight, but sleep would not come. There was a tight sensation in the pit of her stomach which made sleep impossible; some hot milk would help. Quietly, she slipped out of bed without disturbing Richard. The moonlight coming in the window was such that there was no need for a lantern and she made her way to the door and down the hall toward the kitchen. Near Albert's room she paused. There was a light coming from beneath his door, meaning he was still awake and had a lantern burning. How could he stay up so late when he knew he must get up at five for the milk route with Ann? Quickly she moved on down the hall to the stairs and went below.

A short while later, now with a lantern in one hand and a pitcher of milk in the other, she came up from the cool cellar to the kitchen where she put a pan of milk on the stove and waited for it to warm. How often did Albert stay up this way with lantern burning? She knew he wrote a lot; was this what he was doing now? There had been a temptation to look in on him, but better judgment told her otherwise. They'd had enough adventure at the pond this night. The kiss was well remembered. There'd been a gentle affection in it.

The milk was now hot, Catherine drank it slowly, returned everything to its proper place, and made her way back up the stairs. The light still shone below Albert's door, but she hurried by to her own room.

The DeGraf's had picked their first good crop of strawberries and Richard would take them into market early the next morning. Dick felt that if anyone could get a good price for them, it would be Richard. Albert had asked to go with his brother, but that was out of the question; choir practice would keep him out too late. Albert had insisted that Richard needed help. This surprised and pleased Dick, and convinced him that perhaps at last the brotherly feud was dead. Still, Albert needed his rest. Dick said that little Govert would go, and Albert would run the milk route, taking Ann with him—so that settled the matter.

Albert came down for breakfast at five, stretching and yawning as he sank into a chair. His mother was busy in the kitchen, but Ann still hadn't gotten up.

"You seem sleepy this morning" Ella commented. "Didn't you have a good night?"

"Oh, I'll be all right. Just a little slow in getting started this morning."

"You stayed up writing again?"

"Sort of."

"You do too much of that. You need your rest."

"Oh, I'll make out."

"How was choir practice last night?"

"Fine."

"Do you think you are going to enjoy it?"

"That depends on how long I'll be staying here I guess. You haven't said any more about . . ."

"I've been meaning to speak to you about Philadelphia. Your father and I have talked about it again. He feels you should stay here until this fall. You'll go in time to start school there."

"Oh," Albert gave a visible sigh of relief. "I'm glad."

"Yes, but I'm still concerned about you and Catherine. I hope you've remembered what I've said."

"Oh, Ma, you fret too much. I haven't done anything that I'm ashamed of. Honest!"

"I believe you. It's just that I worry that you're going to get hurt."

"You make too much of it!" He shot at her bitterly. "First thing you'll have me making too much of it, and then there <u>will</u> be trouble."

"I— I'm sorry. I won't mention it again." Ella turned back to the stove. He glanced from his food and saw wet streaks down the side of her cheek. It had been the first time he could remember that he'd ever spoken so crossly to her.

"Oh, Ma! I didn't mean that! It's just that you seem to be pushing at me so hard lately." He went over and put his arms around her. "I can take hounding from the others, but not from you. We've always been too close."

"I know. I haven't meant to. I promise, I won't bother you about it any more. Now you'd better go out and load the wagon. I'll get Ann down for breakfast." She started off for the stairs muttering to herself. "That girl is so hard to get up mornings. I pity Peter after they're married."

chapter

10

Albert brought the milk wagon by the house, picked up Ann and went on out the drive. The moon had gone down below the horizon and the sun wasn't up yet, so it was much darker than when they had come home from choir practice. Ann was still half asleep and her head bobbed loosely to and fro as they bounced along. The mists were heavy and Albert could not see beyond the horse's head. The wetness of the air hung over them like a huge saturated cloth, which made breathing difficult, and he let the mare set her own pace. They would make up any lost time when they were over the ridge and out of the valley. Ann could hardly keep her head up.

"What's the matter? Was last night too much for you?" he jibed.

She opened one eye and looked crossly at him.

"Don't bother me."

"Maybe you got too much exposure at the pond." He thought maybe that would wake her up.

Ann half heartedly swung a small fist at him, missing him by several inches.

"No more out of you, Little Brother! Let me sleep. I'll talk to you later!"

"All right, all right. Don't be so touchy." Albert was feeling sleepy himself. His late evening writing was not making him his brightest at this hour of the morning. Ann snuggled toward him, put her head against his shoulder and soon was sound asleep. He leaned back toward her and stared at the horse's head; there was something hypnotic about the animal's slow rhythmic movements that made his eyelids feel like lead. Although he fought it, soon the reins ran slack and his head slumped forward.

A sudden bump in the road brought Ann out of her slumber and when she opened her eyes, she could clearly see the morning light shining across the mare's chestnut mane. She and her brother were leaning against each other at the center of the seat; he was sound asleep.

"Albert! Wake up!"

Albert gave a start and looked about him.

"Well, how's my bright-eyed, bushy-tailed little brother this morning? Do I remember way back there someone talking about me being sleepy?"

"Gee, I must have fallen asleep myself."

"That's rather obvious."

Albert looked towards the sun which had broken clear of the horizon, and then about the roadside to see where they were. They were out of the valley and on the road headed south toward town. Fortunately, the mare knew where they were going, but by the position of the sun and their location, she certainly hadn't been in any hurry. Since he'd fallen asleep, she must have come the whole way at a slow walk with even a few stops along the way.

"Good gosh. It's gotten late."

"Don't blame me. I wasn't driving. I'm only a passenger here, you know."

"Don't rub it in."

"It's nice to have one up on you. How'd you like me to tell Pa you can't even sit behind a horse any more."

"You wouldn't do that!"

"Maybe not, but then again, what's it worth to you?"

"What do you mean?"

Albert hustled the mare along now. The road was level and they would have to make up for lost time. The milk cans rattled and banged and he could hear the "slush-slush" of milk in one can that was only half full. *He should have put its contents in a smaller can*, he thought, *they might have butter by the time they got to town.*

Ann looked over at him shrewdly. Even though she'd been half asleep earlier, her mind had been going over last night's pleasant events with Peter at the pond. The moon had been bright and she wasn't sure just how much Albert might have seen.

"Well, I think I've got some things on you that you might not like the folks to hear about. Just now is only one of them. You figure maybe we can make a deal?"

"I still don't get you." A sudden flash and Albert's face lit up. "Oh, of course, last night!"

"My, your mind must be foggy this morning. Yes, last night."

Albert broke into a chuckle and slapped the reins several times loosely over the mare's rump, making her break into a fast trot.

"I get it. You're trying to blackmail me so I won't tell on you."

"That's right, little brother."

"Don't call me that! If you want to make a deal, that's going to be part of it."

"All right, Al. Now, how much did you see last night at the pond?"

"Plenty!" Albert grinned.

"What do you mean, 'plenty'?"

"I learned a lot about girls last night." The grin now broadened. He could see that Ann was uncomfortable, and he was going to make the most of it.

"You didn't see anything. You're just trying to needle me cause of what I know about you."

His smile quickly faded for she might have the edge on him. The thought flashed through his mind that they could just as well have seen Catherine and him up on the hill.

"Aha! that took the silly grin off your face. Now maybe we can settle down to business."

"What've you got on me, besides this morning?" he asked, hesitantly, for fear of what she might say.

"Not sure I should lay my cards on the table first."

"We've got to start somewhere."

"All right. For one thing, I saw you getting real cozy with Bella DeKamp last night. Don't tell me you're finally getting interested in girls?"

"Not with her!"

"Bella's a good friend of mine and sits next to me in choir. She spotted you right away and was asking about you all through rehearsal. She wanted to meet you and I told her I would speak to you about it. Then, when I was going to, I saw you'd already met."

"Ah-h!" Albert gave a groan. "So you put her on me. I wondered why she latched onto me the way she did. Thanks a lot!"

"What's the matter? Don't—you like her?"

"Na!"

"She's a nice girl."

"She's loud and big—fat!"

"She's not fat! Just big and well rounded. I thought boys liked girls to have plenty of curves—and stick out in front."

"Not _that_ much—least not me."

"Well one can't please everybody, I guess. I thought you were real interested." Ann was visibly disappointed, but then brightened quickly. "Well, what _were_ you doing over there?"

"I was trying to talk with another girl, but Bella kept getting in the way!"

"Aha! Who?"

"She's new. You probably don't even know her."

"I know most of them. Who?"

"Her name's Margie."

Ann pursed her lips, trying to think of a Margie in choir. She knew a Mary, a May, but no Margie.

"What's her last name?"

"Don't know."

"What's she look like?"

Albert described her. Ann thought a minute, then smiled broadly. "Long dark hair, huh? Would you say she's about Kate's size, only thinner?"

"Uh-huh."

"That must be the girl. Let me see—now what was her last name?"

Ann was still thinking when Albert pulled into the long shady drive at Ridgewood's old people's home. This was the first stop on their route. The house, or more properly, mansion, stood atop a small hill and was surrounded by gigantic oak trees that hid it from view until one was into

113

the circular drive that went by the front porch. This had once been owned by a wealthy Dutchman, who had much of what was now the southern part of the town as his estate. Originally, it had contained 2500 acres, but all that was left was the hill with its five acres, and the buildings; the rest had been divided into small farms and the building lots of outer Ridgewood. The house had thirty-eight rooms and when Dick was still a small boy, green from Holland, the people of Ridgewood were determined to tear it down, for no one had use for such a monstrosity. Then, an enterprising businessman from New York passed through that way and bought it for next to nothing. Craftsmen came from the city and reworked the house into an old people's home. Except for management, the home was run by residents of Ridgewood, but the patients are all city people, whose children no longer want to take care of them during their remaining years. As for the country folks, they've no need for the home, for they take care of their elders themselves, having neither the desire nor means to put out for care of their own aging relatives.

Albert pulled past the front porch to a small drive that led to the back of the house. He was bringing the first can in when a large brown woman met him at the door.

"Mornin', come right in, boy," she said.

"Good morning, Mam, how are you today?

"Ah's fine, jus' fine. Great mornin' dis is!"

Ann was right behind her brother with two pails of milk.

"Com' in fo' some tea an' cake—an' set a piece," said the woman.

"We'd like to very much," replied Albert, "but we're a bit late this morning."

"Jes' take a minute. Tea's hot an' got de' cake right heah!"

Albert glanced at Ann and she nodded her head in approval.

They couldn't rush away.

The woman was equally wide as she was high. She reminded Albert of the picture of "Aunt Jemima" on the box of pancake mix. She was head cook for the home and had a staff of three women working for her in the kitchen. Albert had never seen her, but she was jolly; laughing after every two or three sentences as though she continually remembered some new joke. Her laugh was refreshing and never seemed to grow stale. *She must be great for the spirits of these old people,* he thought. *How could anyone be glum for long with this huge barrel of mirth around.*

"Haben't seed yo fo' quite a spell now, boy. My, you is growed! You gonna' be quite a man one o' dese days."

"Most of the time I stay home and do the milkin'," Albert replied. "Hurt my back, so now they figure it best I come in on deliveries instead."

"Oh? I was beginnin' to tink yo' didn't like comin' ta town," she let out a peal of laughter that bounded around the huge kitchen.

"It's not that. Just I'm needed more at home."

"I tink yo mamma wants ta' keep yo' away from all des wild town gals. Dat's what I tink!" Another roll of laughter.

Albert blushed and busied himself with his tea and cake. He glanced over at Ann who was sitting taking it all in with a smirk on her face.

"Man, but da' gals must go crazy ober yo'. Look at dose blond curls!" She brushed a big brown hand across Albert's forehead pushing his hair back. Albert started to back away, but her hand was already there rumpling up his hair. "Heah, I is as brown as a cinnamin roll an yo' is as fair as a angel. Lawdy man, I ain't seed one like yo' in a long time." The rolls of fat around her middle shook convulsively as she burst out laughing again.

Albert was completely flustered, his face turned brilliant crimson. He gulped down the last of his tea and as diplomatically as the circumstances would allow, he and Ann excused themselves. It was a quick retreat out the door and into the wagon, with the big brown woman following behind them. As Albert snapped the reins on the horse's rump, the huge woman called after them, "Com' back real soon now!"

Albert took the horse off at such a fast pace the right wheels left the ground as they cut around the front of the house. Ann was laughing so hard she couldn't see where they were going for the tears. They brushed past the front of the house and were on down the lane when she sat upright and yelled to her brother.

"You forgot the empties!"

"Oh God!" Albert reined the horse to a stop. "Do we have to?"

"You've got to get them or we'll be short on the next delivery."

"Now more slowly, Albert turned the wagon around at the end of the drive and headed back to the kitchen steps.

"Hold the reins for me. I'm going to make this fast," he said.

"What's the hurry? You've got a real lover in there. Want me to go on alone?"

"Don't be ridiculous!" Albert scrambled up the back steps and grabbed the empty milk cans that were standing along the edge of the porch. He turned and was headed back towards the wagon when the door burst open and she was there again, filling the doorway.

"Boy! Ah said com' back soon, but ah sho' didn't expect yo' dis' quick!"

"Just forgot our empty cans," Albert stammered and fled for the wagon.

Again, the milk wagon shot out the drive and all Albert could hear was the boom of laughter following him. He still thought he heard it when they were out on the main road, but then realized it was Ann who was laughing beside him. A half mile down the road she got control of herself.

"I've never seen anything so funny in all my life!" she burst out, between spasms. "If you could have seen your face when that big fat mama ran her hand through your hair. It was a howl!"

"You sound just like her now!" Albert said disgustedly.

"How I wished I had my box camera back there!"

"I didn't see anything so funny. It was downright embarrassing."

"Man, but da' gals must go crazy ober yo'!" Ann mimicked the brown woman.

Albert bit his lip and slapped the reins over the mare sending her along at a faster pace.

"I never realized you were going to give me such a good time this morning!" Ann quipped. "We'll have to do this more often."

"Not on your life. Next week I'm going back to milking!"

"Just wait 'til I tell everyone about this!"

"You won't dare!"

"Oh, won't I? Now I've <u>really</u> got you!" Ann was elated, but just as quickly as complete joy arose in her, it subsided. "Darned!" she muttered half aloud.

"What now?" he asked, exasperated.

"This is really <u>too</u> good for blackmail. I'll never be able to keep from telling no matter what you promise me. I'm too weak. I just know I couldn't keep it a secret."

"Oh, come now. Have a heart, will ya?"

"Well-ll. We're going to have to make it real good. You know I've got you."

"Yeah," dejectedly.

"All right. We'll bypass all the <u>little</u> things I have on you. This is my ace in the hole. Let's get down to bare facts."

"Ah! Bare facts! Very appropriate!"

"About last night."

"For one thing, you had your dress up almost around your neck, when you and Peter were wading."

"I did not! You're exaggerating!"

"Oh! I don't know about that. You do have very nice legs."

"Oh, stop that!" Ann blushed.

"No, I mean it. I thoroughly enjoyed the view."

"My dress was hardly above my knees."

"Like heck it was! You had on white underpants with a lace ruffle. Also" and he placed special emphasis on the words. "You weren't wearing the usual bloomers. These were very brief. Is this something new with young girls I should know about? Remember, there was a bright moon— and I've got good eyesight!"

"Oh God! I'm lost! Ann drew in a deep breath. "Only Peter was ever meant to see them." Promise you won't tell Ma."

"Why should I tell Ma?"

"Well, you're Mama's boy."

"I resent that!"

"It's true. Everyone knows you're her favorite."

"I still wouldn't tell. Did I say a word about your getting married after I promised I wouldn't?"

"No, I gotta' admit, you didn't."

"Well, then? Why don't you trust me? What you do when you're with Peter is your business. You can take care of yourself, I know that."

"I think you really mean it. You promise then you won't say anything about what you see between Peter and me. Not just last night but in the future, too?"

"Only if you do the same for me."

"Agreed."

"Shake on it?"

"Shake."

"Good, that's settled then."

The wagon pulled in at Mrs. Wagner's rooming house, their second stop. This they did quickly and were soon on their way again. Ann felt relieved in having made her pact of secrecy with Albert, for he and Catherine would continue to accompany Peter and her on Thursday nights and she'd felt he cramped her freedom. Now, if she could only reach some agreement with Catherine.

"You know, I think you've grown up a lot this summer. It's time you went out with a girl."

"Why?"

"You'll find it lots of fun, and it's kind of exciting, in spite of what old VandenTill says. He makes everything that's fun sound like it's bad. I don't believe half of what he says."

"You'd better not show your feelings too openly. Remember, you'll be spending the night before the wedding at his house, just like Catherine did."

"I know, and I dread it. You think Pa will make me? After all, not all the brides do."

"All who get married in our church do. If you want a church wedding, you'll have to go through with it."

"Oh, I guess I can be pious for one night!" She gave a stifled giggle. "The next night will be worth it."

Albert gave Ann a shocked look. For her to think it was one thing, but for her to say it to him was another. He was no naive boy who knew nothing of what went on during the first night. A farm boy learned about these things long before even starting school, for animals know neither modesty nor inhibition. It was mostly the way she said it. She was looking forward to that night with great anticipation.

The milk wagon rumbled up to Dumen's bakery, their last stop. As Albert backed the wagon to the platform at the rear, Mr. Dumen opened the double doors to receive the morning's delivery. A burst of warm air from within the building surrounded them with the smell of fresh baked bread, cakes and rolls. Mr. Dumen's simple action threw a switch in Albert's stomach—he was hungry—instantly, ravishing hungry, for this was an ambrosia to the nostrils that brought tears to the eyes.

118

Mr. Dumen was a heavy set man with a completely bald pate, dressed in white pants and shirt, covered by a long white apron that started just below his neck and came to within six inches of his shoes. He often said that the lack of hair on his head was a distinct advantage in his trade, for his customers never had to worry about fallen hairs in their bread or rolls. The hair on his arms he didn't mention, yet there the hair was as thick as a hay field and always white—from the flour that covered them from morning 'til night.

"Good morning to you," came a resounding voice from the doorway.

"Good morning," Albert returned, climbed back on the wagon and started unloading the cans of milk onto the platform. Ann came to watch. Her part in the milk route effort was over after they'd made the many house-to-house deliveries, completed since leaving Mrs. Wagner's boarding house two hours earlier. The milk unloaded and the empties put on the wagon, they followed Mr. Dumen into the bakery where his wife was wrapping bread fresh from the oven. Mrs. Dumen gave them a cheerful smile and commented that Albert had grown since the last time she'd seen him.

Mrs. Dumen, a women in her middle fifties, was thinner and taller than her husband. The many hours of working next to hot ovens had dried her skin and brought premature wrinkles to her face. Her long salt and pepper hair was brought tightly into a bun at the back of her head and in this respect, she reminded Albert of his grandmother who wore her hair, though now snow white, in this same fashion.

"A growing boy like you must be very hungry by now."

"Yes, Mam!"

"How long has it been since you had breakfast?"

"About four hours."

"Now I know you're hungry. Come, we'll fix you something." She took Albert by the arm and with Ann following, they went into the store at the front of the bakery. Mr. Dumen grinned and went back to his baking, letting his wife take over the visitors. With Albert still in tow, Mrs. Dumen marched up and down in front of the show cases.

"You pick out what you'd like to have."

There were rows and rows of all kinds of bread: white, rye, sourdough, currant, raisin, pumpernickel, and cinnamon loaf. There were pastries, cakes, honey kuchen, and pies of every description. The more Albert looked the greater was his hunger, but the choice seemed endless. Mrs. Dumen saw his plight, looked over at Ann and winked.

"Can't you make up your mind?" she coaxed.

"Well, I don't want to put you to any trouble," he stammered.

"No trouble at all. You just say what you'd like and I'll fix it."

"I think I'd like to try the pumpernickel."

"How about a piece of pie to go with it? I've got some blueberry pie that's still hot out of the oven."

"That'd be fine!"

Mrs. Dumen took a loaf of pumpernickel and they followed her into the adjoining kitchen.

"Have a chair. Coffee is on the stove. I'll get the pie."

Ann got the coffee pot and set four cups on the table. Mrs. Dumen was back with the pie, a large bowl of homemade sweet butter, and a jar of gooseberry jam.

"Well now, I guess we have everything. It's nice to have new young ones make the deliveries once in a while - - and how's your mother and father?"

"Just fine. Is Mr. Dumen joining us?" asked Ann, before she started to pour the fourth cup.

"No, he's got a batch of rolls he has to watch. I've been wrapping bread for almost two hours, so I need a rest. He'll have his coffee when he gets through." Mrs. Dumen cut up half the pumpernickel loaf, buttered and jammed the slices, and then cut up the pie. Ann noticed that Albert's piece was twice as big as the other two.

"I haven't seen your mother in a long time now. It's mostly the men folk that come into town—except for this one." Mrs. Dumen nodded toward Albert.

"Yes, it's mostly Dad and Richard, who come into town," Ann said. "They stop by often. If not on deliveries, then on their way home from market."

Without warning, Ann reached over and punched Albert on the arm. "Wagenvoort," she said.

"What?"

"Wagenvoort," she repeated. "That's the name. Remember it. We'll talk about it later." Mrs. Dumen gave Ann a quizzical look, and Ann knew an explanation was in order. "I was trying to think of a girl's name earlier this morning and it just came to me."

"Oh," Mrs. Dumen raised her eyebrows, "his girl friend? But no, he would know her last name, yes?"

"Just a girl I met last night at church," replied Albert sheepishly and hoped this wasn't going to lead into something.

"I hope she's a very nice girl," Mrs. Dumen started.

"How many loaves of bread do you bake each day?" Albert asked before his sister could answer, wanting to change the subject.

"Three hundred, four hundred on Fridays," she replied. "I want you to take the rest of the blueberry pie with you."

"Mom would like us to pick up five loaves of bread; three white and two rye, a honeykuchen, and some rolls," spoke up Ann. "And, we should be going now, they'll be expecting us."

Ann paid Mrs. Dumen for her mother's order, and received several extras without charge. They bid Mrs. Dumen goodbye and were on their way home at last.

PART III
FIELDS OF GOLDEN GRAIN

11

lbert and Ann were home for over an hour when Richard returned
from the Paterson market. Things had gone very well at first and
he'd sold over half the load of strawberries at a good price. Then
a late shipment came in and flooded the market. Reluctant to sell the rest at
a very reduced price, he had brought them home.

Dick was pleased on the one hand, but exasperated that they now had
all these strawberries on their hands. So much time and effort had gone into
raising and picking and now this.

"Why didn't you sell the rest for what you could get? There's nothing
we can do but dump them out to rot."

"They just didn't want them, Pa," explained Richard. "I'd have had to
practically give them away, and I wasn't about to do that. I thought we
might sell some to our milk route customers."

"Why don't we make preserves out of them?" suggested Catherine.

"What would we do with so much preserves?" Dick shot back.

"Sell them when the market's good. They keep, so we wouldn't be
affected by a temporary glut as there is now." Catherine looked over at Ella

for approval.

"We could do it," replied Ella. "It'll be a lot of work and we'll need help from you men. We can't just dump them! We'll do it out in the cookhouse. Much like Ann and I have done with peaches over the years." She would be in charge and there was no question in her mind any longer. The men would get a good fire going and plenty of their largest pots. "Then get all the jars you can find out of storage and bring them to the cookhouse." The women took the necessary kitchen utensils they'd need and the wagon was brought to the cookhouse and unloaded. Richard and Albert were set to washing and boiling jars. Dick stood by helplessly and watched the three women take over.

"I hope you know what you're doing," Dick said, amazed at the women's sudden takeover of the situation.

"If we can't sell 'em fresh, then we'll sell 'em as preserves," retorted Ann.

"You go about your business in the barn," Ella told her husband. "You're no good to us here. The rest is women's work."

The cookhouse was soon filled with jars, pots, and strawberries in various stages of processing. Steam from the boiling water clouded the air as they settled down to an efficient routine. Ella wanted to know how everything went at choir practice and whether Albert seemed to enjoy his first session. Before Ann could reply, Catherine answered with a question of her own.

"Did Albert tell you about the girl he met during the choir social?"

"No! All he said was that he had a good time."

"I guess he did! He met a very pretty girl and I could hardly tear him away to come home."

"Oh?" Ella brightened at the news.

"He really surprised me. And we thought he was so shy. His first night at choir practice and it looks like he's got a girl friend."

Ann sat decappng strawberries in silence, but listening. Either a lot more went on that she wasn't aware of, or else Catherine was making a big story of almost nothing. Why Catherine was doing this, she didn't understand, for she'd never figured her as an idle gossip.

"You really think so?" Ella beamed with intense interest. "What's her name? Do I know her?"

"Wagenvoort! Marjorie Wagenvoort!" Ann volunteered and gave

Catherine a sarcastic smile.

"My!" Ella broke in. "You both seem to know all about her and yet he didn't say a word to me."

"Why should he, Ma?" broke in Ann. "He's not a child anymore."

"Yes, I know. He's grown up a great deal this last while," Ella sighed.

"You've got to face it," Ann continued. "He's no longer your little boy."

"I didn't say he was," Ella snapped back. Ann had hit a tender spot and it hurt.

The women worked until noon. Ella broke off from the preserves to make lunch, while her daughters continued in the cookhouse.

"Why did you do that?" Ann asked, belligerently.

"What?" replied Catherine in apparent surprise.

"If I didn't know you better, I'd say you set Ma up before."

"You mean about Albert?"

"Yes, about Al. You think he's going to appreciate your blabbing about him meeting that girl last night?"

"Oh, I don't think he'll mind. Did you notice how Ma brightened up when I told her?"

"Yeah, I noticed. I was a little surprised. She's tried to keep him under her wing. I was sure she'd object when he tried for a little freedom."

"You know, it was her idea that Al join choir so he could meet new people—a girl, that is."

"I suppose so. Maybe she does feel it's time he left the nest and tried to fly on his own a bit."

"Of course. He needs to get out more, we all know that. I hope to see that he does."

"You gonna tell Al that you told Ma?"

"Think I should?"

"Definitely! And soon, before Ma gets to him. The least you can do is warn him so he can be prepared."

"Why are you so concerned that I tell Albert?" remarked Catherine, as they started for the house.

"I try to watch out for my little brother when I can," was all she'd say.

———◆·▶◀·◆———

Catherine asked to go on the milk route with Dick the next morning, and he agreed. It would take some doing, but she was convinced he would go along with her idea and if he had any doubts, she should be able to handle them during the morning's run. They would pick up the city cousins at the train depot along the way, and for Catherine's part, she wanted to stop at the printer's and order some good looking labels for the strawberry preserves. She was so sure they'd make out well with selling the preserves, that they would also want to buy a large supply of jars for subsequent pickings. They wouldn't be just regular jars, but should be fancy and set off the preserves to their best advantage. Dick would have to be persuaded, but she was confident she'd overcome whatever objections he might have.

The train pulled into the station ten minutes late, and they watched from under the paint-peeled overhang of the produce transfer platform for Beatrice's children to disembark. Freddy was carrying a tattered suitcase, while Sara carried a cardboard box tied up neatly with string, with a homemade handle. Between them walked Mary and Raymond. There was a year difference in age between each of the four starting with Fred at twelve and progressing downward to Raymond. These represented the last of Beatrice's flock of nine; there had been no children since Raymond for Beatrice had at last stopped the procession of annual increase.

"There they are!" mentioned Dick, pointing toward the next to last car. He and Catherine waved to them and hurried over to greet the newcomers.

"Have any problems on the way?" Dick asked, taking Fred's suitcase and Sara's box, as they headed for the wagon.

"No problems, Uncle Dick," replied Freddy, "but it's an awfully long ride and the train made a lot of stops. I thought we were never going to get here."

"That's because it serves as a milk train," Dick explained, tossing the luggage up in the wagon beside the empty milk cans and the preserve jars.

128

"You must be hungry. Have you had anything to eat since you left home?" asked Catherine.

"We had a few sandwiches," spoke up Sara, "but we ate those long ago."

"And I'll bet you're tired too. Did you sleep on the train?" Catherine moved the youngest two in between them up front while the others sat in back.

"Not very much," returned Sara. "It was too bouncy and noisy. All it did was go clickity-clack, clickity-clack, all the way."

They were on their way home, following a brief stop at the printer's to pick up the labels. Catherine fed the cousins from the basket of food she had brought with her. Ella had insisted she bring plenty for them to eat— she knew they'd be hungry. They wolfed down everything as though they hadn't eaten in days; several of the hot rolls Catherine had gotten at Dumen's went the same way.

The food gone, the children fell asleep; the jouncing of the wagon apparently was less disturbing to them than that of the train. *It was no wonder they were exhausted*, Catherine thought, she knew they'd been up before 2:00 AM to catch the early train out of Philadelphia. They rode on in silence but there had been much to talk about earlier; it was as if she and Dick were all talked out.

Dick was humming to himself, and she knew why; it had been an interesting morning, especially their stop at Dumen's. Several times from Dumen's to the train depot she had glanced across at him and seen the pleased expression on his face. Mrs. Dumen had made his day.

Her father-in-law, always so austere and strict, had shown another side of himself. He was vulnerable to flattery, if not toward himself, then towards his family. It'd been a small incident, but it showed that beneath the cold, hard outer shell, there was some warmth.

This had all come after the long talk they'd had on the way into town, which was pleasant enough in itself. Dick had slept on her idea as he said he would, and agreed they should give it a try. He had pointed out that if and when word of this reached church, their actions might be frowned upon as being improper, especially by the Reverend. However, he saw no harm in it, and wasn't about to be concerned about the Reverend's thoughts on a matter which wasn't any of his business in the first place. He'd even agreed that they should buy new jars, not a big supply, but at least enough to handle the next picking. If all went as well as she predicted, there would be time enough to get additional supplies. They would try her scheme next Monday, he had said, then Albert should be well enough to help Richard with the milking. By the time they'd reached their first stop, she knew that nothing would dissuade him from exploring its possibilities. This had set the tone for the rest of the morning—next had come Sullivan's livery stables and the horse.

Dick wanted to see the horse that Richard had mentioned the day before. She'd gone with him when they'd looked the horse over. Richard had not exaggerated. The strawberry roan was beautiful, but mean! No one could handle him, and the owner was willing to reduce his price. Dick would think it over and go back again.

The stop at the Dumen's was never a short one, but this morning they'd had to watch the time so they'd be at the train depot at nine. Catherine had been there once before, but that'd been long before her marriage. It was as they were sitting drinking coffee with Mrs. Dumen that the episode began. She had noticed an odd expression on Mrs. Dumen's face when Dick introduced her, but its significance was obscure. What followed she played back through her mind as it occurred, much like a phonograph needle plays back a choice recording.

"I don't understand you, Mr. DeGraf," Mrs. Dumen said. "You have these beautiful children and you've kept them buried away out there on the farm. Shame on you! I'm glad you're finally letting them come in and see our little town."

"What's this now?" Dick asked.

"Yesterday, I met Albert with his pretty sister. Ann is no stranger to me, but Albert was only a boy the last I'd seen him. My, how he's grown and such a handsome lad. Now, today, you bring another surprise—this lovely young woman. You must be proud to have so many good-looking children."

"We can't take credit for Catherine here," Dick replied matter-of-factly. "But for the others, their mother was a beautiful woman in her younger days—before the fire."

"Oh, I'm sorry," Mrs. Dumen gasped. "I didn't think about your wife's tragedy when I praised the children."

"There's no need for apologies," Dick continued with some emotion. "My wife may have lost what was a lovely face, but in these last years she

130

has gained an inner quality that has more than made up for what she lost."

"Oh, I'm so glad," was all Mrs. Dumen could say.

Later, Dick charged Catherine not to repeat what had been said at the Dumen's. He returned to his stern old self—but not quite, for he had exposed himself briefly in that unguarded moment.

◆·▸×◂·◆

A red-winged blackbird suspiciously eyed the intruder and kept silent where he sat hidden in a scraggly swamp birch near the edge of the pond. The soft footfalls along the path were cause for only moderate concern, so he tried out a few preliminary trills, waited a few moments, and then encouraged by the apparent harmlessness of the new occupant on the scene, launched into full morning song. Another blackbird, at the far side of the pond, unable to let this go unchallenged, answered the first, but improved on the melody by adding new notes and crescendos. Every artist loves competition, and soon the intervening waters reverberated in an oral contest.

Albert pushed the boat from shore and hopped in as it glided out across the quiet waters, slid the oars in the locks, and quickly moved the boat forward. His grandfather had taught him many years before how to feather the oars so as to move along without creating so much as a ripple.

He had told his mother he was going to do a little fishing and his equipment lay in the bottom of the boat, but what he'd said was only partly true. The fishing would wait until later, for his first interest was to sit and unobtrusively watch the activity that was always going on out here. To the casual eye it was a place of nothingness, but he never found it so, for nature was at work here as much as in an ant nest or a bee hive. The secret was to become an undisturbing part of the scene—silence was essential.

On the opposite side, the pond joined the swamp; here the shoreline, if such a thing existed, was shallow and the cattails grew in abundance. He pointed the bow in that direction, gave several quick strong strokes of the oars without breaking water and let the boat glide forward on its momentum. He thought he'd seen a great blue heron among the bulrushes, but wasn't sure and wanted a closer look. The boat moved without making a sound, gradually slowing as it went. The blue heron was there, standing knee deep in the water and perfectly still. There was a quick movement of its head downward and up it came with a small fish, which it deftly tossed in the air, opened its bill under the falling object, and the fish disappeared.. He was so close he could see the bulging ripple in the bird's neck as the fish slid down. The heron turned, saw the approaching boat, and with slow lazy wings took to the air and glided away deep into the swamp.

Behind him a small mouthed bass broke water as though to remind him that he'd come to fish, but that would wait a little longer. A few more strokes of the oars and the boat was among the cattails. Dragonflies zipped in and out among the reeds and every so often seemed to momentarily land on the water, only to shoot off again in another direction. Just before him, straddling several stalks, was a huge spider web and he quickly backwatered to keep from breaking it. Mrs. Spider was making out just fine as he could see; she had a goodly supply of insects ensnared within her web. Looking closely he saw that many were mere shells, their body juices having long since been sucked dry, while others were encased in heavy webbing for future use. As man puts his savings in a bank for a rainy day, so Mrs. Spider had her cache for possible lean days ahead. Albert was about to back the boat away without disturbing her, when a dragonfly hit the silky filament making the whole web vibrate violently upon contact, and Mrs. Spider quickly went to work trying to secure her latest victim. This would be a tremendous meal, if she could but web it down. Each time she added a series of silken threads, they were broken by the flies' violent struggle, but then she would try again. This went on for several minutes, until with one especially convulsive movement, the dragonfly broke free leaving a gaping hole in the web.

"You can't have them all," Albert said to himself, and pulled strongly backwards on the oars. He could see Mrs. Spider repairing her damaged web as he glided away.

The pond was alive today as it always was. A group of turtles sunning themselves on a half exposed log finally decided to take to the water in front of the approaching boat. Further in the reeds the frogs croaked in several octaves and one deep bass voice sounded far to the left; a very large bullfrog, perhaps the granddaddy of them all. Ahead, a mound protruded topped by a cluster of brilliant blue irises, and nearby a black masked Maryland yellowthroat flitted in the bushes. Albert decided it was just about time to move out for a little fishing when he saw a mother muskrat and her young and redirected the course of the boat so that it came near. The young ones were playing together like a group of kittens rolling over one upon the other, but this still was not getting any fishing done, so he headed the boat out to deeper water.

As he sat and fished, he now watched nature's circus of events from center stage for here he could observe the shoreline on all sides. Swallows swooped low across the water cutting curves in the sky. Their erratic flight, as they dove and soared catching insects on the wing, fascinated him so that he didn't see her until she was almost at the boat landing. It was Catherine. He threw up his hand as a signal and she waved back. The fishing line was reeled in and with strong easy strokes he headed in her direction.

"May I come aboard, Commodore?" she called, while he was pulling to the dock.

"Your Majesty! Of course. Welcome to the H.M.S. Pinafore." Albert stepped ashore, bowed low, took her hand, kissed it with a grand flourish, and assisted her into the boat.

"Clear the way! Pipe us aboard, Captain," he called to an imaginary crew.

"Why, thank you, Commodore. How gracious of you," she exclaimed with all the dignity and pomp of a queen.

"Have the troops arrived, your Majesty?"

"Troops?" she asked, not sure at first that he was referring to Aunt Bea's children arriving for the summer.

"The reserves from Philadelphia. Have they arrived?"

"Yes, they're here. They came in by special transport and are now making a reconnaissance of the battle area."

"Fine! I hope they are being properly billeted and provided for."

"They are presently under the care of the Duke and Duchess of yonder castle," she made a grandiose gesture towards the house.

"Good. I'm glad to hear that all is well and there is no need for our assistance. Therefore, let us embark. Heave to." He took to the oars and they glided off across the water. "What are the orders, your Majesty? For what part do we sail, what distant lands explore—Trinidad, Cape of Good

Hope, Rangoon, or Singapore? It is but for you to say. The world is yours."

"Your choice, Commodore. The helm is yours. Show me all the seven seas, its lands and islands too, but be sure we're back in time for lunch, one hour hence." Catherine was caught up in the spirit of the game. The dreams and fortunes of her girlhood days flooded over her. It was grand to be alive and young, for indeed she felt young just now—radiantly young and carefree, and well pleased with the world.

"So be it. Your wish is my command. We sail upon the wings of light, and time will stand as naught 'til we are back." He paused and looked down towards the starboard side, turned the boat and headed for a group of ducks. "Before we set our course for foreign lands, we must inspect the frigates ere we go. The wonders of the orient must wait—for duties of the navy and our state." He guided the boat silently to within yards of the ducks, before they became alarmed and in a great rush of beating wings took to the sky.

Catherine broke into a fit of laughing at the scattering ducks. "Albert, you amuse me. You became so engrossed in our make believe. Do you realize your talk just now was metered like a poem? It's like a fairy tale."

"What's wrong with fairy tales?" he asked defensively.

"They are for children."

"Are we not all children, at times."

"I suppose so. I used to make my own dreams when I was growing up, but no more. That time is past."

"Why should it be? You are still young— and beautiful."

"Oh, come now. Let's not spoil things. No, like many little girls who read too many fairy tales, I used to dream of a knight in shining armor. A gallant, but tender prince who would take me away to grand adventures in mystic lands beyond the seas."

"That knight never came?"

"No, instead I found a husband."

"You had to settle for reality. That's my problem, too. My dreams seem to conflict with reality. Yet, I continue to dream."

"As an adult one has to set aside these fantasies."

"Why?"

She had no answer. He saw a cloud pass across her face. Then finally in a more subdued voice, "Oh, let's get out of this world of fantasy and back to reality."

"You started this, I didn't."

"How so?"

"You called me Commodore."

"A single word."

"That's all it took to get me started."

"Do you enjoy doing it?"

"I need to sometimes, to retain my sanity, I think. Perhaps I overdo it at times and lose perspective of my surroundings. I sometimes dream I am a student of Socrates. The dream becomes so real that I wonder if I am a farm boy dreaming about Ancient Greece, or in Ancient Greece dreaming I am here. Which is the real me and which the ghost of my imagination."

"I do not think it good to dwell too long in the unreal world. We'll get nowhere if we continue to talk like this. It is a practical world and we have to live in it day by day.

The boat had been motionless near the center of the pond; conversation had replaced travel, and Albert had made no effort to move on. She looked about and became aware of their stagnation.

"Come, come Commodore. You have not shown the world to me as you promised, and time has not stood still." Her voice now had returned to normal.

"I'm sorry. I do not have the power here that comes to me in my dreams."

"From what I've glimpsed of your fantasies, perhaps it's best that things are as they are." Her laugh told him she was again enjoying their little excursion.

He leaned forward and put a finger to his lips. "Let's be quiet for awhile. I want to show you something— if we're lucky."

Albert eased the boat forward and headed for the far end of the pond with mute strokes, the oar blades never breaking surface on the forward stroke and slipping up and over for the next with such fine precision that they hardly knew they'd left their liquid home. At that end of the pond there was a high grassy bank which sloped directly down to the water. This point was clear of water weeds. Thirty feet beyond this the water again ran shallow and the cattails began. Albert detoured so they came up around and behind the cattails, where they could watch the grassy bank and yet not be seen. Catherine noticed there were several trails up and down the bank where the grass was flattened down, all pointing toward the water. She heard a splash and then another.

Well behind the cattail screen, Albert eased the oars inside the boat and pointed to the water's edge. Catherine looked and saw nothing, but then two furry forms broke the surface and scurried up the bank; they were silky brown and glistened in the sun. Up the bank they went each trying to out-scramble the other to the top and then, with one grand shove, each in turn came slipping and sliding down to go 'kersplash' back into the water. Catherine had never seen such animals before and thought they must be beavers.

Albert moved his position next to her and whispered, "They're River Otters. How and why they're here I don't know, but they must have come over from Saddle River and decided to settle here. There's just a pair as far as I can tell, I've seen no others. I'm sure no one else knows about them, certainly not my brothers, for they'd have set traps for them for sure."

"They're cute. What are they trying to do?" she whispered back.

"They're playing, just having fun sliding down the bank."

They watched the repeated climbing and sliding of the two furry creatures; sometimes they slid on their stomachs, sometimes on their backs, which showed the silvery sheen of belly fur. Albert pointed out the larger one's right foreleg, where the hair was thin and the skin showed through.

"I found that one at the other end of the pond early this spring caught in one of Richard's muskrat traps. Wouldn't he have been surprised if he'd gotten there first. Mr. Otter would now be just a pelt. I let it go and got bit several times for my trouble. They're little scrappers when cornered, but so playful when free."

"You do this often on your brother?" she grinned. He knew she didn't disapprove.

"More than I'd care to acknowledge."

"Doesn't he catch on?"

"How can he? I always reset the trap, although it disgusts me to do it. I don't think he'll catch the otters again. They're smart, not like muskrats."

"What do they eat?"

"Mostly fish, but I never feed them. They should not get used to human scent. They're wild creatures, and best they stay that way. For them to lose their wariness is to make them vulnerable. It's enough for me to watch them from a distance. Have you seen enough?"

"Yes, I think so."

Albert took an oar and banged it against the side of the boat when the otters were half way up their climb upon the bank. Each took a quick flip backwards and all that remained were two widening circles of ripples in the water. The bank was deserted.

"Why did you do that?"

"To keep them wary of intruders. Now we again tour my watery estate." He leaned forward into the oars and saw the wide-open smile on her face which he returned to her of equal kind.

"You do odd things, I think, but I like the way you do them," she said.

"You will not tell about the otters, please."

"Heavens, no. It's <u>our</u> secret."

chapter

12

Sunday morning decided it in Dick's mind. He had vacillated all Saturday and been on the knife's edge. It was just a matter of a small push to put him on one side or the other. The discussion started at breakfast as to who was going to ride to church in what that morning. There wasn't room for everyone now that there were four extra children in the house. Dick, Ella, Sarah, and Clara would ride in the large carriage and no one questioned this, but who else would ride with them? Normally, Albert, Ann and little Govert would squeeze in the rear seat, while Richard and Catherine used the two seated buggy. That left no room for Beatrice's four, so the produce wagon would have to replace the buggy.

No one cared much for the wagon, which was slow and uncomfortable. Richard and Albert had cleaned it thoroughly Saturday afternoon, so it wasn't dirty, it just wasn't the kind of vehicle that one cared to ride in to church. Ann wanted no parts of getting stuck with her city cousins and the idea of riding to church in a produce wagon was downright demoralizing. As Albert often said, Ann could be extremely vocal at times and this morning she was in good form. She was no longer afraid of her father, and when he mentioned it was no disgrace to ride in the wagon, she stalked off to contact Peter. She would ride with the Vandenbergs.

Ellen said nothing, but only shook her head and smiled. She would never have thought this scene even remotely possible a decade ago; for then Dick ruled the house with an iron hand; his word was law. Now, such things were settled by debate–a far cry from the old days.

Albert said he'd drive the wagon and take Govert and the cousins. Govert was the only one who wanted to ride with them; he was starved for companions his own age and had been in his glory since their arrival. That settled the matter for this Sunday, but there would be others. Dick rationalized that a new horse and carriage wasn't such a luxury as the practical side of his mind had kept telling him. The long years of semi-poverty had taught him a degree of conservatism no longer necessary. Yet, it was difficult to shake. The DeGrafs were no longer poor. The family's harangue that morning caused the inner stirring that had plagued him ever since he'd ridden in Cornelius' new automobile to break forth. Although he wouldn't go as far as Cornelius had, he became determined to have the best darned horse and carriage in the area. The strawberry roan he'd seen Saturday morning was as handsome as he'd ever seen; if only it could be broken for carriage use. There'd been wild fear in the stallion's eyes and kicked-in stall boards. It would be no easy task to handle him. He'd agreed to take Catherine and Ann into town Monday with the strawberry preserves. Now he was certain that Albert should go with them, for the boy had a keen sense about animals. He wanted Albert to have a look at the stallion before the final decision was made.

———◆•×•◆———

Monday morning everyone pitched in with the milking. The men-folk finished loading the wagon and were having coffee, when Ann and Catherine came downstairs dressed in their Sunday best.

"You two look more like you're off to a wedding than selling preserves." commented Dick.

"Now Pa. This is what we said, remember?" Catherine reminded him. "You agreed to put on some good clothes, too."

"How about me? Where do I fit in?" broke in Albert.

"Since you're going along, that goes for you too," Dick remarked. "If these girls insist on me being duded up. I'm not about to let you off the hook."

"But all I'm gonna' do is look at a horse."

"Never mind, now get to it," Dick motioned Albert toward the stairs and followed after him.

Albert sat in back of the wagon with the preserves. Here he could watch the countryside go by and reminisce. There was Saturday's excursion at the pond, which was enough to occupy his thoughts for quite awhile. He wasn't sure why he'd shown her the otters, for he'd never intended to tell anyone about them. Their furs were valuable, far more than any muskrat, and if his brothers ever heard, they'd be sure to get them, one way or another. Yet, he trusted Catherine to keep his secret.

When they arrived at the stable, Dick told Ann and Catherine to drive over to Dumen's bakery, pick up Ella's order of baked goods, and see if the Dumen's might be interested in preserves. The owner was away, so the stable boy showed them the horse.

"I wouldn't get too close if I were you," the boy said. "He's a mean one."

"Oh, we'll be careful," Dick replied. "I just want to show him to my son. You can go about your chores."

It was a young stallion, probably not more than three years old, beautifully marked, good withers, long legs, and about 17 hands high. There was fire in his eyes. Even stalled as he was, he was checked with bit and bridle, and Albert could see where the bit had chaffed the sides of his mouth to the point of bleeding. A hobble was attached to the front left leg.

"He's sure been kicking up a fuss in here." Albert leaned over the side of the stall and looked in. The horse reared back and then charged towards him. He quickly retreated. "Look at how he's kicked those stall boards to splinters."

"He's done most of that since Saturday. They'd just brought him in and the stall wasn't nearly as bad."

Dick reached over to take hold of the lead rope but the horse reared back, snorted and shook his head violently from side to side.

"Hmmm! He looks a lot meaner than when I saw him before," signed Dick. "Maybe we'd better forget about him."

"No harm in looking him over, Pa. He's been mistreated! Still, he's a darned good looking animal." Albert took several cubes of sugar from a paper bag, set them on the top rail, and stepped back. The horse watched them closely and when they made no attempt to come forward, he reached over and took the sugar.

"Think they've ruined him, beyond hope? Maybe we're asking for a heap of trouble." Dick was becoming less sure of the idea he had been stewing about over the week-end.

"Could be, but it would be interesting to try to bring him around. Another week of the kind of treatment he's had and he'll be no good to anyone. I'd hate to see that. The way he is now, I'll bet we could get him real cheap. Let's buy him, Pa. It'd be a shame not to. I think we can handle him. Did they say Saturday how much they want for him?"

"A hundred and sixty dollars."

"Gosh, that's a lot for a horse."

"He's supposed to be from pure blood line, but I'll never pay it. Now that I see him again, I wouldn't give half of that."

"Well, you can at least bargain for him. You've nothing to lose."

"If we can handle him" Dick paused thoughtfully, "we might have a time just getting him home."

"You weren't thinking of getting a new carriage today too, were you?"

"I was, but not any more. It'll be enough to just get him home."

The stable owner came around the side of the building and hailed them while still at some distance. He was a huge burly man with a massive black mustache and thick hairy arms.

"You two gentlemen lookin' for a good horse?"

"Well, if you've got one," Dick replied. Albert just nodded, his father would do the talking.

"You're lookin' at him. Best damned horse in the stables—or anywheres else in these parts."

"That's not saying much for horse flesh around here then."

"What's the matter? That horse's a purebred."

"Any horse you've got to hobble in a stall to keep him from kicking someone's brains out, ain't exactly good!"

"He's a bit temperamental, that's all. Got fine spirit. Now, if you're lookin' for a plow horse, you're in the wrong place."

"Looks mean to me. You've had a whip on him plenty, haven't you? Bet you can't even walk him without half choking him to death, let along hitch him in a carriage."

"He's not a carriage horse. He was brought here for the Fire Company. He's a fire horse, and you know they've got to be the best. They're bred for speed, strength, and stamina."

"Then why ain't he up at the Fire House?"

"Well, they had some trouble with him." The burly man was sizing Dick up and deciding this wasn't going to be an easy sale. "But proper training will fix that."

"Trouble! You're damned right you've had trouble. We can see that. As for training, the whip marks, hobble, and bloody mouth speak well enough for that."

"God damn it! I didn't ask for your opinion on our handling," the burly man raised his voice in irritation. "You interested in buying him or not?"

"I might be interested, that depends." Dick was enjoying himself. This was more his kind of bargaining than selling strawberry preserves. "How much you want for him?"

"A hundred and sixty dollars, and that's a bargain."

"Too much. We're not even sure we can use him. He looks mean as Satan."

"All right. A hundred and twenty."

"I'll tell you what I'll do." Dick squinted at the horse and then looked directly down at the stable owner. The burly man was broader and heavier than him, but Dick towered over him a good six inches. "If you take the hobble and the bit and bridle off him, put a halter on, and walk him around out here on a lead rope for us, I'll give you what you ask. And no whip on him, either."

The burly man ran his hand across his mustache several times, hesitated, and then stepped over to the left side of the stall. He reached over and took hold of the bridle; it was barely in his hands when the horse tried to rear on its hind legs, but the check rope stopped him. The stallion then dropped back and let fly its hind legs in swift succession, knocking out a section of the back of the stall.

"Can't do it," chuckled Dick. "I thought not."

"All right, so he's a little mean. Just needs more training."

"Yes, and if you have any more sessions like this one, you'll likely wind up with a horse with a broken leg. I'll give you forty dollars for him and take him off your hands."

"That's giving him away!"

"I don't think he's worth much to you. He's been ruined. Not sure he's going to be worth anything to us either, but I've got a boy here who has a way with animals. He'd like to try."

"You're crazy if you think this kid can handle him!" the burly man stormed. "That horse needs a strong arm. He'll kill this boy!"

"I think not. I've a lot of confidence in him."

"All right, you can have him for that price. I take no responsibility for anyone getting hurt or any property damage."

"No, we'll be responsible. We take him as is—no comebacks."

"I want the money before you touch him."

"We're taking a big chance." Dick took out his wallet, counted out the money, and handed it to the stable owner.

"It'll be worth it to see what you do with him." He put the money in his pocket. "You've got a lot of horse there, but handlin' him's gonna' be another matter. Frankly, we haven't been able to."

"We know that. Now we'd like to be left alone with him."

"Gladly," replied the burly man. He had no desire to be around when the fireworks began.

Albert looked towards the driveway and saw that the ladies had pulled up in the carriage and were waiting for them. "Catherine and Ann are here," he told his father.

"Well, how're the two horsemen doing?" asked Catherine as they strode up.

"We bought ourselves a horse—a wild one. Albert and I were just going to work on him when you drove up."

"We can always leave again and go shopping," remarked Ann, half expectantly.

"We've still got strawberries to sell," reminded Catherine.

"We've got problems," remarked Dick. "The preserves on one hand and the horse on the other."

"Pa, why don't you go with the girls and leave me stay with the stallion. I'll see if I can get him settled by the time you get back."

"I don't like you with that horse alone," returned Dick. "Not safe!"

"I'll just talk to him and calm him down."

"Don't you get in that stall with him! He could kill you!"

Albert shook his head. "I'll be careful."

"Just get him used to you, 'til we get back." Dick looked uneasily from the stallion to his son. He now regretted not having Richard along to help. The stallion was meaner than he'd figured and they'd need all the assistance possible. "Better yet, if we're not back in a couple of hours, go over to Dumens. She'll give you a bite to eat and we'll meet you there."

"Yes, Pa." Albert walked back towards the horse, turned and waved as the carriage pulled out, but his mind was on the strawberry roan.

Albert went back to where the stallion was stalled and stood watching the horse for several minutes before making any attempt to approach him; he knew all his movements would need to be done slowly and quietly. If he was going to befriend the stallion, it would have to be done with gentleness and patience. He guessed the others would be gone for several hours—but he'd need every minute of that time.

His first job was to replace the bit and bridle with a simple halter. To have a horse harnessed like this while stalled was a miserable way to keep an animal, but apparently they had no other way to control him. He'd have to get rid of the harness before he could put the halter on, which meant the stallion would be free within the stall unless he roped him fast. He must think through thoroughly each step ahead of time. To begin with, he generously disposed of one lump of sugar after another, and the horse began taking them readily; he'd never known a horse that didn't have a sweet tooth. All the while he fed, he talked to the animal in low soothing tones as though preparing a small child for bedtime.

Finally, he put his hand to the horse's cheek and gently scratched him. The stallion flinched at the human touch, but took the sugar anyway. He decided against the rope and the next time the horse lowered his head for sugar, Albert unbuckled the throatlatch, slowly reached for the check piece and eased the harness over the horse's head so that it fell to the ground. The stallion was free to move about the stall with only the splintered boards and hobble to retain him. There was no way to get the horse to come to him except by coaxing.

Albert slipped his arm through the halter and fed more sugar from his open hand. Each time he held the sugar lower than before so the horse had to bring his head to within inches of the halter.

When the horse came down for the next lump, he brought the halter up around its head; the horse began to rear back, but a quick flip and the halter was in place. On the next cube of sugar, he snapped the buckle and the job was done. He'd used up his whole bag of sugar but it was worth it. Albert leaned back from where he stood at the stall railing; there was a tenseness in his chest as though he pulled a great weight.

The grocery store was down the street, but before heading in that direction, Albert stopped and spoke to the stable owner, told him what he'd done, and asked that no one go near the horse while he was away. When he returned, he was fortified with more sugar, apples and carrots. They were green cooking apples, and he quartered each before offering it by hand. They lasted longer that way, and he'd heard of horses getting a whole apple stuck in their windpipe and choking to death. That was the last thing he wanted. For the next half hour he stood at the railing and talked. What he said wasn't important, it was the tone of his voice that counted. The horse accepted his presence.

The stallion had reared his head, rolled the whites of his eyes and stomped when he'd first approached the stall, but now there was none of this. His manner and voice were having their effect and he was able to bring the horse's head around to him gently with the rope and halter; the cutting bit was gone, and the horse didn't seem to mind the slow easy pull. Albert patted the forelock but when he touched the withers a quiver ran through the stallion's body.

"You're going to get yourself killed!" the stable boy yelled from behind him. The horse reared, kicked at the stallboards and lunged forward, knocking Albert back; he caught himself and quickly jumped to the side.

"Get away from here! You're spooking the horse! Leave me alone with him!"

"It's your funeral!" the boy slurred, leaving abruptly.

"That kid must've beat you, ol' boy. I can see you don't like him." He spoke to the stallion as though it were another person, and returned to the railing. He remembered his father's parting words about not taking chances. "Never get in a stall with a wild horse—he can crush and stomp you to death in an instant." But that was long ago and had become blurred with other thoughts until it lost its meaning. He eased himself down inside the stall. With slow cautious movements he loosened the hobble on the horse's left front leg. The stallion stood and quivered. When the hobble was free, Albert stepped back, allowing the horse to put its foot down. It suddenly fell forward nearly crushing him against the wall, but quickly righted itself and stood on three legs with the other dangling.

"Circulation's gone, huh?" The horse backed off abruptly and then stood still. Albert rubbed the leg and moved it up and down until finally the stallion could put his weight on it.

It was getting close to noon and he'd been with the stallion over three hours. The feeding of sugar and apples had been replaced with oats and hay; anything to gain the horse's friendship, and he wanted to save the tidbits. They'd be needed later on. The decision was quick and rash, but it seemed the best at the time. Albert left to see the burly man again.

"I'm going to start walking the horse home," he told the stable owner.

"You're gonna' what?" exclaimed the stable owner, as though he hadn't heard properly.

"When my father comes for me, tell him I'll be on the north road out of town. I'll be walking the stallion."

"Now wait a minute! I sold that horse to your father, a grown man. Do you think I can let a mere boy try to take that wild beast out of here?"

"There'll be no problem, if everybody stays well away from there. I'd like to take a gunny sack with some oats, if I may."

"Take what oats you want. But I can't let you take the horse. If anything happens to you, I'd never forgive myself. And I'd have your father to face."

"My father knows what I'm doing. That's why he left me here alone."

"You're sure about that?"

"Quite sure."

"Well, all right then. I told your Dad I took no further responsibility."

"That's right, so what I do is our business, not yours."

Albert went back to the strawberry roan. He was by no means sure he was doing the right thing, but if he waited for others, there would be the problem of the stallion getting used to them. It'd taken him all this time to gain the horse's confidence and there was no telling how he'd react when the others arrived. It was best he do this alone. Anticipation made him hungry, but there was no time for eating. The apple he chewed on nervously would have to do for now.

Fortified with sugar, apples, and oats, Albert was ready for the biggest test. He talked to the stallion again, and then unlatched the stall gate, letting it swing open. All that kept the stallion from freedom was the rope from the halter to his hand—a very thin thread for a horse like this. Holding a pail of oats in front of him, Albert backed out into the sunshine of the yard and the stallion followed him. Once out in the open, he let him finish what there was. The pail empty, the stallion raised his head and looked about. Albert had no doubt the horse knew he was free; the animal's muscles quivered just below his hide. This was the moment of decision. At any instant the stallion could race off down the road and Albert could never stop him. To hang on the lead rope would be suicide. Words of reassurance flowed in an unending stream as he slowly led the horse out the yard and down the road. The stable owner stood some distance in the shadow of the building and watched, and shook his head in amazement, nervously stroking his mustache. A mere boy, less than half his weight, had done what he, with all his experience, could not. He'd never seen anything quite like it before.

Albert took all the back roads and alleys out of town, for the traffic on the main roads was one thing he wanted to avoid. It was slow business. When the stallion stopped, Albert stopped. Then he'd coax him on with a tidbit from the gunny sack he'd fastened to his waist. He'd feed only while they were walking—there was no reward for standing still. Twice they got lost before they reached the edge of town.

Now that success seemed assured, Albert thought about the others—his father and the girls. He wondered what his father's reaction would be when he returned to the stables and found him gone. He'd lied to the stable owner about his father's permission to take the horse. It seemed a small lie, but his father might not think so. He'd face that when it came. The success of his decision would make it right.

When they reached the north road, they were at the outskirts of town and open countryside lay ahead of them. Albert relaxed and was feeling quite pleased with himself, for he'd won perhaps the biggest test ever imposed on him. Self-assurance is a wonderful thing, but it can also lead to carelessness. A horse and carriage, which he should have heard, came up from behind at considerable speed, and before Albert knew it, the carriage was almost on top of them and bearing down. The stallion heard the commotion at his heels, danced sideways pulling Albert into the ditch at the side of the road. The rope was still in his hand when the stallion reared on its hind legs and bolted for the open fields dragging Albert a dozen yards before he let go. The driver never stopped. Albert picked himself up from the grass where he'd been thrown and looked about. The stallion was gone.

He followed through the field along where he thought the horse had traveled. To have come this far only to lose him was ironic. His father would never forgive him. Over-confidence had been his downfall. Doggedly, he pushed on through the tall grass. He could see disturbed spots of bent stalks. That told him the stallion had passed that way. How could he have gotten out of sight so soon? This, indeed, was a magnificent horse with speed and stamina; a horse that surely could run for miles and hardly be winded. All the foreboding thoughts that had plagued him earlier at the stables now flooded back on him. Failure was a difficult thing to face, even in the bright sunshine of an early afternoon. It would be far worse when he met his father empty-handed. Then tonight alone in bed; that's when troubles were always their worst.

At the far edge of the meadow was a rise beyond which he couldn't see; the scant marking in the grass skirted this. Instinct told him to head for the top of the small hill, where he should have a view down the other side. At the top he looked in all directions and saw nothing but fields and small patches of woodland. Dejectedly, he sat down and felt he wanted to cry. What a stupid fool he was. The words kept coming to him over and over. "Stupid fool, stupid fool! You were so sure of yourself."

How long he sat there he wasn't sure. His brain had become fogged and he didn't know what to do. The stallion could be anywhere–miles away and traveling further all the time. He'd have to retrace his steps and pick up the horse's trail—if it left the grasslands it would be lost for good. He sat thinking, wondering what to do, when something warm and wet touched the back of his neck. Turning, he glanced upwards and saw the stallion towering over him. As quietly as the sunlight that shone down upon them both, the roan had come up behind him and stood.

Albert and the horse were walking along peacefully, fully two miles out of town, when Dick and the girls came along. Albert had learned his lesson; when they were still some distance he took the stallion off the road and tied him to a tree. Then he returned and waited.

Dick had been ready to scold the boy. He was much more worried than angry, for he knew the risks that had been taken, despite all his warnings. Now that he saw his son was safe, it was easy to forgive. Albert waved and grinned broadly at them when they drew up.

"How'd the preserves sales go?" he asked, as though that were the important topic of the day.

"Never mind the preserves," Dick roared. "You didn't listen to me very well this morning. I told you just to get acquainted with the horse; not take foolish chances."

"Nothin' to it, Pa. It was easy as a breeze." He tried to make his voice sound casual and unconcerned.

"That's a lot of stuff!" retorted Ann, eyeing him up and down.

"Look at your clothes! You look like you've been dragged through a plowed field!"

Albert looked down at the front of him. He'd never realized what a mess he was, his pants were torn in several places and they were smeared with mud. He'd been so concerned with the stallion, after he'd landed in the ditch, that he'd never thought about himself.

"Oh, I had a little accident, but everything's all right. The horse is waiting to go home." He waved in the horse's direction in a grandiose manner.

"All right, son, you've had your day. Now, what do you propose to do about him?"

"I'll sit on the tailgate and keep him company while we lead him on behind. Just take it slow at first 'til he gets used to it. He scares easy." Albert went over and retrieved the stallion, hopped up on the lowered tailgate and they were on their way home at last.

———◆‣)◉(‣◆———

The new horse was turned out to pasture as soon as they arrived home. Albert left the halter on, but otherwise the stallion was free to feed and wander among the cows in the quiet country pasture. No one approached him for the rest of the day, and the cows would have a settling affect on him. It would be slow tedious work to get him to trust a human hand and respond to a human voice. Dick and Albert agreed it might be a month before they could hitch him to a carriage. There was no need to rush; everything would come in its own time.

The whole family admired the strawberry roan. He was handsomely built with good muscular development and long legs for speed. This was no common carriage horse; he had style and grace of movement. Dick already envisioned driving him to church, for there wasn't another horse on the road that could match him. Perhaps this would be far better than a new automobile. That was a foreign thing, which amazed and shocked people, but the stallion was something they knew about—something men would admire and envy. Not a very Christian attitude Dick admitted to himself, but scoffed at when suggested by others.

———◆‣)◉(‣◆———

That evening after the others had retired, Dick sat at the kitchen table figuring out the profits from the sale of the preserves while Ella finished her chores. They would have their second picking of strawberries the next day, which by the looks of it would be larger than the one they'd had last Thursday. The children from Philadelphia would be on hand to help. Dick was well pleased with the day's receipts; he hadn't realized his daughter-in-law had such a good business head and he minced no words in telling Ella about it.

"That's only part of it," Ella remarked. "She wouldn't have made out nearly so well if she'd had to sell those preserves to women."

"Why so?" Dick raised his eyes questioningly.

"Oh, come now. Why do you think she insisted on their getting dressed up like they did. I'll wager every sale she made was to a man, middle-aged or older."

"I suppose so. Most merchants are."

"You men are a pushover for a pretty face and figure. Catherine knows how to dress—and how to hold herself to make the best of a situation."

"She's a fine lookin' woman," Dick admitted.

"Well! I'm not surprised you've noticed. It's hard to overlook."

"Richard is very fortunate." Dick glanced up quickly at his wife. He was not completely insensitive to his daughter-in-law's attractiveness, nor to the sounds of jealousy he thought he detected now.

"Beauty alone does not make a good wife. It can be a distraction, too."

"Meaning what?"

"Oh, nothing," she caught herself. "I was generalizing, that's all." She turned and busied herself with her work.

"I don't like that kind of generalizing, as you call it," he said gruffly. "Let's hear no more of it. She's a good woman, and we're fortunate to have her in the house."

"Of course, I never meant otherwise."

Dick went back to his figures, but a chord had been struck and he found he couldn't concentrate. He knew Ella was sensitive about her face. Every once in a while there were signs that those scars ran deeper than her skin. Jealousy of Catherine was not becoming to her, but perhaps she couldn't help herself. Women worked from a different set of values than those he understood. Clumsily, he got to his feet, went over to her, put a massive arm around her waist, and drew her to him.

"We have so much to be thankful for, let's not waste it with bitterness." The scar flamed red on her cheek, he bent awkwardly and kissed her. It was the best he could do, but he would make it up to her in other ways.

Dick decided that they would follow all their options for the sale of the strawberries. The best of the crop would be sorted out for fresh sales at the produce market and also, possibly, for retail to their milk route customers. The remaining berries would be processed for preserves. He realized the preserve market was limited, as even Catherine's best efforts would not prevail over a saturated market. Richard remained their best salesman for the produce market.

chapter

13

On Tuesday, the milking done, everyone went out and picked strawberries. Govert paired up with his cousin Freddy and it was a question whether between talking and eating, they were getting more strawberries in their stomachs or in the baskets. Finally, Dick put a halt to their unproductiveness and made them settle down to the job at hand. The eating tapered off, but the talking was difficult to subdue. Govert was anxious to hear about Philadelphia, and Freddy was more than willing to tell him. Albert was not above eavesdropping on Freddy's conversation. He felt too proud to ask direct questions and admit he knew so little about city life. They weren't going to call him a green country boy before he ever left the farm. Freddy's stories of city life grew to tremendous proportions and it was obvious that his tales would need to be screened for truth and fiction. Not knowing the subject matter made it difficult to draw the lines of distinction. Albert thought city life couldn't be all this wild, or could it?

"You seem intent on Freddy's conversation." He'd been so engrossed in listening, he hadn't noticed Catherine come up beside him.

"Trying to learn what you can about Philadelphia?"

"You guessed it. But I'm not sure how much I can believe. It sounds fantastic."

"I believe the boy has a vivid imagination, but don't think too harshly of him—so do you."

"True, though of a different kind."

"But even more fantastic. Our experience at the pond proved that."

Directly after ten o'clock coffee, the ladies moved to the cookhouse and set up for sorting the berries, while the rest of the family continued to pick. Sarah joined them. Albert brought her rocking chair from the porch and got her comfortable in the shade outside the cookhouse door. She was too arthritic for the bending and stooping necessary in picking, but insisted she wasn't so bad off that she couldn't help sort berries. It gave her a feeling of usefulness.

Cousin Sara said she felt hot all over and wasn't hungry. Ella noticed a pinkish rash around her neck and shoulders.

"Looks like you've been eating too many strawberries," she said. "You help Grandma sort berries and stay out of the hot sun."

Sara claimed she hadn't eaten nearly as many as the boys, but Aunt Ella's suggestion suited her fine. She wasn't used to working in the fields.

About an hour later, Sarah came in the cookhouse and asked Catherine to have a look at Sara. The girl was not well. Little Sara's forehead was hot, her chest was covered with small flat pink spots, and the glands at the back of her neck were swollen.

"I'm afraid it's not strawberry rash after all, Ma," Catherine commented. "Looks like German measles to me."

"Good grief!" exclaimed Ella. Ann stood in the doorway and smirked. "It's not funny!" she snapped at her daughter. "They're very contagious. Lord knows who else will get them now—and how'd she come by them?"

"No doubt she caught them while still in Philadelphia," replied Catherine. "It takes about two weeks to show up."

"Well, I won't get them," laughed Ann. "I've already had them."

"Govert's never had them and what about her brothers and sister?" wailed Ella.

"Maybe we'll have an epidemic. They've got to get them sometime anyway." Ann thought it was very funny. "If they all come down with it, we'll have some peace and quiet around here for awhile again."

"Oh shush!" Ella scolded. "That's no way to talk about a thing like this. Are you sure it's German measles, Catherine, and not chicken pox? I'm never very certain at the early stages."

"Quite sure. Chicken pox are darker and by the number she's got, some of them would be blistered by now. These spots are mostly on her chest, chicken pox would be up in her scalp. Besides, this is the wrong season for chicken pox."

"Well, that's a relief," Ann sighed. "I've never had chicken pox, have I, Ma?"

"Makes a difference, doesn't it?" retorted Ella.

"Are you women going to just stand here and talk while my poor grand-daughter suffers?" Sarah broke in. Little Sara had been named for her, and she wasn't about to see the girl neglected.

"Yes, Ma. We'll take care of her," replied Ella. "Will you take charge of her, Catherine? You're the nurse around here."

"There's not much to be done. Just get her to bed and see that she get's plenty of liquids. You could use a break, Ma. We'll manage here." Ella took Sara by the hand and headed for the house.

"Ma always takes everything so serious," Ann chided after her mother was gone and they'd gotten back to the job at hand.

"She's had a lot of trouble in her life," retorted Catherine. "I'd think you'd be more sympathetic."

"I try to be, but it still gets me. There must be more to life than looking at the dark side of everything."

"What makes you say that?"

"You know what I mean. Surely you notice the difference here from over at your place. Your folks aren't so somber and glum. I'll bet your Dad was a gay blade when he was young. You were pretty lively yourself ... before you got married. I don't see how you stand it. Sometimes I'd like to scream."

"We can't be laughing all the time. Even that would get dull after awhile."

"Hump! I'd like to experience a little of that dullness for a change. I never heard of a little fun being bad for anyone, except at church. Pa and Richard are so concerned about sin that they're half afraid to even crack a joke." Ann slammed a bowl of strawberries into the pot on the stove with a vengeance.

"Pa's not nearly as stern as he used to be. I've noticed his lighter side at times."

154

"He's improved, I admit, but Richard's more and more like Pa used to be. I'll bet he kicked up quite a fuss about our selling the strawberries the way we did. Right?"

"He did at first, but then came around to the idea."

"Now there was a case where the prospective dollar won out over righteous indignation." Ann let out a boisterous laugh.

"Well now, I wouldn't say that. Pa made the decision and Richard abided by it."

"Don't try an' kid me. I know my brother. God shines bright in his eyes, but the silver dollar glitters more. The deacon in him will look the other way if it puts money in his pocket."

"You do Richard an injustice."

"I expected you to say that." Ann eyed her sister-in-law as she bent over to fill a group of jars. "You've changed, Kate. You used to have a lot of fire in you. Now even your protests are lukewarm. Does marriage do that to a girl?"

"I'm no different than I used to be," defensively.

"Yes you are! You used to be a lot of fun, but you've become as deadpan and somber as the rest of them. I'm glad I'm getting out of here soon."

❖◆❖

By Thursday afternoon, the three remaining cousins were down with German measles, and it was only a matter of time before Govert would have them. Ann had been right in her jesting prediction of an epidemic. Ella was beside herself trying to keep them all in bed, for they were too sick to be out and not sick enough to want to stay in. Catherine said she'd stay home from choir practice to tend the ailing ones; Ella had about worn herself out. This meant that Albert would be chaperone for his sister, which he didn't like one bit. They were barely out of the yard when she began working on him.

"I hope you're not going to be a prude tonight. Let us have our fun, and don't go peeking at us every five minutes."

155

"Well, let's not get too wild. I'll have to give an accounting for tonight."

"It'd better be a good one. Remember our agreement. I'm holding you to it."

"Yeah, I know."

Peter was surprised when he saw that his sister wasn't accompanying them. "Looks like we've got a new watchdog tonight,' he grinned and punched Albert on the arm as he climbed into the back seat next to Ann.

"Yeah," replied Albert, "and I'm not taking any nonsense from the two of you."

"He's bluffing, Pete. Al's only a mouse in cat's fur."

"I don't know," laughed Peter. "I've seen some pretty mean mice in my day."

"I didn't ask for the job," retorted Albert, feeling outnumbered.

"Don't let us rile you, Al," Peter returned. "I appreciate your position. Remember, I had the same job a number of times with Richard and Catherine."

"That must have been interesting," chuckled Ann. "Dear proper Richard. I'll bet he never got out of hand."

"Matter of fact, it was generally a pretty dull affair."

"Poor Kate. Well, let's not make it too dull for Al. Are you lookin' Al?" Ann taunted. "Come on, turn around and look at us." Albert did and Ann drew her arms around Peter and gave him a long passionate kiss.

"How's that for starters?" she teased.

"Don't push me too far," Albert warned. "I could make one of you sit up here with me."

"You wouldn't dare!"

"He could," Peter exclaimed. "He's the boss. Your Pa cue you in on your responsibilities, Al?"

"Yeah, we had a long talk right after supper."

"Ha! I thought so! Pop did the same with me."

"I don't want to be unreasonable, but it's going to be a long evening, so let's not start off so fast, huh?" Albert continued. "Suppose you want to stop in at the pond on the way?"

"We'll be glad to skip it, if you'll agree to stop coming home," Ann replied politely. Her younger brother had suddenly gained considerable stature in his new role. It would be best to use sweetness to get her way with him.

They arrived at church in plenty of time to do a little socializing before rehearsal. Bella DeKamp was nowhere's to be seen, and Albert hoped she wouldn't show up tonight. Catherine's words rang sharply in his ears. If he was to have peace at home, he'd have to hunt out Margie and try to make the most of it, even if it was just enough to introduce her to his mother next Sunday. *It seemed both women were pushing him unreasonably hard and he resented it.* Desperation took the place of forwardness, and when he saw her come in the door with an older woman, he went up to them without hesitation.

The girl's companion saw him first and smiled in his direction; there was a striking resemblance, and he realized this must be her mother. Not quite ready for meeting the mother so soon, he momentarily froze.

"Good ... good evening," was all he could stammer.

"Why, good evening, young man," the older woman replied. Margie turned and when she saw him awkwardly standing there, gave him a startled look as though she hadn't expected to see him.

"Do you remember me?" he blurted out. "I'm Albert DeGraf. We met briefly last week."

"I know," came a small voice, "but— but I didn't think . . ."

"That's why I thought I'd try to see you before rehearsal tonight."

"Mom, this is Albert—Albert. . ."

"I know, Margie," replied the older woman. "He just introduced himself."

He could see that Margie was even more nervous than he was, which gave him added confidence. "I'm very pleased to meet you, Mrs. Wagenvoort. Do you also sing in the choir?"

"Yes, but mostly to accompany Margie, since there is no one else to bring her."

"Oh?" he turned to Margie. "You have no brothers or sisters?"

"Well,..yes," Margie answered in a stronger voice than before. "I have two of each, but they're all younger."

"I, too, have two brothers and two sisters," he returned. "But only one that's younger."

Mrs. Wagenvoort excused herself, saying she needed to talk with one of the ladies of the choir before rehearsal, and left the two of them standing there facing each other. It was a painfully slow conversation, which was abruptly cut short by the announcement for everyone to take their places for rehearsal, yet he managed to say he would meet Margie during the social.

Practice was not as long as it had been the previous week. He was congratulating himself for the progress he'd made with Margie, but couldn't understand what had made him so nervous. She seemed nice enough, but he certainly wasn't infatuated with her, so why be nervous? It was her mother; he hadn't expected that encounter and the older woman's piercing eyes, he felt, had looked right through him. They'd agreed to meet by the refreshment table and as the choir filed out to the next room, he glanced ahead to see if he could spot her. Before he realized it, Bella DeKamp was next to him and overflowing with conversation. He kept on walking and told her he had to meet someone but she didn't take the hint. He looked for Ann in hopes she'd rescue him; but when she saw him signal, she only smiled broadly and waved back at him.

Margie was already waiting for him, but when she saw Bella tagging beside him, he could see she was hurt. Confused, he introduced the two girls to each other, although they'd met before. There was a coldness in their second meeting and he felt squeezed between them. He told Bella that he had talked with Margie earlier that evening and wished to speak to her again, but it came out all wrong. The way it sounded, it was as if Bella were an old friend and Margie but a recent casual acquaintance. From here, things went from bad to worse and he could see he was rapidly losing ground with Margie, yet making no progress in getting rid of Bella. Mrs. Wagenvoort came upon them suddenly and in a cold, steely voice announced that it was time she took Margie home. She swept her daughter with her out the door. *They must think I'm some kind of gigolo,* he thought, *playing one girl against the other.*

In desperation, Albert headed off to find Ann and Peter, and Bella was right there with him when he finally caught them with the couples group. His second night at choir and he had joined the couples group with a girl at his arm. The thought never occurred to him until it was too late. God, what a precedent he was setting, now everyone would think that Bella was his girl. Albert's mind reeled and tossed like a kite in a windstorm, while the others chatted and welcomed Bella to their group. We must be leaving, he told Ann several times, but she didn't seem to hear. Then, he reminded her that it was a long ride home and they had to make an important stop along the way. That did it, for then the farewells were brief and the three of them departed abruptly.

It was a dejected driver who reined the horse out of the church drive and onto the north road. While gloom sat in the front seat, jubilation abounded in the rear.

"Al, you never cease to amaze me!" Ann teased. "Here we thought you were bashful and all the while you're probably the fastest fella in the community. Don't you think he's set some kind of record, Pete? In one short week, he's in the couples group."

"That's pretty fast, I have to admit," said Peter.

Albert just stared ahead of him, saying nothing.

"Yes, and look what he's after. Nothing small for him." Ann was looking for a response, but got none, so she tried to make up a little jingle.

"Oh, Albert's amorous, over Bella's big breasts. Oh, Albert's amorous, over Bella's big breasts."

"Oh, shut up!" came from the front seat.

"Take it easy, Ann," cautioned Peter. "He's not in a jokin' mood tonight."

"What do you think causes Albert's attraction to big breasts? Is this what comes from milking so many cows? Have mammary glands become an obsession with him?"

"Will you lay off?" Albert growled. "She trapped me. I told you the other day I didn't like Bella."

"What's all this now?" Ann exclaimed incredulously. "You were trapped? You seemed a pretty willing prisoner to me."

"Well, I wasn't. I tried to get your help back there. Couldn't you see I was trying to get rid of her?"

"No, we didn't see," said Ann. "Maybe you'd better explain yourself."

"I've had enough from you," Albert shot back defiantly. "You won't understand anyway."

"Oh, come on little brother." soothed Ann. "If we've misjudged you, how are we going to know about it unless you tell us. We thought you were making out just fine with Bella. We're only teasing you about your accomplishments."

"She's a leach! She clamped onto me and I couldn't shake her loose!" He bit his lip in the dark. "She messed up everything. It was a real disaster."

"Good grief!" exclaimed Ann. "You know, Pete, I think I still have a little brother. What we thought was a fast worker, was just a green kid caught by calculating, scheming Bella. Wait 'til I get my hands on that bitch!"

"Now! Now! Let's calm down. Seems to me Al's got a problem that's gonna take some calculatin' and schemin' on his part. After what happened tonight, everyone's gonna' think Bella's his girl. Maybe we should try to help him."

"You're right," she admitted. "It makes me mad to see Al taken advantage of."

"Maybe you ought to fill us in on the details, Al." Peter commented. "Just what <u>did</u> happen back there?"

Albert explained both the previous week's events and those of earlier that evening.

"Things really got turned around on you, didn't they?" remarked Ann. "No wonder you were upset at our teasing. We're sorry about that, really we are."

"Good ol' Kate," Peter said. "Things would have been different if she'd been along tonight."

"We'll get her to join forces with us," put in Ann. "Between us all, Bella won't have a chance." Albert didn't see how any of them were going to get him out of his predicament. "Let's celebrate! To our pact to extradite Al from Bella's clutches. Turn in up there, that's the lane in the pond." she ordered.

"All right, I promised," Albert answered. "I'll sit up by the carriage and think this thing over. I won't bother you."

"And have you broodin' by yourself!" exclaimed Ann. "Not tonight, little brother. We had some mean tricks we were going to pull on you, but that's all off. Tonight you're one of us and we're going to show you some fun. We're all going swimmin'!"

"But..." Albert stammered.

"Oh, come on now. We'll swim in our underwear." Ann grabbed Albert by one hand and Peter by the other and ran down the bank to the shore line.

"Last one in's a skunk!" challenged Peter and removed his shirt.

"Can you imagine the fit the folks would have, if they could see us now!" Ann bubbled over with mischievousness.

"If some of the others knew it," returned Peter, "we'd get kicked out of church."

"We'd blame it on our chaperone," giggled Ann.

"Like heck you would!" shot back Albert. "I'd say you overpowered me. We're all in this together."

"That's my boy," laughed Ann. "Peter, help me with this snap on the back of my dress." Peter gave her an assist, she wiggled her arms, let the dress slide down to the ground and stood in her underwear, her long bloomers almost reaching her knees.

"Now, what's so horrible about a girl being seen in her underwear?" she taunted and rolled her eyes at Peter. "You can't see much more of me now than you did before."

"That's true for now," Peter grinned. "But just wait 'til you come out of the water wringin' wet."

"Don't I know it!" and she plunged into the water ahead of them with Peter and Albert close behind. All three swam briskly toward the center of the pond, where they treaded water.

"Now, isn't this better than sitting up in the carriage wondering what mischief we're up to?" Ann teased her brother.

"It does have its good points."

"Pete, I think the boy's ripe for corruption. He's now a partner in crime and would never squeal on us."

"Wouldn't have anyway, you know that." Albert turned over on his back and looked up at the stars. It was a magnificent refreshing feeling which made him forget all about the sorry events that had occurred earlier.

"We trust you, Al," Peter commented.

"There's no question about it, Pete. You know Al and I made a secret pact, sworn in blood." She burst out giggling so she swallowed a mouthful of water. "Neither one of us will tell any tales on the other. Right, Al?"

"Right you are!" Albert spoke to the sky. "It was pretty thin blood, but we shook on it. That kind of puts me at a disadvantage as a chaperone."

"You bet it does," she chided, "but we won't take advantage of you ... this time!"

"Thanks!" Albert rolled over from his back and swam towards

the opposite side of the pond, turned and leisurely stroked back again. Time passed quickly, and finally. "I hate to say this, but we will have to be going soon."

"I suppose you're right, Al," remarked Peter. "Let's take one swim around the pond and then we'll go in." The three struck off and slowly made a large circle and then headed for shore.

"Let's stop a minute," called Ann when they were able to touch bottom. "I'm getting cold feet. My modesty is catching up with me. I can feel my underwear clinging to me like a glove and I know what I'm going to look like when I get on shore. We've corrupted Al enough."

"Sis," broke in Albert with a big grin, "I was just getting interested."

"Oh, shush little brother," she giggled. "You two go on ahead, take your clothes up to the carriage. I'll be along shortly."

Peter and Albert did as they were told and waited for Ann at the carriage.

"Your sister's a lot of fun." remarked Peter, as they changed into their clothes by the carriage. "I'll bet you never figured her like this."

"Oh, I suspected she had her wilder side," clucked Albert. "It's showed before in many ways."

Ann joined them carrying her wrung out underwear. "We'll stuff these under the seat," she said. "I'll take care of all of them when we get home and see you get yours next time, Pete."

"You know, we're not going to be especially late tonight."

Albert set the horse off back in the main road for home. "We left church early."

"Good!" remarked Ann. "We won't have to figure out any excuses then."

chapter

14

Sunday morning Albert looked out from the choir loft, past the back of Reverend VandenTill's head to the rows of congregational faces, all seeming to stare straight at him. It had given him an uneasy feeling the previous Sunday, but he was gradually getting so he could look directly at all those upturned heads and not see them as individuals, but as pieces of an impersonal conglomerate mass. This was not always so; the eyes played tricks with the mind, or perhaps it was the other way around. The vague congealed form would periodically crystallize into individuals, or at least certain individual faces within the mass would come into focus while the others blurred into obscurity. The faces of the DeGrafs, seated in the rear most pew on the right side of the center aisle, frequently came into focus. Perhaps this was because there were so few of them this morning, leaving blank spaces in that pew.

There'd been no problem in finding room in the carriage this morning, for three of the city cousins were still confined to bed, and although Sara was up and about, she was not yet ready for church. His mother had stayed home to take care of them, saying that one of the girls could take her place for the evening hymnal service.

This morning was communion, which meant an extra long service. Dinner would be late today. The communion table stood directly below the pulpit, decked in blood-red velvet with a gold embroidered cross on each of its four sides. Set in neat rows were twelve loaves of unleavened bread and twelve goblets of wine. Beyond the table sat six elders and directly behind them six deacons; advisors to the minister and ruling body of the church. Richard sat in the second row, third seat from the left. He and the other consistory would serve the sacraments to the congregation.

It was the choir director's rule that when a member failed to attend Thursday night practice, he was not to sing on Sunday. An exception had been made the Sunday following the big storm, when hardly anyone showed up. Thus, Catherine sat in the DeGraf pew next to his father, with Govert and his grandmother on her other side. She now sat where his mother had for so many years, and it seemed strange to see her there.

Before the choir assembled, he had tried to see Margie to apologize for Thursday night, but when she'd seen him coming she'd turned the other way. Bella hadn't bothered him as yet this morning; that, at least, was something to be thankful for.

The Reverend was finishing up a rather long prayer and they would sing next, and then would be the communion. "....in the name of the Father, Son, and Holy Ghost, Amen." The choir piece was specially for communion. One of the elders rose, approached the table, and broke bread. The pieces of bread were torn by hand much as Christ had done. He first went to the Reverend and then to his fellow elders and deacons. The Reverend cautioned that only those members in good standing, and who had an untroubled conscience, should partake in Christ's sacrament. The congregation watched as minister and consistory partook; there was a moment of silence, and then the consistory served the bread to the congregation. This done, the goblets of wine were dispensed in like manner. Albert remembered one previous communion sitting next to Catherine during the passing of the wine. When she had passed the goblet to him he had placed his lips at the rim exactly where she had placed her own, and said a prayer for her. He later wondered if this was wrong in God's sight. Some members objected to the passing of the goblets among the congregation, for they did not care to drink following certain other members. The Reverend paraphrased Christ and said they should concern themselves less with that which passed <u>into</u> their mouth as <u>out</u> of it.

The communion over, the Reverend settled into his sermon with his usual vigor. He was never as preoccupied as when he was preaching the gospel of Christ and the damnation of man. Sin was his favorite subject. Albert sat and listened with a detachment that he had never experienced before. From his present position, it was as though he were a mere observer, with the sermon directed toward those in the congregation. Here he could observe the expressions on the faces before him.

Sin was a terrible thing according to what he heard now and had heard so many times before. No man was without it. Only Christ was perfect. Albert thought, *If we are so miserable, why does God even bother with us?* He had looked up at the stars too often not to realize how puny and insignificant was the life of man, and from what he read, the stars he saw were but a small fraction of what lay beyond. Surely, a God who controls all this must have more important things to do than be concerned with man's petty little ways. Christ had said this himself. "What is man that thou art mindful of him." *Is God concerned with every little thing we do,"* he wondered. *Is God like the Reverend, who thinks all fun is sin*? They'd had fun Thursday night at the pond. It was a glorious feeling to swim free below the stars, and no harm had come from it. Yet he knew the reaction of many here if they had but been aware. These thoughts confused him, so now his ears closed out the words and he dwelt upon his own quixotic fancies. One face in the congregation was clear to him, that next to his father, while all the others became swallowed up into a muddy pool of nothingness. This too was sin, but yet he studied each line and feature of brow, eyes and nose again, of mouth, chin and throat again—memorized—still again and again . . . ceaselessly through the rest of the sermon.

Albert had made it a habit of going to the pasture every day to visit the stallion. At first, the roan would come to him reluctantly and only after bribing with sugar and apples, but now the stallion would come when he approached. Dick had given orders that no one else should try to go near the horse.

Directly after milking, Tuesday morning, Albert took a short piece of rope and asked Catherine to join him in going to the pasture. The cows had not been released from the barn as yet, so the stallion grazed alone.

"You stay by the fence," he suggested. "He's gotten used to me being alone, but I think it's time there was a second person." Albert brought the horse over to Catherine. "Have you noticed how gracefully he moves?" he exclaimed, elated with the powerful smoothness of the animal.

"He seems to flow like water," she said.

"You're not afraid of him, are you?"

"Not as long as I'm on this side of the fence."

Albert handed her a fistful of cube sugar. "Try offering him some." Catherine placed a lump in the palm of her hand and extended it across the fence. The stallion took it with no hesitation.

"Have you thought of a name for him? Certainly, he needs a name."

"Well, I thought of 'Pegasus'. You know, the winged horse from Greek mythology. But, I'm afraid people will start calling him 'Peggy',"

"Not if you train him to the name. After all, only Pa and Richard will be handling him, besides yourself."

"Hmmm, probably true." Albert reflected a moment. "All right, 'Pegasus' it is!"

"You have such a way with animals," she said. "It's too bad people don't respond as well. There I think you need some help."

"You mean about Thursday night?"

"Yes, Ann told me all about it. I'm sorry now I didn't go. I might have helped."

"Everything went wrong."

"You're too much of a gentleman. Bella took advantage of you. We'll take care of her, so she won't give you any more trouble."

"I don't see how you can say that. Nothing's going to help. Margie won't talk to me anymore, and as far as her mother is concerned, I'm afraid it's hopeless."

"That does present a problem. You've got a lot to learn about girls, I see that." Catherine had exhausted her supply of cube sugar.

"He's gotten used to you quite quickly. He's as calm as I've seen him.

Think Ill try riding him."

"What if he throws you? You're just being foolish."

"Maybe. I'll just take him around the pasture a couple of times." Albert tied the loose end of the lead rope on the other side of the halter and brought the horse close to the fence. Stepping up the rails, he swung to the horse's back.

His legs hardly touched the roan's flanks when the stallion leaped forward almost throwing him to the ground. Catherine let out a shriek. Albert recovered himself and clamped his legs in tight. Fortunate for him, the roan was a runner, not a bucker.

In an instant, they were halfway across the field and picking up speed with every stride. As the stallion neared the far fence, it never veered, but cleared the top rail by more than a foot, landing in the vegetable garden. There wasn't any choice and straight through they went, with tomato plants flying in all directions. Although he tried to direct the roan, it was useless. He was riding astride a cannon ball— passenger, but nothing more. When the stallion reached the road, he headed south. Albert glanced back and could see Catherine frantically waving her arms for him to stop. Unfortunately, he had no way of doing that.

In a matter of what seemed mere minutes, they were halfway down the road to the Vandenbergs, still at a full gallop. Albert's legs were beginning to cramp. There was a little slackening of speed as they approached the Vandenbergs' drive. He tried to direct the roan in that direction. For the first time the roan responded.

Neal was returning to the house when he saw them coming. He stuck up his hand in greeting, expecting Albert to pull up and stop. The stallion continue to charge forward. Neal jumped clear as horse and rider thundered by in a shower of flying gravel.

"Can't stop! See you later!" Albert yelled, and they were gone. A half mile down the south road, the stallion began to slow. Albert vigorously patted the roan's neck, talked to the animal, and gently pulled back on the rope. Finally, the stallion settled down to a trot and began responding to his touch in a rough sort of a way. He still lacked much control, but his frequent visits and patience had paid off. He'd won. Pegasus was his.

Albert was halfway back to the Vandenbergs when Neal came riding up.

"What was that all about?" Neal asked. "I thought you were in trouble."

"I was! Everything's fine now." The stallion nosed the mare, and they headed towards home.

"That's a hell of a horse you've got there. You went through our yard like a streak of lightnin'"

"You should have seen him when we first took off. He'd slowed down when you saw him." This was downright bragging and they both knew it. The stallion was dancing sideways periodically so that Neal kept well to the side to give them room.

"He sure is a scary brute. Sure you can handle him?"

"I have up to now. See no reason why I shouldn't from here on out."

"How come your ol' man let you take him out this morning?"

"He went into town, so he doesn't know about it. I'd better be heading back. They'll be looking for me. Care to join me?"

"Might as well. I've finished milking."

"Fine. I'd like to stay on awhile and give him a good workout."

They were approaching the DeGraf farm when a horse and carriage appeared ahead, coming their way. It was Richard, Catherine, and Ann, looking for him. *What'd they expect,* he thought, *to see me lying along the road somewhere?* As the wagon pulled up, the roan started to prance again. Side to side he went, swinging in large figure eights. He was putting on an even bigger show than he'd made for Neal earlier, and Albert had trouble staying astride the animal. The stallion had accepted him, but not the others.

"You tryin' to kill yourself?" yelled Ann as the carriage rolled to a stop.

"Not really, but he's got more spirit than I figured."

"You had me half scared to death," scolded Catherine. "Why did you do such a foolish thing?"

"I had to try him out sometime," Albert replied, "and this morning seemed as good a time as any."

"Wait 'til Pa hears about this!" retorted Richard.

"Pa wanted me to train him. That's what I'm doing."

"He's not going to like what you did to the vegetable garden."

"I suppose not, but it couldn't be helped."

"Oh, let Pa take care of Al himself when he gets home," Ann protested. "He doesn't need any help from you two."

"Now, if you all don't mind," Albert exclaimed. "Neal and I are going to ride south and meet Pa on his way back from town."

"Crazy fools!" muttered Richard, as Albert and Neal turned and headed south.

—◆»✕◆●—

By mid-week Ann's so-called epidemic had run its course and Govert was down in bed with the German measles. None of the children developed complications, so Ella's concerns were groundless; it had been a bothersome inconvenience, but nothing more. The cousins were up and about and with only one ailing child, there wasn't the disruption there had been the previous week. When Thursday night came, Catherine was free to join the others for choir practice.

The little group arrived at church early. Catherine excused herself, and Albert didn't see her again until they were called to take their places. He knew she and Ann planned to extradite him from last week's troubles, but even if they diverted Bella, it would hardly do much good, for he now recognized her persistence for what it was. It was he, not they, who would have to stand up to her. He had wanted to stay home tonight, but the women of the house wouldn't hear of it. Why couldn't they leave him alone; they were all pushing and prodding, each with her own real or imagined motives. Catherine, too, was trying to manipulate his life, and he resented it.

During practice he set about planning how he'd handle Bella when the time came, but then, a sudden feeling of rebellion welled up in him and he abandoned all his previous ideas and set on a new course of thinking. *Perhaps it was a coward's way out,* he thought, *but it just wasn't worth the fuss and bother.* When practice was over, he held back as the others headed for the next room and, instead of following, he doubled back through another door into the cloakroom, past the Reverend's study, and out the back door. He plunked himself down in the dark on the steps where he convinced himself he'd wait out the social hour by himself. Let the others wonder what happened to him.

A light breeze was coming up from the meadows bringing with it the

169

warm sweet smell of new mown hay. It was an odor familiar to every farm boy, but it still had a refreshing newness— a heavy headiness— in the warm evening air. As his eyes became accustomed to the dark, the outline of a white picket fence took shape; the fence which surrounded the small graveyard where his grandfather had rested now some ten years. There were perhaps not more than four dozen gravestones in the yard, and he knew exactly which was that of the senior DeGraf. Some day, perhaps, he too would rest here, and the thought was not depressing. The young can look upon such stones more dispassionately than the old. There was a movement in the air about the graveyard; a quick erratic fluttering of dark, noiseless wings, as several black objects swooped and rose in quick zigzag fashion. These, he recognized were bats. He knew they were feeding on gnats and mosquitos, and must live up in the bell tower. No respectable church should be without them.

The seemingly haphazard flight of the bats so preoccupied him he didn't hear the footsteps behind him and gave a start when a small voice called his name.

"Albert, is that you?" It was Margie's voice. Abruptly he turned to see the girl and her mother standing directly behind him. Before he could reply the older woman spoke.

"Mr. DeGraf, I believe we owe you an apology." Albert instantly got to his feet and faced them. "Your sister-in-law explained to us what happened last week and we're sorry we drew the wrong conclusions."

"Catherine has talked with you?" was all he could say.

"Yes, she told us everything."

"How did you know where to find me?

"She told us that, too. When you didn't appear at the social, she guessed this is where you'd be."

It was obvious Catherine had been busy. If she could do this, then why was he afraid of Bella. Now he knew he'd been a coward.

"Shall we go in?" he said to the ladies. "If you will bear with me, I believe I can face Miss DeKamp."

"She must be a very brazen woman," the older woman said as Albert opened the door and let them lead the way. Mrs. Wagenvoort took her daughter's arm and he heard her whispered instructions. "Now don't you shrink away if that hussy makes a scene."

They had made their way through the cloakroom into the sanctuary when, with a loud commotion, Bella stormed past them and out the front door. In the dim light Albert wasn't sure whether she had recognized them or not, it happened so quickly. When they entered the room where the social was held, Albert saw his sister and Catherine by the refreshment table. Ann was standing with her hands on her hips laughing, while Catherine was cleaning up something on the floor. Catherine looked up, saw them, and came directly over. There was a faint upturn at the corners of her mouth and her eyes glowed mischievously. He could see all he needed to know— everything was under control. Catherine escorted Mrs. Wagenvoort over to meet Ann and Peter, leaving Albert alone with Margie. He noted how willingly Margie's mother left them alone. Women! They were always scheming with, or against each other. It made him wonder how many decisions he'd thought were his, really were.

———◆◆◆◆———

They were still in the church drive when Ann and Catherine wanted to know how he'd made out with Margie.

"You had your chance tonight!" Ann exclaimed. "Hope you took advantage of it."

Albert assured them that everything had gone smoothly.

"We went to a lot of trouble for you," Ann continued. "You'd better appreciate it."

"What are you talking about?" broke in Peter. "You both were having the time of your lives. I watched you."

"Do you think Bella will ever speak to us again?" questioned Ann.

"I doubt it," Catherine smiled.

"You did the dirty work," Ann returned, "but she'll know I was in on it."

"Just what did happen back there anyway?" Albert asked. "We heard a commotion and Bella rushed past us like a wild bull."

"My clumsy sister spilt a whole pitcher of cream down Bella's dress front," drawled Peter. "In this heat, I'll bet she smells rank as a sow by now."

"Didn't you notice that everyone was having their coffee black tonight, Al?" chimed in Ann.

Albert glanced across at Catherine. She was not bubbling over with mirth like Ann, but her face expressed her satisfaction well enough. Ann, who liked to talk, had done but little as far as he could tell. It was Catherine who had done the devil's work. In the darkness he reached over and gently squeezed the small hand. She turned her head towards him, nodded ever so slightly, and squeezed back with a strength that surprised him.

"Let's celebrate this evening's teamwork," giggled Ann. "Let's all go for a swim like we did last week."

"All you ever think about is celebrating," Albert remarked. His eyes flashed to Catherine's face and saw the smile quickly fade; his gregarious sister had told Catherine about their evening swim. Catherine instinctively drew her hand away and he now half expected to see his world close in on him.

"Just because Albert was lax last week, is no reason to believe I'll consent to such going's on," Catherine shot back abruptly at her sister-in-law.

"Humph!" Ann pouted. "Why all the fuss now? You didn't act shocked when I first told you."

"Do you think I could go swimming like you did?" Catherine admonished. "Remember, it's different for me."

"Don't be so priggish, Sis," chided Peter. "Rich will never know."

"You're as bad as Ann," scolded Catherine. "I don't know which of you is the worse, and look what you're doing to Albert."

"He was very easy to corrupt," teased Ann. "You really enjoyed it, didn't you, Al?" Albert sheepishly admitted that he had.

"I'm surprised at you, Albert." Catherine turned on him sternly.

"Aw, Sis, have a heart," pleaded Peter. "You never used to be this way. What happened to my carefree sister?"

"That's very well for you to say, but if I did, and they heard at home, what then?"

"We'd never tell on you," responded Ann and Peter together.

"And what about you, Al?" Catherine asked. "What about you?"

"I can keep a secret as well as those two," Albert responded and pulled the horse to a stop at the usual spot just above the pond. Ann and

Peter clambered out and started for the water.

"Wait a minute, you two!" Catherine called them back. "I was expecting this might happen. We'll go swimming, but not like last week." Catherine lifted up the back seat and took out two bathing suits and threw one at a very surprised Ann. "You and I, young lady, are going to be respectable, whether you like it or not."

"Oh, but that takes half the fun out of it!" complained Ann.

"I don't care," Catherine remarked calmly. "You boys go down to the pond's edge, we're going to change here. We'll be along shortly."

Four swimmers splashed about in the pale light of a half-moon, disturbing the nightly ritual of a colony of serenading frogs. Catherine cautioned Peter and Ann to behave themselves, and then she and Albert swam to the opposite end of the pond, where they stopped to rest. Her red hair was piled carelessly atop her head. She put her arms around his neck and gazed up at him. "My protests back there weren't so much that I objected to you seeing me in my underwear, as that I don't trust them."

"I rather guessed that. At first I thought you were indignant, but I soon realized it was an act."

"We have too much to lose. If I'd done as they'd asked and it ever got out, neither of us would ever hear the end of it. Ann talks too much, but since I've taken away the glamour, she's not so likely to say anything."

"Ann and I have a pact of secrecy you know," Albert tried to console her. "We've each sworn not to tell on the other."

"You think she'll honor it?"

"She has so far. Except for telling you about last week's swim, and then I don't think she felt she was telling on me as much as herself."

"It's still best not to give her cause for gossip. What may seem innocent enough to her could be misconstrued by others," she continued.

Albert stared uneasily into the water. "I think I have mixed feelings about what happened tonight."

"About taking care of Bella? I thought you wanted to be rid of her."

"Of course! She's a leach. But it also set me up with Margie and her mother."

"That's what you wanted, isn't it? I thought this was what we discussed to calm your mother's concerns," she exclaimed with a puzzled look.

"I'm not sure how I feel about Margie. Certainly nothing like the way I feel about you."

"That will come in time." She gave a slight sigh.

"But, you know it's really you I love."

"I wish you wouldn't speak of love so much. Say you like me a great deal, or are very fond of me, but be careful how you speak of love. Love runs deep. It's beyond the depth we dare go. Let's not make an idle word of it."

"You don't feel the same?"

"I didn't say that. It's just that I think we should talk of other things."

"It's a subject that's often on my mind."

"You know you scared me half to death the other day. Why did you take such a chance in riding Pegasus so soon?" she asked, wanting to change the subject.

"He needed to be ridden, and the time seemed right."

"Was it because I was there? Were you trying to prove your manhood to me?"

"Well....I suppose so. We did give you quite a show." He tried to make the remark a casual one, but it smacked of bragging.

"It is one I won't soon forget. You're lucky Pa wasn't harder on you for ruining the tomato patch. One of these days you're going to go too far."

"That's why Neal and I rode towards town to meet him. After he'd seen how well Pegasus responded and I told him how Neal and I planned to break him in for carriage work, the tomatoes didn't seem very important, I guess. You told Margie of my exploits with Pegasus, didn't you?"

"I mentioned it, in passing."

"Indeed you did. All we talked about was horses. I'm afraid you gave her the impression I was a wild horse buster."

"Well, aren't you? Pegasus certainly was wild."

"I guess so, but it was all a romantic adventure to her. I could see it in her eyes."

"You try to read a lot in people's eyes don't you?"

"In some people the eyes are the most expressive part. I first learned this from my mother, but now it's your eyes I seek out most."

"I know, and I also yours. We've developed a sign language, I think."

"Yes, and let's keep it that way. Don't ever close me out when I search out your eyes at home. It's my only way of communicating at times."

"Were you trying to communicate with me in church last Sunday? I felt you looking at me during the entire sermon."

"It was more than mere communication."

"I thought so. I think the Reverend was wasting his words on you. I doubt that you remember much of what he said."

"I guess not, but I <u>was</u> thinking religious thoughts."

"While looking so intently at me? I'll bet you were!" she chuckled. "I would guess they were more inspired by the devil in you than any Godly notions. Your look is very penetrating at times. I think you mind's eye sees me as your regular eyes cannot."

"Meaning my mind's eye is not discreet?"

"Very indiscreet! Though fully clothed, I feel quite naked when you look at me sometimes. Is this just a young man's curiosity, or should I feel there's more to it?"

"It's all part of knowing you better."

"Under the circumstances, you know me well enough, I think. You're very persistent you know, and I don't do much to discourage you, which is very wrong of me."

"Do you really want to discourage me?

"No, that's the trouble. Earlier tonight, I did what I could to get you back with Margie, but here I let you kiss me when you should be showing that affection to her."

He ran his hand through her hair and it tumbled down from where she'd piled it high. They weren't interested in swimming anyway. The kiss was a long one which rose and fell and rose again. Catherine finally broke away, gave a small gasp and looked out across the black waters. "How're we ever going to manage this way?"

"I don't know."

"Nor do I." she said resignedly, almost hopelessly, put her arm across his shoulder, head against his chest and looked longingly into the darkness for what she could not see. Was it possible to love two brothers, but in different ways. One in the real world, the other part of her fantasies. Richard was her husband, she could never betray him. Yet, in a way, she was doing that even now.

chapter

15

Hot, humid days with but little rain occurred during all of July which made for poor pasture and an even poorer vegetable garden. The profits they'd made from the strawberries and preserves were offset by the poor bean crop. Tomatoes sunburned in the field before ripening. Only the corn thrived in the lower ground near the swamp. Dick swore he could almost hear the stalks growing in the bright sun. It was corn that would pull them through, which again proved the value of being diversified.

Neal became a frequent visitor to the DeGraf pastures. He and Albert spent many hours with Pegasus, training him by easy stages for carriage use. Starting him with just the harness and traces, they later had him dragging a board around the pasture. Often, Govert and the city cousins would sit along the fence to watch the fun. Things sometimes got a bit exciting with the still half-wild stallion— lines would get tangled, or Pegasus would rear and dance on his hind legs, or let fly a rear hoof to smash the board to kindling. Dick watched the progress and, although free with advice, he rarely interfered.

Finally, the board was replaced with a sulky and then they took to the roads, one riding ahead on a mare as a teaser. The open road was a welcome change from the confinement of the pasture. Pegasus loved to stretch his long legs, and his speed was hard to contain. His stamina was far beyond that of any of the mares—so it became routine to switch mares during every workout. Both the DeGraf and Vandenberg mares got plenty of exercise during that first week of sulky riding; after that, Pegasus was on his own and his speed was beyond that of any horse on the road. In early July, the roan was introduced to a carriage, and Dick got his first ride behind the stallion.

"Tomorrow we'll go into town and get a new carriage," he told Albert. "A fine horse like this deserves the best." The stallion was still enjoying his run when Dick got off at the house.

"I'll work him a bit longer," Albert said. "Be back in time for coffee." He moved Pegasus out the drive at an easy pace to the road going south. He was on his way to see Neal.

Dick stood and watched him go, and Ella joined him on the porch.

"That boy sure knows how to handle horses!" Dick said as he and Ella watched the circles of dust swirl from the back wheels, churning the dry powder that was a road. Pride swelled within the gruff voice, and this was music to her ears.

"Yes, he has a gift that brings him joy in its fulfillment," she said in admiration.

"Next week we'll ride to church in style." Dick turned and headed toward the barn, with a spring to his gait she'd not seen in a long time. *The stallion was as important to him as anything he owned,* she thought. *Strange how one animal could have such an effect upon a father and son.* The roan had drawn them more closely together, and she was glad.

Albert had been a different person these last weeks and she prayed this change would be a lasting one. He no longer brooded and withdrew within himself. She wasn't sure of the reason, and it could be the stallion, but she liked to think that it was Margie. This quiet, unassuming girl now sat with the DeGrafs during Sunday evening services. To Ella, Margie was the right and proper girl for Albert—and it was Catherine who'd brought them together– Catherine, who had been the source of so many of her fears. Now, she had pangs of guilt that she had so misjudged her daughter-in-law. Yet, how many women, she mused, infatuated by an idealistic youth like Albert, could gently turn that attention to a younger girl. Such affection as he'd shown might have turned many a young woman's head, married though she may be. But then, perhaps Catherine never knew how deep his thoughts had run. His poems had laid that bare. Thank God she, and not Catherine had seen them.

Albert stopped by the Vandenbergs to pick up Neal for the second leg of the morning's ride. Neal was wide-eyed with excitement, and blurted out his news in such rapid fashion that Albert could hardly keep up with him.

"Have you heard? War's broken out in Europe!" Albert hadn't. "Germany declared war on Russia on August first. German troops have marched into Luxembourg, seized the railroads, and are moving West. Yesterday, the Germans declared war on France, and already they're moving troops into Belgium. Holland has got to be next."

Albert was dumbfounded. "Where'd you hear all this?" It was difficult to fathom the significance of what Neal was saying.

"Pa just got back from town. He said everyone's excited and people were milling in the streets around the telegraph station. More news keeps coming in and they're announcing it to the crowds every hour."

"Where's your Pa now?"

"He said he was going to change clothes and then go over to see your Dad."

"Get him! We'll take him over." Neal ran in and soon was out with his father and Peter.

Dick was surprised to see the carriage back so soon, and more surprised to see the Vandenberg men. Pegasus was turned out to pasture and forgotten. Here was news that would not wait. Ella shooed the children outside and the rest of the DeGrafs gathered in the kitchen to hear what Cornelius had to say. When he had told all the news, Dick was the first to speak.

"It sounds bad, but it's half a world away," he said sternly. "How can all this affect us?"

"Yes, but where will it end?" exclaimed Cornelius. "Look how quickly it has spread in one short week. A week ago today the Archduke Francis Ferdinand, of Austria, was assassinated in Serbia.

Immediately Austria declared war on Serbia. When we heard that news, I thought only that these Balkan countries were just kicking up a fuss between themselves, but see what has followed? Two days later, Russia mobilized against Austria. Then two more days and Germany's at war with Russia. Yesterday, again two days later, we have France and Belgium into it. Where will it go from there? It's like a wildfire."

"Holland can't escape," spoke up Neal. "With Belgium in, she'll soon follow."

"I agree," said Cornelius, "it looks bad."

"Then we should fight for Holland," Neal exclaimed, with firm determination.

"You're an American! Not a Dutchman," Dick stormed at him.

"That's right!" retorted Cornelius. "Dick and I are the only Dutchmen in this room. The rest of you were born here." Sarah who sat by the stove in her rocking chair corrected him on this. Old and feeble as she was, she wasn't about to be overlooked as the only 'real' Dutchman in the group. Cornelius conceded to her graciously. Ella reminded them that Dr. Brabin had predicted, months ago, that something like this might happen. Dick agreed that the old doctor had had an insight. This reminder now shook his confidence that what had happened over there was not of their concern.

"What's all this fuss about?" Richard wanted to know. "United States will not get in it, yet we'll profit by supplying them with food and equipment. This'll mean better prices in the marketplace."

"Perhaps," Dick rubbed his beard thoughtfully. "Yet, this could also mean involvement."

"Look at it this way, Pa," continued Richard. "With half of Europe fighting each other, they'll not be raising food. Someone's got to do it for them. I'll bet food prices go sky high."

"All you think of is profit," retorted Albert angrily. "Doesn't it mean anything to you that men are killing each other over there?"

"Of course!" shot back Richard. "But there's nothing we can do about it. We've got to watch out for ourselves."

"Yeah, and profit by other men's misery and death," Albert bit his lip in frustration.

"Now, let's not get too emotional about this," cautioned Dick. "It might all blow over as quickly as it's started."

"I don't think so," replied Cornelius. "It's gotten too big, too fast. It's still gaining momentum, and I'm afraid it will have to run its course."

The next morning proved Cornelius's words. It was not yet nine o'clock when the phone rang; Dr. Brabin wanted to speak to Dick. Ella talked with the doctor while Ann went to fetch her father. The old doctor was choked with emotion, for Great Britain had entered the conflict. His beloved England was at war, and he was gravely depressed at the fulfillment of his own predictions.

"The world is going mad!" he said. "I'm too old to suffer much, but I greatly dread the consequences on the young. It is they who will pay dearly for this insanity."

When Dick hung up the phone, the eyes of the four women were upon him with questioning stares.

"What has happened in Holland?" Sarah asked, her primary concern.

"Nothing," the simple answer, but he saw this would not satisfy them.

"Great Britain's in it now," Ella answered for him.

"Yes, at midnight last night," Dick finally said. "King Albert of Belgium appealed for aid and Britain answered."

"I don't know. I really don't know." Dick abruptly left for the barn, leaving the women to ponder the question by themselves.

The war became the single topic of discussion everywhere. The Reverend VandenTill dedicated the Sunday's sermon to the Last Day of Judgment. The sins of man were catching up with him and the time was ripe for God's reckoning. The Reverend dwelt heavily on Second Peter who foretold the last days before Armageddon.

"Be ye not deceived," the Reverend roared. "The day of the Lord will come as a thief in the night!" The congregation was deeply shaken and many who had not attended both Sunday services regularly did so now. The war in Europe did not seem to Albert to be like a thief in the night, but he was not about to question what might be the Lord's definition of these things.

By early August the initial excitement about the war had worn off, but news reports came in regularly by way of the milk route and from the frequent calls and visits of Dr. Brabin. Twice a month, someone stopped by his house in town to bring the old doctor for a visit. It was an experience he always enjoyed, and Sarah was her brightest during these times. Ella became convinced that the doctor should stay the winter with them. He was getting too old to live by himself, she told Dick, and he would be good company after Albert and Ann were gone. The doctor could take Ann's room after the wedding. The house would seem less lonely, during those quiet winter evenings she knew were coming.

Ann spent more and more time at the Vandenbergs. Catherine's old room was always waiting, Grace had said, and the welcome mat continually out. Ella did not object, for she knew Grace missed Catherine and it was good to see that Ann had become such a comforting replacement. Each time Ann went for a visit she took more of her personal belongings until Catherine's old room was transposed to her own. Most of the DeGrafs merely smiled at Ann's over-zealous movement and passed it off as the pre-wedding idiosyncrasies of the prospective bride. Albert and Catherine saw in it the normal consequence of Ann's desire for a freer life away from home.

Ella would be losing two of her children within a week, but Ann's premature departure would make the exodus less abrupt. Albert would be leaving soon, but where Ann was flying to a perch in the sun well known to her, he was flying to a strange environment— one that she knew frightened him at times.

Pegasus became more consistent in his response in the hands of his young trainer, and it was no longer a desperate challenge to ride him or have him trot before the new carriage. A beautiful carriage it was, for Dick had spared no expense on this one. The men at church reacted just as Dick knew they would. Admiration of the magnificent steed was hard to conceal, and Dick took in the envious glances when they pulled into the churchyard and relished it to its fullest.

The heat of summer had reached its summit by mid-August and hopefully would shortly begin to wane. There would soon be considerable disruption in the DeGraf household for the day of Ann and Peter's wedding had finally arrived, to be followed closely by Albert's departure for Philadelphia.

Early Saturday morning Albert hitched Pegasus to the sulky and set off for the Reverend VandenTill's to pick up Ann. In spite of her protests, she'd had to spend the previous evening with the Reverend's family. Ann's verbal objections had been futile; this was the way it was to be, and that closed the issue for Dick. Although the Reverend was a pious man, he was not adverse to work, and was often about his vegetable garden in proper season. Other times he occupied himself about the stable tending the brown mare. That was his own property.

When Albert pulled into the yard, the Reverend was picking tomatoes and came over to greet the boy and admire the magnificent stallion. Advice was free, and Albert heard all about the evils of city life. The Reverend expressed his confidence in Albert's religious upbringing.

This would carry him through the many temptations he would meet in Philadelphia. It was no small matter that his grandfather had been a founder of the church, his father a conscientious religious man, and his older brother a deacon. He must not jeopardize the DeGraf's long-standing tradition by yielding to the frivolous enticements of the pagan life. All this Albert accepted graciously, leaving the Reverend no cause to doubt his dedication to his church.

Ann was waiting, and they made their way slowly out the drive.

Pegasus couldn't understand his master's restraint and was itching for speed. When they were well out of sight of the house, Albert let the roan have his way and soon Ann's hair was flying straight back from a somber face.

"God, was that an ordeal!" she groaned. "I hope I never have to go through an experience like that again." Albert could see the twitch of muscles in her neck from the tension she'd been under.

"I took the sulky this morning," he said. "Thought it might help to blow the gloom away."

"Gloom is right. Catherine warned me what it'd be like, but still I wasn't prepared." She had the expression of one who'd sat up with a dying friend all night. "Can you believe he preached to me for three hours last evening? The man tried to probe all my inner thoughts and the things he told me about marriage you just wouldn't believe."

"He wants you to be a religious dutiful wife," Albert chided. "In your case, that's quite a task. No wonder the Reverend looked exhausted this morning. You were probably more than a match for his religious fervor."

"Oh, you stinker, you!" she laughed and socked him in the ribs.

"I'll bet that's the first time you've laughed since I dropped you off yesterday. Go ahead, hit me again if it'll make you feel better." She did, and it helped.

"You're all tensed up. You need a good workout. Maybe I ought to let you run alongside of the sulky for awhile."

"I'm not one of your horses, thank you. I'll manage without that," she protested.

"Just tryin' to be helpful. I want you all rosy and cheerful by the time we get home. You're over the worst of it now."

"Ha! Listen to my little brother talk. The voice of experience, and he's not even dry behind the ears."

"Peter's asked me to act as your chauffeur today. I'll be taking you to town after the reception."

"He didn't say anything to me about that," she exclaimed, half in protest.

"You're only the bride. This is strictly an arrangement between the groom and best man. After all, you didn't consult me about asking Margie to be Maid of Honor. What'd you do that for? She's got enough ideas about me as it is. It's not fair. After all, I'll be leaving for Philadelphia next week."

"I thought you'd be pleased. Since you've gotten so sweet on her, it seemed quite appropriate." Ann snickered. "Besides, Ma suggested it."

WOMEN! Here again, they were conspiring and manipulating things toward their own interests.

————◆◆◆————

Reverend VandenTill was well into the wedding service before Albert came out of his daze regarding his surroundings. Here he was standing directly behind Peter and Ann with Margie at his side in their roles of Best Man and Maid of Honor respectively. The whole situation seemed so unreal as to be part of one of his fantasies. However, this fantasy was not much to his liking. He had a feeling of being hemmed in, confined and put upon.

Here he and Margie stood, one step behind the bride and groom. Was this an omen of things to come? It had all come about so fast! To others it might seem but a normal sequence of events. Yet to him a wide chasm yawned before him, into which he felt himself being pushed. Foremost among those pushing, he seemed to feel the hands of his mother. A gentle squeeze on his hand brought him out of his self-imposed stupor. It was not his mother's hand but Margie's. She was looking across at him with a puzzled look. It must have been his expression, or lack of it, while his mind was pre-occupied. Snapping back into reality, he turned, smiled back at her and returned her squeeze with one of his own. Here Margie was warm and appealing, yet his feelings toward her were mixed and confused. How could he transfer the love and affection he had for Catherine to Margie as his mother was hoping for. What kind of miracle was she expecting? His feelings for Catherine had developed over many years going back to his boyhood. She was the only one who had encouraged him to join in games, while he was rejected by the others as too young. What began as a childhood affection matured into what he considered love— a love his rational mind realized was futile but still lived on in his fantasies. Margie however, was real and he could feel her arm pressing against his own. It was not an unpleasant sensation. Perhaps he should try harder to live in the real world with Margie as part of it.

———————

The tables in the DeGraf yard were already decked with the china and silverware of a dozen families when the wedding party arrived. Albert and Margie sat at the head table along with the bride and groom, Reverend VandenTill and senior members of both families.

Albert could see Neal at the far end of the gathering: a location they shared during Richard and Catherine's wedding. He wondered what mischief Neal would be up to this time. In some ways he would have preferred to have joined Neal rather than be in his present situation.

Dr. Brabin was also at the head table as Sarah's guest. Arrangements had been made that the good doctor would move into Ann's room now that she was leaving. Everyone agreed the doctor was too old to live alone over the winter.

Sarah, on the other hand, would have someone close to her own age to talk to during those bleak months. She was still full of stories about her youth in the old country. Whereas, family members had heard these tales many times, here were new ears to listen. Weddings these days aren't nearly as interesting as in the old days in Northern Holland. Family livelihood for many was totally dependent upon dairy cattle. This in turn carried over in many of their festivities, including weddings. In her native area it was customary that when a farmer's daughter reached puberty he would give her the very best heifer in his herd for her to raise as her own. She would be fully responsible for its feeding and care from that time on until her wedding day. The heifer would become the center of attraction during the wedding ceremony. A bride was often more closely judged by the condition and appearance of the heifer than her own wedding apparel.

The dutiful bride would have curried and fussed over her cow so that its coat shone to perfection. Decked in ruffles, bows and ribbons the heifer would have a special place at the head table.

Many tavern room jokes, she'd been told, centered on which was the dairy farmer's most valuable treasure— his wife or his best cow.

Sarah had no idea whether this custom still prevailed, but hoped it did. It was a good custom in many ways. First, it helped teach young girls responsibility and the fundamentals of caring for the animals. It was a much better form of dowry than that followed in some other areas. It helped distribute the best dairy animals among a range of farm families following the custom.

Dairy maids were noted for their beautiful blemish-free complexions in those days and frequent escape from the ravages of small pox that periodically swept the country.

Margie asked her mother if she could go with Albert when he took the newlyweds to town. He'd be leaving them at the railroad station in Paterson and would bring her directly home from there. Mrs. Wagenvoort was apologetic in her refusal. It wasn't that she didn't fully trust Albert to take good care of Margie, but her daughter did have to be careful of her reputation. The long ride home unchaperoned would be a subject for gossip, and Margie's name would be worse for it. Albert said he understood, but moisture welled up in Margie's eyes. She knew her romance had only just begun and soon he'd be leaving to live with his Aunt. She had to make the most of what time was left, for her greatest fear was that some fast and possessive city girl would grab him for her own.

Margie went along when Albert left to get Pegasus. They walked out to the pasture where the big roan was grazing with other horses. Margie wanted to be sure that Albert would write. He agreed. The thought occurred to him that he'd be writing to many people and certainly Margie must be one of them. At the barn they met Neal who only grinned when he saw them.

"Up to some tricks, friend?" asked Albert.

"Not sayin', buddy," he drawled. "Seems you've changed sides. Now you're with them, sittin' at the head table, all fine and pretty."

"Don't hold that against me," he said as Margie held firmly onto his arm and looked crossly at the intruder. Neal ignored her as though she didn't exist.

"All right! We'll go our separate ways today," Neal turned on his heel and was off.

"Shucks, you just don't understand!" Albert yelled after him.

"What was that all about?" asked Margie.

"I'm afraid he thinks I've deserted him" Albert muttered dejectedly.

"So, you haven't done anything wrong."

"That's just it. I'm spoiling his fun." He hitched Pegasus to the carriage, making sure to check everything carefully to see if Neal had been tampering. It was unlikely that Neal would try to pull the same trick as last May, but he had to make sure. He started to lead the stallion out when Margie pulled at his sleeve.

"Wait, don't go yet. Please!" He turned and saw a pair of big brown eyes which had turned moist again. "We've had so little time alone," she sniffed. "I'm going to miss you."

"I'll miss you too, Margie," he said, and looked at her intently. "But they'll wonder if we stay too long."

"I don't care if they do!" she exclaimed more forcefully than he'd ever heard her before. "You like me, don't you? You've never really said."

"I like you a great deal," he said cautiously. "You've been a very good friend."

"I'd hoped you thought of me as more than just a friend." She pressed against his arm. "I'll wait for you and won't see any other boys while you're gone."

"That's not fair to you. I'll be gone a long time. You should see other fellas', I think."

"I...I suppose you'll be seeing city girls once you're gone— and forget all about me?"

"No, I'll be studying at college. There won't be time for them."

"You promise?"

"Of course. There'll be no city girls for me!"

"Oh, good!" A sudden wave of relief swept her face, and she tucked her arm in his as they led Pegasus out of the barn.

Albert headed the stallion out the road with Peter and Ann in the back seat. There'd been the usual rice throwing, but no tricks, and no further signs of Neal. It was not like Neal, to give up this easily, and he wondered if their set-to in the barn had anything to do with it. He felt guilty, but couldn't imagine how he could have acted differently.

They had reached the top of the western ridge, and Albert was about to swing onto the south road to town, when a horse and rider thundered out of the woods and came abreast of Pegasus. He grabbed the reins and brought them to a stop. It was Neal astride one of his father's mares.

"Well, well. What have we here?" he shouted. "I'll be damned if it ain't a weddin' party!"

"Now, Neal, don't go messing things up," Peter protested.

"Not messin' things up at all, brother Pete. I'm just gonna' correct your bumblin' errors, that's all. It's pretty bad when the likes of me has to correct his brother's etiquette." Neal released Pegasus, swung his horse back towards the carriage and leaped into the back seat beside Ann. Ann was speechless, for a change.

"What do ya mean...." started Peter.

"Why kiss the bride, you dope! You never let me kiss the bride!" Neal pulled Ann towards him and gave her a big slopping wet kiss. She tried to fight him off, but his strength was too much for her.

"Now, I feel better!" He dropped back in the seat as though exhausted and winked at his new sister-in-law, whose mouth stood half open trying to form words. "I no longer feel neglected," and he let out a boisterous laugh.

"Now, wait a minute!" started Ann, finally catching her breath. "You can't...." She got no father, for Neal gave her another kiss— that shut her up.

"Now, be quiet!" Neal scolded. "Each time you open your mouth to protest, I'm going to repeat that. If you were my wife, it'd be a regular treatment." Looking over at Peter," Let that be a lesson to you, Pete. Treat 'er rough and she'll love you for it." Neal settled down next to Ann intent on staying awhile.

"Hey! You up front!" Neal called to Albert. "Chauffeur!....Boy....What'd they call you? You've got a new passenger to town. How about shaking that flea bitten nag up a bit!"

"Yes, Sir!" Albert yelled back, with a new enthusiasm and snapped the reins over Pegasus's back so that they sped away with a vigor that was more in the stallion's liking.

Peter and Ann got off at the railroad station a bit shaken up by the fast ride. Albert helped Peter with the luggage while Neal reclined in the back seat and watched them with a pleased expression on his face. When everything was ready, and they were saying their farewells, Neal joined them.

"I hope I didn't offend you, Ann," Neal said contritely. "I really meant no disrespect. Forgive my wild ways. Sometimes, I just can't help myself."

"Why, Neal" Ann exclaimed, surprised at this sudden change in attitude. "Of course, I forgive you."

"You really forgive me?" almost pleading.

"Why, of course!"

"You are truly a gracious lady." Neal bowed low and kissed her hand with a flourish. "As a representative of my father's household, it gives me great pleasure to welcome you into the distinguished Vandenberg family." Neal raised his eyes as he straightened up and looked directly into Ann's now smiling face. He could see she was flattered by his little speech. "I would ask but one small favor of you, dear lady, before you go."

"And what is that?" Ann drew back, still not completely trusting him.

"Take it easy on my poor brother these next couple of nights. He's had no pre-marital experience that I know of." Ann's face turned crimson and she yanked her hand back from where he held it. Neal let out a hoot and a holler, slapped his sides, and ambled back to the carriage. "Come on, boy. Let's get this manure wagon on the road!" he yelled to Albert.

Albert and Neal set off from the train station leaving the newlyweds on their own.

"Pull down Clancy street!" exclaimed Neal. "I could stand a beer or two."

"Well...." Albert started to object, but stopped, for he wasn't about to risk a quarrel. The tavern was almost empty. Neal motioned Albert to a table in the corner, ordered two mugs of beer and joined him.

"Bet you never had a good mug of draft beer before," Neal said, and pushed one mug over to his young friend. "Try it, it won't hurt you." Albert raised the mug, took a swallow and pulled a face. "You've got to develop a taste for it. It grows on you after awhile."

"Not sure I want it to," Albert replied, but he took another sip anyway.

"Did you see Ann's face when I made that last remark?" Neal hooted all over again. "Boy, she must hate me right now."

"Humph! More'n likely she's already forgotten you."

"Probably so," Neal exclaimed, with a shrug of his shoulders.

"Well, it was fun for a while anyway." Then, in a complete change of voice, "So you're headin' for Philadelphia next week. I'll miss you. You know, I have very few real friends around here. Most of them are religious cranks as far as I'm concerned."

"I'll miss you, too," Albert answered. You're the only one I truly trust to take care of Pegasus. It's a lot to ask, but would you look in on him regularly to see he's all right?"

"Gladly, no problem at all." Neal was still grinning, remembering Ann's expression as they left.

"I'll speak to Dad about you taking him out for exercise. He has a great respect for your horsemanship."

"Handling Pegasus will be a pleasure. You know that." Neal watched Albert closely. He could tell there was more to come.

Albert took a large gulp of beer, which almost choked him going down. He looked uneasily at Neal, then at the ceiling.

"I have another request: a real serious one!" Albert then went on to explain that while in Philadelphia he wanted to write Catherine, but dared not do it directly for fear of the gossip it would create.

Neal looked at him questionably, but said nothing.

"Since we've already agreed to write each other," Albert continued, "I'd like to include notes to Catherine which you could pass along without the others knowing."

"Don't know what the hell's going on between you and Kate, and I'm not about to ask." Neal's eyebrows came down in a frown." If Richard gets wind of it he'll kick the shit out of you." A pause. "Then again, after your session with him about our prank at his wedding, you're probably not much afraid of him anymore."

"How'd you know about that?"

"Oh, come on now. Ann was there, remember? You think Ann could keep something like that under wraps. Why everybody in church knew within a week. From there it spread like wildfire. It bounced around on the gossip grapevine for weeks. Surprised, none of it ever came back to you. It was a perfect tale for that church crowd. A real David and Goliath story. Anyway, you know you can count on me. That is, as long as I stay in this area."

"How's that? Albert's head jerked up in surprise. Neal as the oldest son at the Vandenbergs would eventually inherit the family farm. It was clearly in his best interests to stay close and protect those interests.

"I'm gonna' join the Canadian army—cavalry."

"Oh, come on! What you wanna' do that for?"

"I'd like to get into the fightin' before it's over. This place gives me the creeps!"

"Still, can't see it."

"What's there here for me? Nursemaid to a bunch of cows and long faces on Sunday? It's God damned dull. I crave a little excitement. Maybe I'll come back a hero!"

"Yeah, and maybe get killed!"

"That's a chance I'll take. Can only die once, and this here just ain't livin'."

chapter

16

$\mathcal{B}$efore dawn, Albert and old Gin moved the cows into the barn. Dick had asked if he would handle the milking by himself and he'd readily agreed, welcoming the chance to be alone. It was quiet in the barn with only the even steady breathing of the animals and an occasional low moo or snort. The nose-stinging ammonia of fresh manure mingled with sweaty cow flesh and the heavy aroma of seasoned hay. These were odors he knew he would miss and they were already becoming nostalgic. The purr of warm milk into the half-filled pail was another sound that soothed his mind. Philadelphia loomed within the confines of the barn and a new life with all its unfamiliarity, imagined ramifications occupied his thoughts. Now and then he was vaguely aware of the rumbling of wheels in the drive and identified each in turn; first, the heavy wheels of the milk wagon with Richard and Govert then later, wheels of the sulky with his mother and Catherine. Wheels he wouldn't hear were those of his father's wagon going to market, for they had rumbled out the drive long before. After the last rumbling of wheels was gone, he was only faintly aware of new noises around and above him, faint noises that did not fully penetrate his consciousness.

First there was a slight tickle at the back of his neck, and he brushed a hand absently across the spot and then went back to his milking. There it was again. He repeated the motion and had returned his hand to the cow's teat when he heard a giggle from above; his eyes shot upward and he saw a movement in the faint light. In three strides he was going up the ladder two rungs at a time. The loft was dark except for the faint glow through the opening from the lantern below, so he felt his way over to the huge double doors and flung them open. Pale silvery light from a nearly full moon tip-toed into the loft as though searching the dark corners for him. The faint fuzzy outlines of piles of hay along the sides of the vast upper room gradually came into view as his eyes accustomed themselves to the semi-darkness. Still, there was nothing in sight that he hadn't expected to see. Then, half way down one side he saw a slight movement in the hay. Quietly, he moved over to where it had been and knelt down to have a closer look. With a burst of laughter, Catherine jumped from her hiding place, sprang past him, and onto a large pile on the other side. He was after her in an instant, but she dodged and was gone as though in thin air. Again, there was nothing but hay and pale moonlight. *My mind is playing tricks with me,* he thought, *Catherine is on her way to her folks with my mother.* He struck his forehead with the palm of his hand as if to awaken himself, when again he saw a movement in the shadows. This time he leaped directly into the hay and encircled a wiggling, scrambling body that was solid— not a fantasy.

"Fooled you, didn't I?" she giggled. "My, you were deep in thought! I almost had to throw the whole hay loft down to get your attention!"

"What are you doing here?" he gasped. "I thought you went to your folks with Mom!"

"I'm supposed to be sick."

"You don't act sick!"

"I just put on that I was. I had to see you alone once more before you leave."

"I'm glad," he smiled broadly into the darkness and, although she could barely see his grin, she knew it was there for it showed in his voice.

"Oh, about going to Philadelphia next week. I don't want to go."

"I rather guessed that. Is it because of me you want to stay?"

"That's my main reason."

"Will it surprise you that I also dread the thought of your leaving?"

"You do? You're not teasing me?

"No, I'm serious. You've grown very close to me, in a very pleasant way."

"I've already learned to hate Philadelphia."

"Don't be like that! You have a bright future ahead of you, and you'll meet many interesting people. You'll soon forget all about me."

"Never! I'll never forget you, no matter where I go," he blurted out, emotionally. "The city can be a very lonely place."

"Who told you that?"

"Well— no one, but I'm sure it is."

"Nonsense! You'll not have time for loneliness."

"Will you write me when I'm gone? I'll write you often."

"Do you think that wise? How will I explain letters from you? Soon, the whole family will suspect something."

"I've already arranged that with Neal. We'll be writing each other and I'll enclose notes to you, which he'll then get to you without the others knowing."

"Doesn't he wonder what's going on?"

"He <u>did</u> raise an eyebrow when I mentioned it, but he'll never tell anyone. He thinks we're playing a prank on Richard. Besides, he's always felt ostracized by the others. He and I have become close friends, thanks to Pegasus. I know I can trust him."

"I'll write you and mail the letters in town. No one will know."

Albert reached for her hand and pulled her toward the open doors. There they sat on the floor with their feet hanging over the edge. It was lighter here and he could see the outline of her face in the moonlight. The lines were soft and touched with muted tones like a Rembrandt painting. Here was a somber beauty that was different from what he'd remembered. The night rides to choir were not like this; here was a sultry glow of the hushed pre-dawn hours that took his breath away. She noticed the change in him and was about to ask, when he kissed her.

"You take things for granted, don't you?" she chided gently. "You kiss without asking now. You used to ask."

"It was a brotherly kiss."

"Unhuh! Have you kissed Margie like this yet?"

"A couple of times, on the cheek."

"That's all? You've never kissed her like you have with me?"

"I've never kissed anyone like with you."

"Why not? You're not too shy, I know that now."

"No, I just don't like her well enough. We're friends, that's all."

"Oh!" Catherine exclaimed thoughtfully. "I was hoping you'd learn to care for her. She could give you a love that's impossible from me."

"You want to get rid of me then?" his voice choked up. "Is that it?"

"You put it far too bluntly, but sometimes I think I cheat you by not discouraging you more than I do. You talk of love in idealistic terms, but your actions speak differently. I can't love two brothers equally, while married to one. You've grown up a great deal these last few months and it frightens me."

"I scare you?" he asked, incredulously.

"Perhaps I've become more afraid of myself than you. We tread on dangerous ground, you know."

"But I've never asked for what I know's not mine, although I begrudge my brother all he has of you. I'm satisfied with just being with you— in kind of a spiritual way."

"Can one exist without the other?"

"I think so."

"Perhaps for awhile, but you can't tell me it's just my mind that interests you," she chucked her tongue against the roof of her mouth. "I know better than that."

"Well—no," he had to admit it wasn't. A bawling of cows came from below. "Darned cows! They want to be milked."

"You neglect them and pay too much attention to me. I'll help you with the milking. That way it won't take long."

They went down and took adjacent cows, both diligently setting to work to make up time. *It was best they continue their conversation here,* she thought, *it was safer for both of them and some things had to be settled.* "Tell me, Al, if I were a very plain girl with stringy, straight hair, would you feel the same about me? Would my mind transcend a flat chest and lack of curves?"

"Well...." he paused. "Perhaps it wouldn't be quite the same."

"Then all your talk about the spiritual is just that— talk! It's the physical me that draws your eye and whets your tongue."

"No, it's not like that at all." He could not see her face but by her voice knew it wore an impish grin. His hands moved rhythmically and he stared into the cow's flank seeing nothing as he tried to form the words to explain. "Do you remember last year when a group of us from church went to the New York Museum of Art? You were single then."

"Yes, I remember."

"Remember all the paintings we saw of the old masters and then the modern impressionist school of art? There was such a range of mood and color that it was hard to grasp it all. I'd never seen such beauty of line and form, and yet such contrasts. The dark and somber tones of Rembrandt first caught my eye. To me, this was perfection, but yet there was a foreboding moodiness that made me turn away. So much of life lurks within dark shadows that I looked for brighter, gayer tones than those he used. Later, I saw some works of Renoir which probably weren't as good, but pleased me more. Renoir must have loved his fellow man, for he portrayed them with a delightfulness that shone from every face. There was one in particular that reminded me of you—a girl crotcheting. I remember looking at it for quite some time and then searching for you across the gallery so that I could compare you with what I'd seen in that picture. Renoir had seen in that woman those same qualities I see in you. Beauty as I saw it then and see it now is not just a physical thing. There is something that goes beyond mere flesh and bone. I believe the artist saw the purity of a soul, and the body was only the vessel that held it before his eyes. A quality so intense one could feel it at a distance with a sense that transcends touch and sound."

"You looked at me even then, as you do now?" she asked, and wished that she'd known.

"Yes, I've watched you from a distance for a long time. It has become a habit with me."

"You compare me to the paintings you saw in the museum. Is this what you call love?"

"To see the paintings is to enjoy them and it's the same with you. All the senses do not have to be experienced....sight alone is enough. One does not have to touch or smell a Rembrandt or Renoir to appreciate it. I could love....you without touching at all."

"Ah, but you have! You've embraced and kissed me very passionately. We both know that. Then there's the business of the way you look at me at times. You admitted at the pond your mind's eye is not always discreet.

195

This is earthy, not spiritual. It's more the sport of a lecherous old man than an idealistic youth, I think."

"Not as I see you, it isn't. I think you're teasing me, but let me explain. Going back to the museum, did you see any of the Grecian sculptures there?"

"No, we girls were confined to the paintings and I suspect only certain ones of those. I believe Mrs. VandenTill purposely kept us from seeing what she thought improper. Yet, I think I know what you mean. I've browsed through art books from time to time. Grecian. In other words, nude."

"Unadorned, is perhaps a better word. I didn't find them nude in the 'earthy' sense, as you use the word. There is a special grace of the human body, and truthfully, I saw nothing vulgar in it. What impressed me most was the freedom of expression, unsuppressed by the shackles of constraint which bind us so tightly. It made me aware that all the world is not like we know it here. The fear of God's damnation could not have cramped the minds of those who created these works of art. Here, such things are sin. Yet, I saw no sin in them. What sin there is, is but in our minds, and what we make of it."

"This is why you must go away from here, to find a more creative, freer life."

"And wish to God, I could take you with me."

"Unfortunately, that's not possible. I made my choice and now I'm held to it, for better or for worse." There was a finality in her voice that ran flat with the last words.

Albert had no answer to this. He emptied her pail and his own which finished the milking. The first rays of pre-dawn were lighting up the eastern sky. He extinguished the lantern and let the cows go out to pasture.

"We finished early. You were a great help, which proves you are practical as well as beautiful."

"Now who's teasing who? You're trying to steal my style." Still, she enjoyed the double compliment. Shaking her hair back over her shoulders, she laughed and started for the ladder.

"Let's watch the sun rise from the loft," she called back as she scrambled up ahead of him.

"Albert quickly mounded a large pile of hay just inside the double doors and they dropped down on it to watch the brightening day approach.

Puffy light gray clouds floated high with patches of dark violet blue between. Their upper halves were dark iron gray, still partly clutched in the reluctant grip of night, but their bellies were a rosy pink from reflected rays of the rising sun. The sun itself, half a golden disc, languidly rested upon the trees of the eastern ridge and slowly raised itself from its leafy bed to stretch and yawn towards the open sky.

"Good morning, Mr. Sun, and how are you today?" he spoke towards the ever enlarging piece of bright copper. "You seem sleepy this morning. Have we disturbed you?"

"Do you often greet the morning sun like this?" she asked.

"No, can't say as I do, but I feel especially good just now. Actually, a little silly perhaps in having you here with me." He reached for her hand and clasped it in his own. The copper piece became a copper whole and soon the air was bright and shiny all about the place they sat. Her hair had become strewn with bits of hay making a yellow and red quilty pattern. He stroked them out and ran his fingers through it like a comb. She looked towards the horizon and then towards him, but only smiled at the business of those fingers which moved from hair to cheek to chin and down a graceful throat.

"The sun seems especially bright this morning." she said absently. "It's going to be a fine day."

"Wouldn't it be something if the sun were to get stuck?"

"Get stuck?

"If time were to stand still as of this moment, and not move again for a hundred years."

"With us just watching the sunrise. I think it might get tiresome after awhile."

"Well, perhaps a hundred years would be a long time, but five or ten would suit me fine. Just think of all the things you could tease me about."

"You want me to tease you?"

"That's what you were doing downstairs, wasn't it?

"Perhaps a little, but mostly I was drawing you out. To explore your emotions, I guess. You made a rather pretty speech about comparing me with paintings at the museum, but your reasoning wasn't very realistic."

"It wasn't?" He'd moved over on his stomach beside her and looked down into her dark blue eyes which sparkled with amusement. His fingers paused in their gentle touch along the side of her throat. She was fully aware of the tracing those fingers made as they moved softly, cautiously, like a fluttering butterfly, across her skin. Each time on their downward movement they followed along the fine golden chain that hung from her neck to where it converged and the cleft began. Here those fingers slowed and paused just above the line of her dress and then retraced their path back up along the chain again.

"No, it wasn't," she finally said. "You compared me with the paintings. Did you also do the same with the marble statues? Was it enough only to look, or did you feel the urge to test each line and curve with your fingertips? Here the sense of sight alone was not enough. Am I right?"

"There was a rope between the walk and where the statues stood. Besides, I wouldn't have dared to touch them, if I'd wanted to."

"Ah, ha! I thought so. You didn't, but you would've liked to. Just like you do with me now, you test my lines and curves with your fingers." She took the finely woven chain and pulled the locket from its place between her breasts and dangled it in front of her, swinging it slowly from side to side. "This is not what your fingers sought, but where it lay, I'm sure. Am I then but a work of art to you?"

"Of course not. I just enjoy the soft touch of your skin."

"Still, it is testing; exploring if you will. What new curves would you test if you could?" She took the hand from where it had paused and moved it slowly across her bare shoulder to where the cleft began and then, even more slowly, moved it down first along and over one breast and then the other. "There is new territory for your nimble fingers to explore." His face flushed but he didn't withdraw his hand. He could feel a warm softness beneath the cotton dress that made his fingers ache just from the touch.

"You have very gentle hands," she said. "You do not paw or press, but have a touch much like an artists brush." She raised her arm and brought his head down to her own and he knew what she wanted. He kissed her on the mouth for a long moment and felt the movement of her hands as he did so. When he raised up again, her dress was open to the waist and her breasts exposed to the morning sun. What he'd glimpsed but partially in the shadowy light of his room, now shown before him in pale white splendor. She took his hand and placed it where the dress had been and watched his eyes which would not meet her gaze. A confused shyness returned, but did not extend to the active fingertips that hesitantly moved along a fully rounded globe and brushed a small pink island upon a calm white sea, which turned from soft to firm upon his touch.

"Although one part of you feints shyness, another seeks and explores," she grinned and brought her hand up to make him look at her. "Where would those sensitive fingers lead you if I allowed?"

"No further than you invite them."

"It is I then who judge what's right and wrong? You place a heavy burden on me. Your hands have an appetite which your mind denies, or would have me believe it denies. I know you're not deceitful, but you speak of love as though it were a completely spiritual thing; a God that does not eat. Your hands and looks betray the fallacy of that belief. To me, love is not a ghost, nor does it live within a vacuum, but like a living, growing thing— it feeds. As it grows, so grows its hunger and it reaches out for more and more. That which sustained it in its infancy will not satisfy it later on. These little acts of love we now express will not suffice for long. It will be weaned....and then demand more solid stuff."

"You feel that I would ask for more than this?"

"You will, in time, I think."

"I couldn't! I swear!" and yet he bent and gently kissed the nipple on each breast.

"That's hard to believe! All our fine talk of Rembrandt and Renoir. What you do now isn't the same."

"Is what we do unclean?" He had a worried look.

"That depends. . . not if you believe your own little speech of earlier. Why?"

"Just some words I remember from your wedding ceremony."

"Yet, in spite of that, you persist in your devotion. Love of a painting or a statue is quite different from loving me. Those works of art do not return your love. I'm not canvas and paint, nor cold marble. You show your affection and I respond. We build a golden chain that binds us more and more, each adding links as we go." She grasped the chain that held the locket and held it in a tightened fist. "This was given to me by my mother, passed down through four generations, yet I could break it with a single sudden tug. The chain we build, I fear, in time will not be broken, even by my marriage. What then?" With extreme deliberation she put his hand aside and buttoned up her dress. She sat up and looked at him with large blue eyes that glistened with moisture. "You have no answer?"

"Only that I love you more than anything in the world. It's so intense it hurts me all inside."

"Like a gnawing hunger that will not be satisfied?" He nodded. She gestured knowingly, tried to smile, but the smile wouldn't come. "You remember one time I asked you if you wanted to be my lover?" she said quietly. "At that time I said it jokingly, but now I ask it seriously. Is that what you want?"

"How can you ask that?" His face flushed hot. "Have I ever tried..." He couldn't finish.

"No, you haven't, but you easily could. It might follow quite naturally. You _do_ want me though, don't you?"

"I don't know.. .I don't know!" His voice rose in anguish. "I'm confused." He looked at her longingly, and then broke; dropping his head in her lap, he choked out the words, "I want you! God, how I want you...but I love you too much for that!"

"You love me _too much_?" she said incredulously.

"God would damn you for your infidelity," he sobbed. "He'd damn us both..."

The days following the wedding passed slowly for some, and yet it slipped by entirely too quickly for others. The excitement of the wedding was over, the cousins had returned to Philadelphia, and for some this meant only a return to daily chores and preparation for the coming winter. For Ella and Catherine there was the impending departure of another member of the family.

Richard had been especially congenial during the last weeks and Albert found his friendliness almost embarrassing. His brother had never been exactly solicitous towards him except perhaps for a time after the swamp incident. Now, Richard went out of his way to be helpful, and was more sociable than Albert could ever remember.

He wondered at the cause for the change and, even more, how long it would last. One thing was certain, he wouldn't be around long enough to find out.

Friends and neighbors stopped by to give their farewells to the boy who was leaving the farm for city and college. In the small community there were very few who moved out as he was doing. At church, there was a little party to bid him God's grace and protection in his new life. Margie's goodbye was wrought with restrained emotion, and she gave him a packet of pale blue writing paper with envelopes; a gentle reminder of his promise to write.

Directly after supper the evening before his departure, Ella helped him with the last minute packing. He would be traveling light, for a trunk with his winter clothes and books had gone on ahead. During their chat in his room, Ella gave him all the words of advice she'd given him before. This was a matter of therapy for her and her eyes were moist. The sudden realization of his immediate departure made her question the valid reasons she had known previously, for the mind was left to drift as the heart took over; what previously reason had dictated, now emotion rebelled against.

The evening was spent in playing cards. Dick lay stretched on the parlor couch while Richard and Catherine teamed in pinochle against Ella and Albert. The game was dull, and three of the four played badly. Finally, at nine o'clock, after hot chocolate and honeykuchen, everyone went on to bed—it was that kind of evening.

Catherine had gone into a troubled sleep, but awoke several hours later with a burning sensation in the pit of her stomach. This was something that had been bothering her more and more, and would make sleep difficult. She would have to see Dr. Braben again about it for relief. It was always worse in the middle of the night after a brief sleep, a time when it was least welcome. Then, her thoughts were always darkest and fears magnified a thousandfold. Apprehensions, which in the bright daylight were mere annoyance, became the hills of despair in the black of this late hour. Those hills now rose into mountains in the darkness of the room. Thoughts bubbled forth from subterranean caverns deep within the bowels of suppressed consciousness. This night she relived the evening before her wedding. The fantasies of spirit she'd then pushed aside returned to haunt her. Where she'd not known the substance of them then and only darkly groped, a mere sapling of a boy had thrown a light. Yet, that light could not be sustained. It merely let her see the substance of those fantasies, before it flickered out. The night was closing in again.

Her stomach was so tied up in knots she would never get to sleep.

Warm milk was the only cure. Quietly, she slipped out of bed, put on a robe, and headed for the kitchen by touch alone. With soft steps she moved across the room, into the hall, and down towards a faint light at the other end. She knew the light from other times she'd passed this way in dead of night. There she stopped and stood a full moment. Her hand moved toward the door knob, but was quickly withdrawn. There was a strong desire for a final farewell. Yet, what could they say or do beyond that said and done in the barn loft. Quickly, silently she moved on to the back stairs and kitchen below.

PART IV

HARVEST

chapter

17

To Albert's eye it was really not a house at all, but part of a gigantic edifice that stretched a full block along Dubarry Street. It was just like all other structures for many blocks around. Aunt Beatrice's was the fifth house, or more correctly, entrance, from the corner. Three white marble steps separated the front door from the narrow red brick street. The street was like a corridor, a thin red line, dividing the solid bank of opposing house fronts, which stood like regimental soldiers at closed ranks facing their opponents at bayonet point; the tan brick forces were on the left, the gray brick forces on the right.

The atmosphere was one of economy, with shortages everywhere– of space— of light— of time. Only people were in abundance; people jammed together, with thousands living within an area the size of his father's farm.

The lush green foliage to which he was accustomed was lacking and only hinted at by gaunt trees, two within each city block on either side. These stretched thinly upward for the light and struggled for water below the brick paved desert that was Dubarry Street. Each house front had a single door flanked by a window on either side; above this, three windows upon the second floor, and three upon the third. Yet again, above the upper three were two more, but these could hardly be called windows, for they were only small glass holes within a slanted roof. The small window within one hole was pivoted outward and from beneath it a blond tousled head protruded. Albert was surveying his new world.

After several moments, the head retreated within, and Albert returned to the attic room which was his sleeping quarters. The room, about ten feet square, was but half finished as rooms go, for the exposed rafters were merely prettied with a coat of paint. Two cots occupied opposite sides, a bureau with a broken drawer, one small mirror, a shipping crate converted into a desk, two straight-back chairs, one soiled oval rug. These were the furnishings of the room. There was a naked electric bulb which dangled at the end of a cord from the rafters. Several piles of books were stacked in the corner on the floor. Albert went over to the crate-desk and finished the letter he was writing.

Dear Mom,

Arrived safely and was met at the station by Aunt Beatrice and Cousin Henry. They seemed glad to see me, but I find it difficult, now after two days, to know why. I am just one more person in a very crowded house. It is going to take me awhile to get used to it.

I think Aunt Beatrice realizes this for she has me up in an attic room with Cousin Clarence. Although the room is small and very hot just now, Clarence is off to work most of the time. He's an apprentice mechanic and works twelve hours a day, six days a week, so you see I'll have plenty of time to study by myself. Among the rooms downstairs as many as four children sleep in a single bedroom. That makes me pretty lucky at that.

My winter clothes and books arrived before I did and Cousins Henry and Clarence brought them up here for me. Now I'm studying for the entrance exams I'll be taking next Tuesday. How do I have the nerve to think I can enter the University, when I've not had a formal high school education? So much of my learning is home taught. I feel inadequate about so many subjects— it scares me.

You're probably wondering how well I eat, so to relieve your mind I'll tell you. We eat a lot of cabbage, beans, pork, and brown bread.

Also, there's plenty of milk. Meals are not as fancy as at home, or varied, but no one goes hungry and everyone seems reasonably healthy.

Well, I'd better get back to my studying. There's so much to cover that I hardly know where to begin, and then I wonder if it's all really worth it. I can hear your reply to that right now. Of course it is! So, back to the books.

Give my love to everyone. Hope Pegasus is getting his exercise and I'll bet old Gin misses me. Did you ever hear where Ann and Pete went on their honeymoon?

Love,

Albert.

Albert went back to his books for about an hour and then went down to see Aunt Beatrice in the kitchen. The stairs from the attic to the third floor were narrow and steep. Henry and Clarence must have had quite a time getting his luggage up. These stairs were no place for a fat person that was certain. The other two flights were not much wider but at least not so steep.

His aunt was a large woman, though certainly not overweight for her height and frame. Prematurely wrinkled from the cares of raising such a large family, yet she had a zest for life which defied both age and toil. Hers had not been an easy life, but then she'd never asked for one either.

"Is there anything I can do for you, Aunt Bea——?" he asked.

"Oh, you startled me, Albert. Finished your studyin'?"

"I'm pretty well saturated for now. I'd like something physical to do."

"See what you can do with the vegetable garden, then. Uncle Gordon's back's been acting up, so the weeds've got ahead of him. There's a hoe standin' in the corner of the back porch. Don't touch the petunias, though. they're only for him."

"Fine, that's just the kind of exercise I need," Albert replied, and went out to the back yard.

The yard was the width of the house and thirty feet deep. It was walled by a board fence on each side and across the back at the property line; each fence was common with an adjacent neighbor. This was quite a different kind of garden than he was used to, for at home, a single row contained more than a dozen gardens like this. If he wasn't careful he would work himself out of this job before he would have— as his father would say— "warmed" up the hoe.

It was a curious garden consisting of close rows of tomatoes, cabbage, broccoli, and beans with many dried and withered plants of crops now spent. The weeds had thrived throughout, except for one area of the garden which was clean and well cared for. This was a small patch of petunias surrounding a two foot status of a winged nymph. This was the special section his Aunt had mentioned.

The hoe was dull and rusty so he dug around on the back porch and found an equally rusty file. With a sharpened hoe, he was down the short rows and the job was done before he'd realized it. Pausing before the petunia bed, he looked down at the small terra-cotta statue. It shone in dull redness in the late afternoon sun. It was the only object in the yard that was free of city grime. Statues were something that would haunt him now, whether simple little nymphs or Grecian goddesses, for in their place he would always see one living figure.

"How about letting me hang the clothes out for you?" he said to Aunt Beatrice on returning to the house.

"That's woman's work. You've finished the garden already?"

"Remember, I'm no stranger to a hoe." He ignored his Aunt's other remark.

Albert took the large reed basket filled with wet clothes and returned to the back porch. From the porch column, the pulley line extended to an electric pole set at the back fence line, just like other poles and lines up and down the yards, creating a valley of clotheslines, some filled and others bare. After he'd emptied the basket, he went out the front way to meet Freddy and the others returning from school.

Studying in his attic room, helping Aunt Beatrice when he could, and exploring the city alone on foot were Albert's main occupations during the first week. The day of his entrance exam was fraught with apprehension and dread, followed by more of the same while waiting for the results. Five days later word came that he had passed. Sylvia baked him a cake that evening and he and his new-found cousins celebrated his victory. While they themselves had no opportunity to enter college, they didn't seem to begrudge him the honor. Yet, he noticed that Clarence was more nervous than usual during the festivities, and immediately afterward went to bed. Aunt Beatrice's only remark was that she never doubted that Albert would pass his exam. How she had figured that out he didn't know, but Aunt Beatrice was not one for idle flattery.

———◆·❈·◆———

Albert purposely did not write to anyone besides his mother until after he had the results of his exam. This had been difficult, but it seemed best. He had no desire to express thoughts about his new life which he might be sorry about if he failed, and it was decided that he return home. Midway through the second week, a small pink envelope arrived. It was a short note from Margie; it simply wished him well in his exam and his future in college.

He wrote a second letter to his mother, which was really to the family. He knew it would be read aloud at mealtime when everyone was gathered about the kitchen table. As he wrote the words, they came back off the paper in his mother's soft, clear voice. She was an excellent reader, having a vibrant voice that gave the proper quality of merriment or pathos to any text. Her voice came to him now as it had through the years in her readings of Chaucer, Shakespeare, Dickens, Longfellow, and Poe. Perhaps the best of all had been her readings of Milton, Byron, Keats and Shelley, for these had sparked his love of poetry.

Letters to Margie, Neal, and Catherine followed.

Dear Margie:

I received your note on Wednesday and realize I should have written you sooner. I hope you'll forgive my tardiness. I have really had my nose buried in my books these past two weeks, and I guess it has been worth it, for I passed my exams. Now it looks as though I'll be a full fledged student at that, in spite of all my worrying.

My adjustment to life here in the city has not been easy, but I guess I'm making progress. It's a radical change from the life I've always known. For me, it will still be a rather sheltered life I expect, since I do not have to go out and work for a living as most do here. I feel as if I were one of the privileged few— a bourgeois among the poor. I say this with no feeling of pride or snobbery, but only with the realization of how lucky I am.

My social life has been confined to the immediate family, with a few exceptions, if one were to call them social. These are the grocery man, the baker, the iceman, the shoemaker, etc. You see, I've become my Aunt's domestic procurer (more commonly called errand boy). I do the family grocery shopping, and although some say this is woman's work, I 'do' know a good cabbage or head of lettuce when I see it. Already, I probably know the current grocery prices as well as most housewives. Cousin Henry says I'll someday make someone a good wife. Cousin Henry jokes a lot— and this is one of them— I think.

Remember me to our friends in choir. I'll bet they sing better without me. I never was a very good tenor. The high notes were too high and the baritone range too low.I was just in between— a misfit, I guess.

I'll write you again, after I've started classes.

Best regards,
Albert

Dear Neal,

I think you'd enjoy city life— if you had enough money to take advantage of it. Most of the people I know here can only nibble once in awhile at the entertainment it offers. Life can be pleasant though, if you enjoy the excitement of being with people. There are plenty of vaudeville theatres, libraries, taverns, and even movie houses, presently featuring Mary Pickford. People flock to the parks to feed the pigeons and see the trees and shrubs; that which we see every day back home and take for granted. Lush green foliage is never missed as much as when you don't have it. Here it is brick and concrete, not trees and crops.

"There is much more talk about the war here than at home. The latest news from Europe is a daily topic of conversation in the streets— and cause much controversy.

Two opposing groups create heated arguments in the market place. On the one side are those in full support of the allies, and on the other the German-Americans, Socialists and Quakers who urge strict neutrality.

"*The newspapers are full of the war. At first, I found it exciting to know so quickly what is going on overseas. I realize now that we on the farm are in a back eddy from the mainstream of life. I once thought this regrettable, but now I find the daily news from Europe depressing. It is not good to be reminded day after day that men are killing each other this hour, this minute— seemingly endlessly.*

"*What I see in the newspapers are mere statistics, but they represent life, and blood, and death. At these times our conversations about the war trouble me. I hope you have changed your mind about enlisting with the Canadians. Why add your weight to that of all those other thousands? It seems such a senseless brutality. Write me that you've changed your mind.*

"*You already know about my fondness for Catherine, from our conversation that day in the tavern. I know I don't even have to ask again that you keep our secret, since she and I alone will suffer if you don't. As per our arrangement I've enclosed a letter I dare not mail to her direct. If you are the good friend I trust you are, you'll see she gets it privately. Do not question my motives too sharply. She means a lot to me, that's all I'll say.*

Your Buddy,
Al

Dearest Catherine,

It is hard to believe that I have been here for over two weeks. Life is compressed with the pressures of people crowded together and there is a greater urgency of time. As yet, I have been mostly an observer in the daily life of my Aunt, Uncle and cousins. They all have been very good to me and it is as though I have been added to this tremendous family which knows no bounds.

Just think, next week I start classes at the University. What a far cry it is from our little schoolhouse back home. I now realize how much my mother taught me over the years, for it was her teachings that made the difference in last week's exam. I have to pinch myself occasionally to make sure this is not just all a dream.

During my exploration of the city, I discovered several libraries. There's not just one, but many. There are more books available to me than I ever dreamed of and it makes me feel so insignificant to have read so few. My mouth waters just to walk among the stacks. There is so much knowledge to be absorbed and so little time— my appetite far exceeds my ability to devour what I know awaits me here. Best of all, there is no restraint on what I may or may not read— no question as to what is proper and what is heretic or obscene. It is a far different world in which I now live.

The first Sunday morning we attended the Presbyterian church. What a real crowd of us—we filled up two whole pews. The minister was not at all like Reverend VandenTill. He seemed a kindly man, plump instead of gaunt, white haired instead of bald, soft-spoken instead of shrill voiced. There was no raving about sin and damnation. Here, it seems, man's sins are treated with a different emphasis. God forgives shortcomings, and salvation is through Christ's grace. A much better approach, I think. The second Sunday, I went to church twice, once with the family and then alone to a Methodist church nearby. To my surprise, no one questioned my going, nor did anyone ply me with questions following my return. Undoubtedly, they think I'm a big boy now, and have a right to do some things as I choose. This new freedom is overwhelming. Can you imagine any of us at home being able to go and come without giving strict account of ourselves?

I think of you always, but it is perhaps in the museum that the feeling and hunger to see you again becomes acute. It is an appetite that paint and canvas intensifies rather than fills. I will not tell you how long I stood before the figure of Aphrodite of the Cnidians, or before "The Kiss" by Auguste Rodin. Lovely, but so chipped from cold white marble as to leave one impressionless except for their inadequacy.

Our last meeting in the barn loft will always be with me. It has been etched deep and permanently into my brain. Enclosed is a poem I wrote that evening. Hope you don't think it too silly.

God be with you.

You dominate my prayers.

Love,
Albert

"The sky above is blue with puffs of white,
While down below mid flowered fields we sit,
Small creatures here we are, but much in love,
A love we pray transcends our earthly bonds.

"We think not of the power that rules us now,
That gives us life but briefly, then we're cut,
Abruptly off the tiny thread we've spun,
To drift away from earth in the unknown.

"Then this thread of life is spun yet anew,
Another form takes shape now that we're done,
Our time then past, we change to something else,
For change is all that's sure to each of us.

"This God of time thinks not how much we love,
But only that we too must pass to dust,
For everything must go and nothing stays
Like all before and all that's yet to come.

"Oh pray with me that the Great God of Time,
Upon his march across eternity,
Now pause and rest awhile, and find it sweet,
Then never again renew his endless trek."

———◆◆◆◆◆———

Albert left the house early the next morning to explore the city in depth, for there would be little chance once classes began. He had offered to help Aunt Beatrice with the household chores, but she'd said he'd come to Philadelphia to be a student, not a housemaid, and shooed him out the door. She didn't seem to see anything wrong in her nephew, green from the country, wandering the streets of the city alone. He could always ask questions if he got lost, and someone would set him straight again.

"I'd stay away from the south end of the city," she'd advised.

"You'll find only slums and foreigners, and there's nothing you'll want to see there anyway. You probably will be best to stay around the business district near Broad Street or take the subway at Market, if you've never had that kind of experience before. Still, if the crowded city gets too much for you, take the northwest trolley out to Willow Grove Amusement Park." So, with a bag of sandwiches under his arm, he set off on foot to see a whole new world.

The Northeast wasn't called the mill town for nothing; here heavy industry was everywhere, from the textile and knitting mills, to the steel works, foundries, and machine shops. He had no problem in finding the garment factory where Cousins Beth and Sylvia worked. It was ten blocks they walked each day to the square two-story red brick building, which occupied half a city block. The windows stood half open letting out the clatter. This was the discord his cousins endured each day at work. What a contrast to the muted tones of a cow barn, where the cry of a crow flying overhead was enough to shatter the quiet of the countryside. Here, a hundred crows would hardly make themselves heard. No wonder his cousins talked hopefully of marriage and having their own homes. Even the most humble of abodes must seem like paradise compared to this.

Beyond the building tops, there lay a heavy cushion of black smoke like a huge greasy finger smudge upon an otherwise blue sky. The smoke spiraled lazily upwards and then flattened out over the northern city. He guessed this is where the steel mills and foundries were...where Clarence worked. He headed in the direction of the smoke.

No matter where he walked, he walked alone, for people paid little attention to one another; each was intent on his own business. Back home, one greeted passerbys no matter where you met, and during his first days here he'd say 'Hello' a dozen times, but with rare response. *And this is called the city of brotherly love,* he thought. No, this must be typical of life in any city. Yet this was not all bad, for privacy gives freedom—and freedom is what he wanted most— away from the restraints he'd known at home.

The machine shop, a division of Baldwin Locomotive Works where Clarence worked, stood just beyond the foundry. Here, the acrid fumes penetrated the streets and shops with a blue haze that hung over the roof

214

tops. So this is where Clarence works! He could envision his cousin inside, bent over a metal lathe turning artillery shell casings. He knew Clarence took pride in the skills of his trade and worked to the point of weariness.

Albert turned away and left the place. He'd rather work in a sweat shop making shirts or underwear than add his bit as Clarence did. The shops and mills swam past him and soon were left behind, but his thoughts would not retreat as did the mills. He was sure Clarence, himself, could never kill another man, yet he was caught in the impersonal act of destruction. In the city so many things were that way; it was a place of strangers. How much easier it must be to help kill strangers. Somehow, the war and killing were not as difficult for him to understand, as before. *It is the impersonal side of life,* he thought, *that leads man down the path to his own destruction.*

A troubled mind can be difficult to live with, and for its own protection seeks relief. With no purposeful thought, Albert's footsteps led him to the museum. Here, he found a peace he could not find among the mills. That part of the city he would not venture into again.

When he got home in the late afternoon, there was a letter from his mother. All seemed well at home. Peter and Ann had been gone a whole week, which was the longest honeymoon any at home could remember. It was a rare farmer who felt he could afford to be away for more than two or three days, even for marriage. Albert grinned when he read the details. The newlyweds had visited both New York City and Niagara Falls. Leave it to Ann to outdo what was conventional. She was making her own break for freedom, he could see that. Ann would add new spirit to the Vandenberg household if Cornelius gave her half a chance.

Further down in the letter his eye struck a paragraph which made him go back and re-read more carefully. It was about Richard. His brother had made a number of very good sales at market which brought in more money than they had expected possible. Now Richard wanted his father to take him into partnership and share equally in the profits of the farm. Albert had been gone hardly three weeks, and his brother was already maneuvering to take over the farm. Apparently, it was not enough that Richard's birthright would give him the farm at his father's death. He wanted to guarantee that right while his father was alive. This was no prodigal son spending his inheritance prematurely; this was a shrewd businessman paving his future in the soil of his birth.

215

The following week, classes began at the University and there were
three letters from home, from his mother, Neal, and Margie. There was
none from Catherine. Almost four weeks and no letter. Could she have
forgotten him so quickly? Even before opening his mother's letter, he quickly
glanced through Neal's. Perhaps he'd been unable to deliver his own
letter to her. He needed some clue as to what was going on back there.

Hi Buddy,

*How's the big city these days? Bet you're really livin' it up now
that no one's got a ball and chain on you, or has your Aunt taken
over for those at home?*

*Say, what's the big idea? You trying to make a pigeon out of me?
I got a big fat envelope from you and two-thirds of it was for Kate.
What the hell you think I am, Cupid? I get the feeling I'm being used.
Damned if I'd do this for anyone else, so I hope you appreciate the
trouble I went through to get it to her.*

*I've been going over to the farm as often as I've time to work out
Pegasus. Your old man has been real decent to me. He comes out to
talk when he sees me in the pasture. Of course, I'm doing him a favor
as well as you, so I guess it's not all friendship. The roan works out
real well. He's sure one hell of a horse. You'd better watch out or one
of these days I'm gonna' steal him.*

*Guess you heard Pete and Ann finally got back. Ol' Pete looked
well dragged out, and after all I told Ann at the railroad station. I
thought sure as hell she'd hate my guts for what I did that day, but
she's settled in here like it'd been her home all her life. She's so down
right cordial with me it's embarrassing. I've decided she's determined
to get along with me, in spite of myself, and I might just let her do
that. I'll say one thing for her, I think she's going to keep the house
lively. Incidently, I'll do as I damned well please about the Army.*

Nobody tells me what I should or shouldn't do. Not even you.

Don't take everything so hard, buddy. We've all got to make our own way in this world and you've got your chance now. Live it up while you can. To hell with tomorrow.

So long for now.
Neal

Albert threw the letter to the back of the desk and immediately opened his mother's.

My Dearest Son,

We were all so pleased to hear that you've passed your exams and will soon be embarking on your college career. We knew you would make it without any trouble. You are the first of the family to enter a University and we're very proud of you. You will be studying hard so I don't expect you to write long letters to me. It is better that you send a short note each week just to let us know that you are well. That will be enough.

I know that it has been a difficult change for you, and I'm sure you realize that it was also difficult for me to have you leave. Sacrifices must be made to achieve those goals that are really worthwhile— I've known that for a long time.

Ann has visited us twice since she returned from her honeymoon. I know she is doing her best to get settled in her new home at the Vandenbergs. Actually, we see more of Neal than any of the rest of the family. He is a strange young man, so restless and abrupt, but he has become more friendly. He stops by the house once in awhile, though he never stays more than a few minutes. then he's off with Pegasus for hours at a time. He rides very well, but not as well as you, I think.

We are all well here except perhaps for Catherine. She has not been feeling well. It seems many kinds of foods upset her stomach and we are all hopeful that it means we will be having an addition to the family next year. It will be pleasant to have a child in the house again.

I hope you will remember to eat well. I know you when you are hard at study. You tend to forget about meals unless reminded. I have cautioned Aunt Beatrice about this, so when she tells you to come and eat, mind her.

Love,
Mom

He pushed the letter across the desk and stared at the two- by-four wall studding. Snatches, only snatches about Catherine. Not enough to know much more than he knew before, but enough to build up his concern that all was not well with her. Was this the real morning sickness that she had joked about in the barn? She and Richard had been married more than five months now, so it was quite possible. What right did he have to be concerned, yet he was, and couldn't help himself. Perhaps she was so ill that she couldn't get into town and mail a letter to him. He could only wait and wonder.

Slowly, he opened the last letter and read what Margie had to say. It told of church choir and hinted that she missed him. She was proud of him, she said, and hoped he studied hard. It was an honor to know a young man from a University. Would he be coming home for Thanksgiving? She hoped so.

chapter

18

In the evenings, Albert paced the small attic room scanning his texts and reciting out loud. Long passages were committed to memory from Homer's *Iliad*, bits and pieces of mathematical equations, and chemical formulas. Each, in turn, received its due attention. Clarence listened from his cot while Albert recited from his Ancient literature.

"What good will that ever do you?" Clarence asked. "That's not how the world is today."

The trigonometry and chemistry seemed much more practical to him. Teaching is a good method of learning, and Albert convinced his cousin that he also should learn something about trigonometry. From that time on, Albert had a student of his own.

The streets between the University and home became familiar ones. There was no longer time nor inclination to deviate from this route. Studies gradually took over Albert's life, and the talk about the war lost its significance; even his thoughts of Catherine became less frequent, until the day her letter came.

Dear Albert,

What you must think of me, for not writing you before. Believe me, if I could, I would have. The letter you receive now is the third I have written. The other two I destroyed because I had no way of mailing them. I considered giving them to Neal for him to mail in town, but thought better of it. Not that I don't trust him, but I couldn't be sure he might not get careless and the letter fall in the wrong hands. We have too much to lose should that happen.

Since your mother reads your letters to the whole family at meal times, I hear of your struggles and successes. It has been my hope that you will understand my tardiness.

One of the reasons for my not getting into town more often is the increasing problem we are having with Clara. She has not been well and has become almost impossible to keep satisfied. It has been wearing your mother down and I have taken over part of Clara's care. Although this is not pleasant for me to write about, there is a positive side to things. Clara's problem has brought your mother and me closer together than ever before. Sharing the burden of Clara has given us a mutual objective and increased respect for each other.

Closeness to your mother strangely makes me feel a certain closeness to you. There is no question, you are your mother's son in temperament, speech, and many other ways. For this, I truly thank God.

Something that may amuse you, but hopefully not too much. Last week, while helping Dad with the milking I faked being nauseous. I told him I needed a bit of fresh air and went up in the loft and sat looking east from the big doors. If you recall, I played sick one time before. Anyway, I sat exactly where we sat and watched the sun come up. I even talked to the sun as you did that day. Silly, wasn't I? Yet, I thoroughly enjoyed it.

I wish I could write you more, but I must go in and see Clara again. Hopefully, I'll be able to get into town, do some shopping and post this letter.

> *Love,*
> *Catherine*

A great wave of relief swept over Albert.

———◆◆✦◆◆———

On weekends, there was the sampling of religion, each week a different church. A thirst that would not be quenched, but groped onward for something new, something more satisfying than that he had as yet experienced. When churches ran out there was the synagogue. Here, the Rabbi drew him aside, and he was embarrassed.

"You are not Jewish! Why do you visit us?" the Rabbi asked.

"Curiosity?"

"It's not an idle curiosity," he replied. "I want to learn how other people think and pray."

"You feel then we are so different from yourself?" A faint quizzical smile showed through the Rabbi's beard. "You would examine us to see what makes us tick?"

"Heavens, no! It's not like that," he stammered nervously. "Your religion is the father of mine. I only wish to see that from which mine came."

"And you think you can learn that by just observing us? It's not as simple as that. You see only the surface, not the roots."

"I only seek the truth, that's all."

"Only the truth!" The Rabbi laughed and slapped his forehead with the palm of his hand. "That's like searching for an honest man. I'm afraid you make a modern Diogenes of yourself."

"But one must try to find the meaning of it all."

"Yes each must try, but so few achieve. I don't mean to jest at your sincerity, nor drive you away. You are welcome to visit us and don't be afraid we'll try to make you one of us. We are not like many of your faith who try to convert the world. You seem to respect our ways. I show no disrespect for yours." The Rabbi shook his hand vigorously and he made his way out into the street again.

He wondered if circumstances had been different, would it have been anymore difficult to believe what he'd heard from the Rabbi than from the Reverend VandenTill? Religion had broadened its base for him, from the narrow concept of his own church at home to the full breadth of the

Christian faith. Now he had reason to question if it should not extend to even greater horizons. The Rabbi sincerely believed in the same God; Christ was the primary difference.

All this was heresy! He could hear the Reverend VandenTill's voice drumming in his ear, but that ear was fast turning deaf. God had given him a brain, a logical brain that questioned what it perceived. At the University, they taught him to probe and question everything he read, no matter what the subject. Then why should he not also question the dogmas of his church? Were these principles so sacred as to be above the cold eye of reason— he thought not. God created a logical universe where everything from the microscopic to the cosmic clicked along with precision. Only a God with a deductive mind could create such a universe. The dogmas of his church were not logical to him, but a paradox. How could they be inspired by God? They must be only man's, to control the thoughts of other men. Question them, deny them...and you are a heretic.

His mother's next letter suggested that Albert might prefer to stay with Aunt Beatrice for Thanksgiving. It would be his first Thanksgiving away from home, but Christmas would be only a month away and they could celebrate doubly at that time. As though this were more than just a suggestion, she enclosed enough extra money for him to buy a large turkey for the family.

Albert resigned himself to wait until Christmas before seeing the family. He was also reminded that this would give him additional time for study before the mid-term examinations prior to the holiday. This, his mother wrote, was far more important than an all-too-brief stay at home.

The next letter from his mother brought up the subject of Clara for the first time. What had appeared as a prolonged nasty chest cold had turned into a deep congestion. Dr. Brabin diagnosed it as pneumonia.

At the DeGraf household Clara sank rapidly in the week that followed. Having lived in a wheel chair most of her life, she did not have the strength to fight the disease. The next Tuesday night while Catherine was keeping watch, she became aware of a silence in the room. The coarse congestive breathing had stopped; Clara had died quietly in her sleep.

The termination of one life released another from bondage, for during the nineteen years since the fateful spinal meningitis, Ella had devoted herself to the hopeless task of caring for Clara. It had been a task that chained her mind as well as her body to this invalid, and now she was free. The feeling of relief was beset with pangs of guilt. Ella could not bring herself to mourn; for how could anyone really mourn the death of Clara? She was now at peace with God.

Three weeks after the funeral, Catherine talked Ella into joining her on the milk route. Ella had been almost a recluse. There'd always been the excuse of caring for Clara that kept her from going to town.

After finishing at the Dumen's, Catherine and Ella went shopping for the rest of the morning. It was noon when they returned with a load of packages, which were whisked off to Ella's room. Directly after lunch the two women retreated to the bedroom and closed the door behind them. Catherine had bought cosmetics, powders and creams, which had never entered this household before.

"No, I couldn't possibly use them," Ella protested. "Paint and powder are only for women of loose morals. Dick will be furious."

"Nonsense!" retorted Catherine. "That might be true for the likes of me, but for you it is not vanity which prompts us." Catherine brushed aside all further objections and set her artistic hands to work on Ella's face and throat. Experimenting with the mixtures, she eventually got the proper color tones to match Ella's skin and in time the old scars were hardly noticeable.

"Now we'll change your hair," Catherine said. "You wear it like a woman of sixty. A few changes here and there will make you look years younger. You've kept your figure, Ma, and that's the important thing. All we need to do is change the rest to match."

The hair that had been tightly drawn to the back of the head was loosened, combed and set in new directions. The store-bought dress was taken out and when the changes were completed, Ella looked at herself in the mirror.

"What will they think of all this finery?" she moaned.

"They'll like it, I'm sure." Catherine smiled. "They'd better!"

"I haven't dressed like this since I was first married." Ella said hesitantly. "I'm afraid to go down for fear of what they'll say."

"Oh, come, Ma," Catherine coaxed. "You look quite proper. Let's go show you off."

Dr. Brabin was reading a book, and Sarah, the Bible, when they entered the parlor. The old doctor immediately set his book down and looked approvingly at them.

"Ella, you look twenty years younger!" he exclaimed. "And the scars are gone. How did you do that?"

"She did it," Ella smiled and pointed to Catherine.

"Doesn't she look wonderful, Sarah?" the old doctor beamed.

"She could almost pass as Catherine's older sister."

Sarah squinted at Ella and motioned for her to come closer. She shook her head as though in approval, but a deep frown came to her wrinkled features. "Does Dick know anything about this?"

"Not yet. I'll go out and get him." Catherine replied. "You stay here, Ma."

Dick was grumbling about being taken from his work when he entered. Couldn't it have waited until later? He took one look at Ella and stood thunderstruck.

"My God! What have you done to yourself?"

"Don't you like it?" Ella asked hesitantly, apprehension flooding over her.

"Isn't it a little soon after Clara's funeral for you to parade in such finery? It's like you was celebratin'."

"Oh, no, Pa!" gasped Catherine. "It's not like that at all. Ma's served Clara hand and foot all these years. Isn't it about time she had a little enjoyment in life?"

"It ain't right! Not so soon." Dick shouted defiantly. "You're pushing your young ideas on all of us, Kate. Now there's not even respect for the dead anymore."

"But Pa, she's still an attractive woman. Must she hide that forever? How long would you have her mourn Clara? A year? A decade?"

"I say it's not respectful," Dick said sternly, his eyebrows pulling down. "What will people think?"

"It's always what people think!" Catherine shot back at him. "Can't it be as Ella thinks? Just this once?"

Ella, who'd stood speechless, suddenly turned and rushed up to her room.

"Now look what you've done!" Catherine raised her voice in contempt.

"You and your new ideas." Dick glowered at her. "You'll bring this household down on all our heads!"

"Dick! Dick! My son!" croaked Sarah, breaking her usual silence. "Stop this arguing and listen to me" Sarah pulled herself up, her gnarled arthritic hands clasped tightly onto the arms of the chair. There was a firm set to her mouth which he'd seen many years before and knew its meaning. "It is *you* who's bringing this house down upon us! I've stood aside long enough! Now listen!"

Dick saw the old matriarch gleam in his mother's eyes. By right, her word was still law in this family, even over his. She was now ordering him for the first time since before his father's death.

"You're wrong!" Sarah stormed at her son. "Your first responsibility is to Ella, not the community and what it may think. She has borne the brunt of Clara's affliction, not you. Your father was a stern man, but he had compassion. I've seen little of that in you these last months. It is not Christian to be so hard."

"But Ma!" Dick started, but she raised her hand, silencing him.

"Go make amends with Ella! Bring her to me. I'll decide what's right about this!" The white-haired woman's voice had an authority that was not to be denied. A fire burned in her that all had thought long dead. Meekly, Dick left and disappeared up the stairway, while Catherine and Dr. Brabin exchanged glances.

Sarah motioned to Catherine to put some pillows behind her back to prop her up. She would settle the matter directly, and Dick would not dispute her word. Several minutes later, Dick returned, his arm around Ella. The scar on her cheek shone in streaks where tears had washed away the makeup. The bright new dress had been replaced with one of her high-necked greys, and the hair was again drawn back as tightly as before.

"Ella!" Sarah addressed her daughter-in-law. "Dick was hasty in his judgment. I hope he's asked your forgiveness." Ella nodded solemnly.

"But Ma!" Dick said defensively. "It wasn't that I didn't approve of what she'd done. I thought she looked fine, but it's too soon after Clara."

"I doubt that any of us recognized approval in your voice or actions," Sarah cut him down. "You talk of respect. Now show respect for me!"

"Yes, Ma!"

"Respect for the dead is one thing, but respect in the living is far more important. Clara's dead, and Ella's sacrificed enough. Now let her live with pride and respect in herself. I would think you would want your wife to look attractive and not withered before her time."

"I do, Ma," he explained, "I do, but..."

"I will decide what's right here," Sarah broke him off. "Perhaps the dress is a bit bright, but I saw nothing wrong with the rest. A month from now the dress too should be proper. You have my blessings, Ella. Now, go up and refix yourself. It's getting time for coffee."

———◆◆◆◆———

Albert found the letters from home disruptive to his studies. First, there was a certain feeling of guilt in not attending Clara's funeral. His mother had written that they all agreed there was nothing he could do and best he stay where he was. Here was a second incident of his not returning home when there seemed reason to do so. Or, was it that he was actually feeling a bit homesick? Finally, there was the letter from Neal which seemed almost defiant in its tone. He was still determined to join the Canadian Army and had had a number of arguments with his father.

Classes at the University became a duty and a chore, instead of the exhilarating challenge they'd been before. Now, he counted the day between Milton and Browning, between Wordsworth and Longfellow. Long days that had lost their zest and went by like mere numbers between trigonometric angles.

The weather turned bitter cold several days before Christmas. The wind was out of the northwest and the temperature dropped into single digits. Albert put on his long winter coat, and as he walked to catch the trolley for school his breath made frosty white plumes in front of him. People scurried along the streets bundled up as best they could, yet it was obvious that some were but ill prepared for the sudden change in the weather. Cold had rarely bothered him on the farm, but here the wind whipped down the streets in such a gale that he seemed short of breath. The hard concrete beneath his feet intensified the biting feel of the worst of winter yet to come.

People said it was going to be a bad year. Those with rheumatism, and other means of prediction, were convinced that this winter would be one to remember. Perhaps as severe as that of '88', the old ones cautioned.

Wednesday morning was bright and clear and warm if thirty degrees is warm; it is, if the day before was only eighteen, with a ten-mile wind. Albert ran the whole way from the trolley to the house. Aunt Beatrice was baking when he arrived. There were rows of pies setting on the back porch and two cakes in the oven. She knew he'd be in a hurry so she had lunch ready for him and a bag of sandwiches to take along. She said she was sorry he wasn't staying over with them for the holiday, but understood his anxiety to go home. He knew she only thought she understood.

The train pulled out of the station and soon it was crossing the Delaware River bridge. Albert looked back at the houses along the waterfront, the factories and mills beyond, and realized how foolish all his worries had been last summer when he dreaded coming here. Now, he was dreading what he'd find at home. Perhaps these worries were just as foolish as those other ones had been.

The train roared through the southern Jersey flatlands. The early afternoon sun shown brazenly on the brown stubble of cut corn fields punctuated by stacks of stalks bundled and standing upright. There'd been melons growing here too, for he could see the dead withered vines laying prostrate in wiggly patterns like so many thin brown snakes parched in a drying sun. Later, there were fields of asparagus, stiff stalks of light tan with slender feathery branches waving in the wind. Putting his face close to the window, he thought he saw a sprinkling of blackened berries on them. They were dead and dried, but had not, as yet, been cut and burned.

The sky clouded, and what had been bright and almost gay turned a shadowless grey under a darkening overcast. The scene had lost its interest, so he turned to a thin volume of H. D. Thoreau and began to read. Some time later his peripheral vision told him that something was flying past the window and when he looked, he saw flakes of white shooting by outside. It had begun to snow.

When the train out of Philadelphia stopped at Paterson, there were several inches of a dry, powdery whiteness over the ground. It crunched noisily under his feet as he walked across the platform towards the station house. The clock on the outside wall showed ten after six. He had no idea who would be meeting him, or how long he'd have to wait. These were details that'd never been settled, but surely someone would come.

It was nearly thirty minutes later, when looking out through the flying fluff drifting lazily past the platform lights, he saw a carriage pull up and the unmistakable frame of his brother. Without ceremony, he waved, rushed over, threw his suitcase in the back, and climbed up beside Richard for the ride home.

chapter

19

"How was the trip?" Richard half grinned as he reined in the horse.

"Rather uneventful, I read most of the way." Albert settled down to make himself comfortable.

"Don't you get tired of just reading all the time?"

"No, it's one way of passing the time."

"We need to stop at Dumen's before heading home." Richard looked straight over the horse's head." I've some business to work out with Mr. Dumen."

"Oh?" Albert's head came up a bit in surprise. "And how is everyone at home?" This was strictly a rhetorical question since he'd talked with his mother on the phone the day before.

"Fine! Fine!" The answer was no more sincere than the question. Then unexpectedly, "You've heard that Neal is determined to join the Canadian Army?"

"Yes, he wrote me about his plans," said Albert dejectedly.

"Darned fool! Several of us have tried to talk him out of it. He's been completely pig-headed about it. Tomorrow before dinner Cornelius wants us help him convince Neal not to go."

"I guess some of us do get irrational obsessions at times." Albert stared straight ahead, not wanting to meet his brother's questioning look. The ride the rest of the way to Dumens was mostly in silence.

Mrs. Dumen met them at the door and on seeing Albert broke into a broad smile.

"Well, if it isn't the <u>Professor</u> coming home for the holidays. This calls for a celebration!" Taking Albert by the arm she led him over to the display case. This was an experience Albert had had on other times but always enjoyed. Here he was directed to select several items and then they proceeded to the back room for him to eat his fill. Albert dutifully provided Mrs. Dumen with all the latest news from Philadelphia. Meanwhile Richard sought out Mr. Dumen and Albert didn't see him again until they were ready to leave for home.

It was fully ten minutes later on their journey that Richard explained his meeting with Mr. Dumen. A subject Albert had wondered about but wasn't going to ask.

"I'm making arrangements with Mr. Dumen for us to open a small shop next spring by converting some unused space near his show room. We'll sell dairy products, fruits in season, strawberry preserves and other things that should go well with his line of bakery goods. This will provide us with a central location where we can sell at retail prices. Much better than depending on the wholesale farmers' market or going door-to-door."

This all came as a big surprise to Albert. His brother was more enthusiastic than he'd ever seen him before. There was a tone in Richard's voice seeming to actually invite Albert's opinion. Again a first as far as he could recall.

"Of course we will still have vegetables suitable only for the produce market, but gradually I'd like to change that."

"Perhaps we'll need to grow more fruits and berries and less beans and carrots," Albert ventured. "Have you talked to Dad about any of this?"

"Only briefly. He's not at all convinced. I'm hoping I can get your support to bring him around. He has a high regard for your opinion. Especially, now that you are a college student."

"I'll help you in any way I can." Albert could see his brother's plan had real potential as an alternate to the cumbersome, labor intensive sale system long established by their father. It was only Richard's last remark that seemed to carry a tone of sarcasm. Was it possible his brother envied him now, or was he being oversensitive, still thinking of old feuds.

Richard dropped Albert off at the back porch and proceeded on to the barn to unhitch and stall the horse for the night. The only light at the house came from the kitchen. Most of the family had already retired since they'd be up before dawn the next morning.

The snow had almost stopped; it was beautiful, and would be perfect for sleighing. He would hitch Pegasus tomorrow, but who would go with him? In the short time since he'd gotten off the train, he'd become aware of changes since before he'd left for Philadelphia. What other changes was he about to encounter?

Old Gin must have heard his step on the porch because he immediately heard her bark from the kitchen. It was her greeting bark and when his mother opened the door, the old dog bounded out to greet him with tail wagging furiously. He dropped down on one knee, grasped her around the neck and got a face washing; a wet affectionate tongue slobbered him thoroughly. Here was one of the family who never seemed to change. Animals are so much more predictable than people.

His mother's smile was more radiant than he'd ever remembered. She had hinted about Catherine's cosmetic remake of her face and throat, but this still hadn't prepared him for the transformation. Along with the near absence of the scars was also an absence of a certain resigned melancholy air that he'd become accustomed to.

"You look wonderful!" was all he could stammer as he folded his arms around her in a gentle hug and kissed her. She insisted he have a bite to eat. Although he wasn't at all hungry, thanks to Mrs. Dumen, he couldn't refuse. This gave Ellen an opportunity to bring him up-to-date on activities.

They would be celebrating Christmas dinner with the Vandenbergs. It seemed especially important for it would give Catherine and Ann the chance to be with the whole family. Ellen then turned to more serious matters.

"I have not meant to censor my letters to you, but there were some things I felt might disturb you from your studies. Catherine is pregnant! There were several false alarms, but now there is no longer any question. It is quite obvious to even the casual eye now. Knowing of your deep feelings, which I hope have now much subsided, I felt it best not to mention.

You will find it has changed her."

"Also, Dr. Brabin has moved into Clara's old room. We've invited him to join our family on a more-or-less permanent basis and he accepted. He makes good company for Sarah."

"I wondered why Pa didn't insist I come home for her funeral," Albert questioned. "Not that I could have done anything."

"That was another thing," Ellen continued. "He at first thought you should for appearance's sake, but then Sarah opposed the idea and your father relinquished."

———◆◆◆———

The next morning, Albert came down in time for the morning milking, although no one had asked him to. Perhaps they thought he would sleep late. His father and Catherine were seated at the table when he entered. This was unusual, to eat before doing the milking, but then he noticed it wasn't really breakfast at all.

"What are you doing up so early?" Ella asked. "We thought you'd be tired after your trip yesterday. You _did_ get in late."

"I went to bed no later than you did," his reply. "I'd like to help with the milking this morning if I may, Pa."

"Glad to have you, son." Dick grinned at him. "Still a farm boy at heart, eh? I thought maybe city life would have spoiled you."

"Not that fast, Pa. I still like the smell of a cow barn. Where are the others?"

"Richard and Govert left a little while ago on the milk route, so's to be back in plenty of time for dinner," Dick replied. "Now, don't just stand there, sit down and join us, boy."

Albert plunked himself down next to his father, who he noticed was having only coffee and a bun. For a brief moment, he looked toward Catherine; she hadn't spoken a word, only given him a brief smile when he'd entered and gone back to her plate. She was the only one who was eating—poached egg and thin oatmeal with hot milk. She looked different, but he wasn't sure just how. It was obvious she was with child but there was more than that. She looked considerably more mature. Whereas his mother looked twenty years younger, Catherine somehow looked considerably older. It seemed that freshness of youth he'd known was being replaced by a haunting elegance of a mature woman.

The ground outside was as white as writing paper, reflecting pale moonlight with its sheen. Dick and Albert stopped by to see Pegasus while Catherine went on ahead to the cows.

"Has he been giving you any trouble, Pa?" Albert asked and went up to the roan and patted him along side of the head. Pegasus whinnied and rubbed his nose against Albert's jacket affectionately.

"A little trouble now and then, but nothing I haven't been able to handle. He still remembers you, I see."

"Yeah, he should. It hasn't been that long. He looks in good shape. Guess Neal's been helping exercise him."

"Neal was a big help while you were gone. I certainly didn't have the time to spend with him that I should. Well, shall we go look after the cows?"

"Let's! See you later, ol' boy." He gave the stallion an affectionate parting pat.

The smell of the barn and sound of cows chewing their cud had not changed, and it was good to be back. Albert set to milking and soon his hands moved with the same rhythmic agility they'd known before. The callouses were gone, but those hands were otherwise the same. Everything was as it'd been before, but not quite. As he moved from cow to cow, there was no sign of Catherine, although he heard her, always some distance away. He worked his way well apart from his father so they could talk if she had a mind to. He'd almost given up when he felt a hand on his shoulder. Looking up, he saw her standing above him with a finger to her lips. Leaning over she whispered "We need to talk, but not here! I've arranged things for Sunday directly after church."

Ella put the turkey in the oven shortly after the others left for the barn. It was a twenty-five pounder and none too big for the combined family feast that was planned that noon. Preparations had been divided between the two families. Ella and Catherine would prepare the meat, which included a large ham in addition to the bird and the vegetables. Grace and Ann would bring the pies, cakes, plum pudding, bread and rolls. It was the first time the two families would be celebrating the holiday together, and it was hoped that this might become a tradition.

The Vandenbergs arrived shortly after twelve noon. Dinner was to start around two, giving the women time to have everything ready. In the meantime the men retired to the parlor to talk. Cornelius took the lead in getting to his problem in trying to talk some sense into Neal's stubborn head.

"The boy insists on joining the Canadian Army" Cornelius blurted out in an exasperated voice. "It's crazy! It's not our war! Why get involved? Maybe you" (he swung his arm to include all present) "can convince him not to!"

Dick explained that Neal had everything to lose and nothing to gain by such a foolish move. As the eldest son he would eventually inherit the Vandenberg farm. It was to his best interest to help his father in every way to improve conditions and productivity for their future.

"I believe we have a good example of what I mean in a recent proposal by Richard. His suggestion is that we establish a new sales outlet for our produce through Dumen's bakery. We were planning on discussing this at dinner time. Neal should be thinking more in this direction than going off to a foreign war."

For a man usually of few words, these were, for Dick, strong statements. Albert looked toward Richard and saw his pleased expression. Perhaps he didn't need as much support in convincing their father as would have appeared the previous evening.

Dr. Brabin was next to confront Neal with a reasoned approach. His beloved England was deeply mired in the conflict and its capacity to furnish food, clothing and other living essentials to its people was being severely taxed. Neal's best contribution would be to help provide those essentials rather than waste himself on the battlefield. All the while Neal sat in silence showing little if any emotion to the barrage he had brought down upon himself.

Finally, Albert felt he must express himself also. Not that he wanted to gang up on Neal, but he had a perspective from his stay in Philadelphia. He repeated much of what he'd written Neal about how at the farm they were in a back-eddy from the main stream of reports about the war. In the city reports seemed to come in hourly and there was the daily posting of casualties. It soon became like a constant drum beat drowning out all his other thoughts. Men were killing and getting killed each day, each hour, each minute. Finally, he immersed himself in his studies, and for a time closed it all out. By the end of his little speech, Albert was near to tears. Although often ridiculed during his youth for his strong aversion to violence and killing, no one did so now. It was during his closing remarks that Ella came, stood in the doorway and when he'd finished, invited them all in to partake of the Christmas meal.

The large dining room had been extended by removing the panels between it and the adjacent sewing room. This allowed for a long narrow table adequate to sit both families. Dick sat at the head at one end and Cornelius at the other. Dick was in charge of carving the bird, Cornelius of slicing the ham. The women sat along the left side, the men along the right.

Except for the brief episode early that morning, Albert had seen little of Catherine. Dick led a prayer, typical for the beginning of all DeGraf meals, but now elaborated to account for the Vandenbergs' presence and Albert's return from Philadelphia.

During the meal Albert looked toward Catherine, sitting diagonally across from him, several times before he caught her eye. She responded as he'd hoped she would. They still had their private method of communication through eye movement. Yet, it wasn't quite the same. There was something missing. Perhaps Sunday's meeting would resolve this.

Following dinner Dick motioned for the women to stay and become part of a general discussion.

"Richard has explained a business proposition to me that sounds promising and could involve all of us. I think we should talk about it and get as many of your thoughts about it as possible." Dick then had Richard speak about renting space from Dumen's bakery.

"The proposal for having a central retail outlet for the products of both the DeGraf and Vandenberg farms was favorably received. The plan included expanding the number of products to such things as strawberry preserves and fruits in season. Everyone was encouraged to think about additional crops or processed food that could be added.

Albert sat back and watched the goings-on with a particular interest. Here his father was conducting an open forum, in which everyone was encouraged to participate. This was in strong contrast to his father's past actions when his word was law. His eyes then went to Richard. It was obvious he was glorying in the enthusiastic reception his proposal was receiving.

The response was spontaneous and vigorous with almost everyone participating. Finally, after more than an hour, Dick brought things to a close. The women had to clean up and had their kitchen chores, while others had the barn and milking duties.

———————

Sunday morning was bright and clear, brisk for the season, but not especially cold. A new snow had fallen during the night and now blanketed the previous one with several inches of fine powder. No one questioned that Albert would take Pegasus and the two- seater sled to church. Yet, there had been no word as to who would ride with him. Normally Dick and Ella took Pegasus, but Dick graciously relinquished that privilege to Albert. As Dick had always said from the beginning, Pegasus was Albert's horse and no one was to challenge that. It was as they were finishing breakfast that Ella informed Albert that she would be his passenger.

They were well on their way in the lead over the main carriage when she first spoke of what apparently had been on her mind. This was the first real opportunity since he'd come home for them to talk freely without interruption. As Albert glanced sideways at her he could sense a new vitality. The burden of Clara had been lifted from her shoulders— her soul. Then, too, she could associate with others without constant awareness of scars she must try to hide. She was unusually talkative and Albert assumed a passive listening role.

The conversation began almost mundane to Albert. The congratulations on his having successfully completed his first semester at the University.

How proud she was of him, that he was the first of either the DeGraf or Vandenberg families to ever go to college. This placed a burden of responsibility on him to not do anything to jeopardize that privilege.

All that said, Ella got into the meat of her discussion.

"Catherine and I have had many conversations about you while you were away." Ella's voice was calm but firm. Albert raised an eyebrow but said nothing.

"Yes, she confided in me about your feelings toward her, but then I was aware of them perhaps even before she was."

"And?" Albert braced himself for what might come next.

"Catherine has convinced me that you two need to talk privately before you return to Philadelphia. I will arrange that she accompany you on the ride home from Church."

Albert found it difficult to believe what he was hearing. His mother, who for months last summer worried about them being alone together was now actually going to arrange for their meeting. All he could do was to stare at the back of Pegasus's head and wonder at this change of events.

Albert sat in Church next to his parents, Sarah and Govert. Richard sat up front with the Deacons, while Catherine, Ann, Peter and Margie were with the choir. He'd seen Margie briefly before church and they agreed to meet after the service was over. In many ways this was all quite familiar and yet somehow different. He couldn't quite put his finger on what it was. Even his meeting with Margie seemed rather distant and reserved.

It was not until the congregation, as was customary, repeated the *Apostles Creed* that he realized that perhaps it was <u>he</u> who had changed more than those around him. Since childhood he'd memorized the *Creed*, but now the words caught in his throat. Even to mouth them without saying them aloud made him feel like a hypocrite. Like words in a song whose melody drowns out the senses, he'd never before analyzed just what these words proclaimed. Doing so now, he could not accept them for himself.

His exposure to other religions while in Philadelphia made him see things differently.

It was either this or the fact that at the University they'd taught him to question everything. Was it possible that in four short months his views on many of his surroundings were being dramatically altered?

These apparent changes were not necessarily a bad thing. His mother's renewed vitality and spirit was certainly most welcome and heart-warming. Had he actually thought everything would be the same as last summer? A static world: like his wish that morning with Catherine in the hay loft, or of his poem to her that evening.

<u>For change is all that's sure to each of us.</u>

chapter

20

ith Richard on one side and Albert on the other, Catherine was assisted up onto the passenger seat of the two-seater sled. An extra blanket appeared from nowhere and was tucked around her legs and lower body. Albert then swung up onto the other seat, jiggled the reins and Pegasus trotted off before any of the others had begun to leave.

His meeting with Margie had been cut short by the apparent emergency. However, they had promised to continue to write each other while he was in Philadelphia. The gossip Ann had whispered to him earlier left him with mixed feelings. He'd think about that later. Now, he had to get Catherine home—or was this all part of a hoax cooked up by the women?

Albert glanced over at Catherine as they left the church drive onto the main road. There was a half-grin, half-smirk on her face. Well out of sight and sound of those at church, Catherine broke into a hardy laugh.

"I never realized until now what power I have over Richard and Dad DeGraf now that I'm with child. All I had to say at the end of service was that I wasn't feeling well and wanted to go home. Ella took over the rest.

"Mention of my delicate condition and the welfare of the future grandchild was enough to send them stumbling over each other to provide me assistance. You know the rest."

"Is there anything I can do?" Albert was still a bit in a fog about things.

"Heavens no! I'm fine. Strong as a horse. After all, I'm not <u>that</u> far along. I told you in the barn, I'd see we got a chance to talk today. You can thank your mother for pulling it off. It may surprise you, but we have become very close friends. She's written you I'm sure of our many conversations about you these last several months. Ma has gained full confidence that our relationship will remain a platonic one. That's why she arranged this time for us to be alone."

"So, here we are all by ourselves." Catherine's voice suddenly turned serious. "A lot has gone on for both of us since you left for Philadelphia. I'm sure you can't feel quite the same about me as you did last summer. Look at me! I'm not the young woman who sailed on the HMS Pinafore, or watched the morning sun come up with you in the hayloft. Unlike in the poem you wrote that night, time has not stood still and everything has changed. Yet, not everything! The experiences we had at the pond and that morning in the hayloft will always be with me. Those moments are permanently locked in my memory. We both lived in a fantasy world, which, lovely as it was, just could not last. You made me feel young beyond my years. For that I will always be grateful."

All this while Albert sat looking directly at the road ahead. Pegasus settled down to a slow even trot.

"You've been very quiet," Catherine continued, then paused. "What are your thoughts about all this?"

Albert cleared his throat several times, while thinking where to start. "Looking back after these past four months, I realize I had an obsession with you. I fantasized all sorts of things, many of which I'd be embarrassed to describe even now. It seems now that it was a combination of love and lust. One side of me saw you a beautiful object of art, the other badly wanted to go to bed with you, but dared not."

"You made that quite clear that morning in the hayloft, and I did little to discourage you. For this I'm sorry. It was wrong of me to lead you on the way I did. Yet, I'd been totally swept up in the fantasy we'd spun together. I felt like a young school girl with her first love. But, where does that take us now? You haven't said."

"I admit, it's not the same. During the first month in Philadelphia, I couldn't get you out of my mind. I thought of you every day. Then I became engrossed in my studies and slowly thought about you less. It was as though my new obsession at the university was gradually replacing that I had had for you."

"It would appear we both had a rather rough period of adjustment after you left. For me, there were many black days—and nights—in that first few weeks. We had become very close, perhaps more so than was best for either of us. You see, I had had a gnawing hunger ever since my wedding day for something missing in my marriage. Call it a certain girlish longing. You seemed to fill that something with our fantasies."

Then, with a decided change in tone of voice, she continued. "Do you remember our discussion in the barn about the essence of love?"

"Yes, I claimed I could love you without ever touching you, but of course, I was wrong."

"I, on the other hand, claimed love was not a ghost, but a living, growing thing that feeds and would be weaned. I also was wrong! We were both wrong."

"How so?" Albert raised a questioning eyebrow.

"I later realized that for life to have meaning, enduring love must go beyond the physical alone. Neither the physical nor your concept of the spiritual will suffice in themselves. Both must be present for full, lasting satisfaction. Where only the physical is present, we are little better than animals. Your own form of the spiritual seems closer to idol worship than love—and I'm no idol. You'll have to admit your 'love from a distance' was not realistic. Your passionate kissing clearly told me that."

"I have to admit the kissing and what went with it had far more substance to it." Albert grinned openly. "Anyway, what I called spiritual had nothing to do with religion. It was merely meant to signify the warm feeling I still get in just seeing you and being with you. The physical contact is just a bonus beyond sight alone."

"Yet, those episodes we had last summer made me aware of what I'd been missing. I pined for release from the mental tedium of life here on the farm. The church has been no relief—in fact, it has had a deadening effect on the mind and soul, which only made my feelings worse. Everything is too constrained, solemn, and rigid." Then, a sudden lighter tone in her voice, she asked, "You remember our excursion last summer on the HMS

Pinafore? Silly, wasn't it?"

"Silly?" he exclaimed, a bit put out.

"Yes, silly! Deliciously so!" I giggled to myself about it for days. One time later, Ma caught me in the middle of one of those gay moments and questioned its source. Feeling you would not mind, I told her all about our little boat ride. I believe that was when she first got the impression that I wasn't about to seduce you."

"You didn't tell her about the otters, did you?" This, his biggest concern.

"Of course not. That was our secret. I will always honor that. My mentioning our pond experience is because of its contrast to most of life around here. It was a mentally stimulating event of a light and uplifting nature. So much else here is cast in heavy gray hues of austerity. I finally realized what I was missing was the challenge of positive mental stimulation."

"What you seek, I found in Philadelphia, and at the university. If only I could take you there, wouldn't that be grand?" Albert exclaimed enthusiastically, but then quickly changed when he realized the impracticality of it.

"Hear me out! I have you to thank for first making me aware of my loss and what followed. Your mother sensed my distress when you left, and we formed a close bond that has filled the spiritual void I was experiencing. I believe I wrote you how closeness to your mother strangely made me feel a closeness to you. That was not an idle comment. The similarity in temperament, speech, and outlook is amazing. In me she found a willing subject to discuss her love of poetry, fine art, and philosophy."

"I look to Ella as my teacher—my guiding sister—not my mother-in-law. She's taken me on as a student to replace the one she lost when you left. Thus, we each fill a need for the other. Every evening, after the chores are finished, we have a study period of selected prose or poetry. Our strongest support is where we might have least expected it. We not only have the blessing of grandma Sarah and Dr. Brabin, but they join us on occasion."

"I realize I am being selfish—like a child who wants to have her cake and eat it too. Yet, I feel I am beginning to experience both. My marriage with Richard completely fulfills my need for physical love. In that respect, he is a good husband. Now, I am also satisfying my craving for mental stimulation through Ella. I have learned to love her truly with all my heart," Catherine brought her arm around Albert and drew him close. She kissed him with a passion beyond that he'd experienced before. "This is in gratitude for letting me first glimpse the light," she grinned, "As a liberated spirit, I feel I can do this without fear of undue complications."

Albert was completely taken back. Although he thoroughly enjoyed the kiss, this was the first time Catherine had actually initiated the act. Indeed, she was a changed woman in more respects than her physical state.

"So, where does this leave us now?" Albert asked. "I realize things cannot continue as they were last summer, but I still enjoy looking at you as I did then—from a distance."

"Even in my present physical condition?" Catherine responded in surprise.

"Yes, you are still beautiful to me. In a different way, of course, but still lovely!"

"My! College certainly hasn't dampened your sense of flattery." Catherine grinned openly.

"You will still continue to live in my fantasies," he continued, "Even as you grow old. I will remember you as you were last summer. For you, all time will stand still." He let the reins go slack and returned the kiss. She didn't mind.

"Last summer I agonized how I could love two brothers while married to one. With a little understanding on both of our parts, I now believe it is not only possible but logical. Are you willing to continue our relationship, knowing there is a point beyond which we dare not go? Actually, I can see this as a three-way love—Richard, Ella, and you—each with a different aspect of that love. You and Ella will fill that gaping void which has so haunted me."

"This suits me fine," Albert exclaimed. "A platonic love with you is better than nothing."

"Now that Ella and I have this special understanding," Catherine continued, "We will no longer need Neal as our go-between for the exchange of letters. I cannot think of anything we might write that I wouldn't be willing to share with Ma. When she writes you, there will always be a letter included from me. You may do similarly in your letters to her."

What a change of events this has become, he thought—*no more need for secrecy.* In response to this last bit of news, he gave a quick jerk on the reins. Pegasus took off in a brisk trot for home.

Albert pulled his overcoat up close around his throat and, peering through the early morning semi-darkness, tried to make out the position of the hands on the clock at the far end of the railroad platform. The falling snow made him squint to distinguish the dirty gray hands from the almost equally darkened color of the rusty face of the timepiece. It was a quarter past six and he still had fifteen minutes to wait before he boarded the train.

Looking down the length of the platform, there were the same objects he had seen many times before. Only now, shrouded in a fuzziness of flying snow, everything took on a fairy-like appearance. Near the platform's edge, a group of milk cans stood double-decked in neat rows like a squad of ghostly metallic soldiers waiting patiently for their sergeant to march them off. Little caps of snow topped each can like hats set squarely in place. For a moment he tried to imagine these as people waiting for the train. He felt the need for company, someone to talk to, but there were only the milk cans that would get on this train. In a way, he was lucky for the milk cans because otherwise the train would not stop here at all. He could see the small patch of yellow light shining out on the snow from the station clerk's office window. He might go in and talk to him, but what would they say? He knew the man only as Mr. Rupert, friend of the Dumens. His mind bussed with the holiday activities and he needed time to digest it all. So many things had happened since last August.

Looking back at the milk cans, he thought of Neal, whom he'd had little chance to see other than at the Christmas dinner. Neal's obsession with joining the Canadian Army bothered him and he felt he should have done more to dissuade him. What good could come of it and what prospect for disaster? Yet, Neal's obsession seemed to carry him beyond reason. Yet, how could he judge Neal, when his own obsession of last summer for Catherine had all the portent for a different kind of disaster.

That, fortunately, had been averted and things had turned out quite well. He no longer begrudged Richard his rightful due. He would be satisfied to express his love in a different way.

His greatest joy was hearing that his mother had opened a whole new world to Catherine with their studies of the classics. They had established their own small island of free thinking, unrestrained by the shackles of constraint imposed by the Church. His mother was expanding those worlds and revealing the substance of the fantasies of spirit she had only darkly groped for, earlier.

A light appeared far up the tracks. The train was coming. He watched the light grow from a small speck to a blinding shaft. Still at some distance he could see the snow swirling down and across its beam along the track. With a roar the train burst into the station disrupting the quietness of the moment before. Now there was activity. The station clerk came out of his office and a group of men from the train started loading the milk cans, swinging them up onto the rubber bumper as though they were paper cartons of air. A sudden gust of wind blew a flurry of snow in his eyes. Blindly he reached for his bag and started up the train steps, but there was a yell behind him. He glanced back, the snow still stinging in his eyes being tears that made it hard for him to see the small figure of the station clerk standing just below him on the platform.

"Why, it's Albert DeGraf," the man cried. "I thought I recognized you. What are you doing boarding this train?"

"I'm leaving," was all he answered.

"Well, have a good trip. Best of luck."

"Thanks, Mr. Rupert," Albert reached out awkwardly and grasped the outstretched hand. Then he went inside the coach and made himself comfortable, determined to get some sleep. The railroad platform was quiet again and the clerk went back to his office. A busy mind is a poor precursor for sleep. Try as Albert would, sleep would not come. So, he sat, oblivious of the noises around him, looking with glazed eyes at the rapidly moving countryside. Now he finally had time to think of Margie. They had had a pleasant time talking at church, but little more had come of it. According to Ann's gossip grapevine, Margie was now seeing a young man, a neighbor, not from our church. Ann hadn't blamed her one bit, saying Margie had to think of herself. Four years is a long time to wait. Yet, here it was only four months. He felt a little put out that she hadn't waited a bit longer. Yet, there was also a feeling of relief.

On the ride from home to the railroad station, Richard had continued to present new justifications for his proposal of their opening a sales outlet at Dumens. Albert had already expressed his approval, as had all of those at the holiday dinner. Yet, Richard would go over and over the details to take every step possible to guarantee the project's success.

The more Albert thought about it, the more it seemed Richard and Neal each had their own obsession, which they followed doggedly. He, too, had his new obsession at the university. It had grown stronger during the past several months until it overtook and surpassed that which he'd had for Catherine. He would still love her, but in a less emotional way—it would augment and inspire him in his studies—not distract from them as in the past.

When he had first arrived at Dumen's the day before Christmas, Mrs. Dumen had addressed him as *Professor.* They both were well aware the title had little meaning under the circumstances. Yet, it had a very nice ring to it—*Professor Albert R. DeGraf!*

For the next four years and more, he would expend all his physical and mental energies to fulfill that goal. As the train roared south towards Philadelphia and his future, he vowed this was now to be his destiny. The destructive hour was past—a bright new world now lay before him.